The Last Sunset
on
Troublesome Creek

The Conclusion of the
Life and Death on Troublesome Creek
Series

Bordes Slone

Dedication

My journey for Hiram Daniels is complete. I hope you enjoy reading my books as much as I did writing them. I plan on writing another book this year if I am privileged to. I might even carry on with more stories from Troublesome Creek. I hope all like the title I chose, with the help from my friends and loyal following. You will never know how much the encouragement from your input kept me going when slow times were around.

So, I dedicate this book to all that bought my books or read them or just complemented on my writing. Thanks!

Prologue

The hardships Hiram Daniels endured in his lifetime matured him into a great orator as he passionately fought for his rights and precious farm on his beloved Troublesome Creek. Hiram's happiness and joy, derived from his love of family, proved to be all he ever wanted and he achieved greatness from experiencing just plain life itself. His daughter, Mattie, brought him such joy, that if that was all he had, he would have been satisfied. But his last, a son, named Jesse, gave him hope for the future of the Daniels clan.

He fought along Troublesome Creek, where he lived and made his livelihood, only to lose most of the time, but never giving up and winning battles when the opportunities presented themselves. He pondered on many points until the answers came for him to finally decide to give or take from any situation that arose. Many sleepless nights he laid awake pondering the future and drawing knowledge from his past to make decisions for not only him, but decisions that would affect all River County.

His third wife took care of Hiram, at first out of loyalty to him for rescuing her from being tied, raising her siblings to adulthood. But as her marriage developed, a love for Hiram crept into her inner being that could not match anything outside her realm of life. She was never more pleased then when she carried his child and gave him a man-child so he could carry on his legacy.

Hiram developed a sense for business and he became quite wealthy, but at the same time managed to leave his farm and land intact for his future generations to enjoy. Hiram didn't let wealth change him as wealth changed others. He remained down to earth and never bragged or boasted foolishly, as the world does. He was proud of his family, even though one carried a wild side until he was changed by death of his son. Hiram loved Cullen and never did understand him until he received salvation from God, who provided more answers in an hour than most people received in a lifetime.

Hiram's life was never interrupted with anything. Whatever the situation, he never lost sight of his up-bringing. If problems arose, he rose to the task, figuring in his head that the answer was there if he could find it, and he did one way or the other.

When Mattie received her braces for her crippled legs, Hiram could hardly contain the joy that sprang from his heart to the outside. Unspeakable joy rose as fog rising from the earth, rising to the sky, the highest point of the universe in his world. Hiram knew from experience the joy of a higher power that was not of this world. A power that was lowly and humble, decisive but sweet to the soul that made a mere mortal body feel weak to His comparison. Hiram was never more happier then when he joined the church. He figured there was two kinds of happiness – one for the natural man and one for the spiritual man – and he had experienced both. His life was a complete circle, returning to the beginning from which it came.

One can not read Hiram's story without trying to put themselves in his shoes for most of his journey. A journey of failures, losses and incredible pain that was overshadowed by triumphs, joys and immeasurable bliss as he lived his life to the fullest. A journey most people only dream about, and Hiram was a dreamer. He made many decisions based on what dreams he had in a given sitting of sleep. At such times he looked toward the Bible and God for his understanding and guidance. He quoted many scriptures from his childhood when his mother read verses around the fireplace, on cold evenings in winter. No matter where he happened to be or what condition his mind rambled, he always turned his head toward his strength: God, family and land. One of his greatest quotes from the Bible was, "I will look to the hills from whence my help cometh from."

-- Bordes Slone

To

Ann,

Life is like a river as it journey's to the sea, never returning. Our life is kind of like that. We can not return after this life = God has been good to me and blessed me good to me and blessed me. Hope you enjoy the journey!

From Daniels Slone

Bordes Slone

2021

Song

On Troublesome Creek, on Troublesome Creek,
Where the water runs clear and deep.
It's as close to Heaven as I'll ever be,
At the forks of Slonetown on Troublesome Creek.

As hollers criss-cross and meander true,
Trees grow tall as they sway and stoop.
The people are honest as the day is long,
That is why River County is still my home.

On Troublesome Creek, on Troublesome Creek,
Where the waters run clear and deep.
It's as close to Heaven as I'll ever be,
At the forks of Slonetown on Troublesome Creek

Seasons

Spring, when the mountains roll and tumble upward
Rising slowly struggling, reaching for the sky
But not able to achieve their goal
That does not keep them from trying
Trees budding, blossoms coming forward
Releasing their beauty in the sun and rain
In spring and early summer, winters but not staying for long
Moving their cycle, going but not yet gone
Petals opening, petals falling, floating to the earth
To bounce lazily with all beauty removed.

Spring buds turn into grown leaves
Hot heat, sun staying in the sky, days longer
Dog days of July set in as the long days of wilting flowers

To be renewed in the early morning fogs
Berries ripe for the picking,
ticks invading lush pastures and fields
Yellowjackets, hornets, waspers nest building all day long
Working for another year but futile in their endeaver,
only to die off
But the queen is saved to bring new life another year.

Leaves full grown veins showing,
colors emerge pigment changing
Colors; yellow, red and a mix, some brown as if dead
Only to begin their downward journey
back to earth, tirelessly moving
onward, piling on the forest floor,
mounding to be crushed underfoot
Enriching the soil for new growth when the time comes.

Winter's frost freezing breath
sticking to whatever it touches
making white dead trees, wind
swaying branches small limbs falling downward,
snow and icicles reaching down from rooftops
Everything white to the frozen earth,
stuck together as white plaster
So cold even the animals fail
to venture out of their barrows and dens
living in cramped places trying to stay warm,
trying to survive nature's hardships,
hoping and knowing it will not be long a new beginning
will take place and it all begins anew for another year.
Spring will surely come.

Poem

Rolly Joe Mountain so tall and grand
The high flats where the chickquapins band
The snow cap in spring so white and bold
With blooms of the honeysuckles all orange and gold.

The oaks growing out of cliffs, ragged and rough
Beech trees hanging from formations with hardly enough
Poplar and hickory amongest the birch so sweet
Bean trees, sasafrass, pines and sarvis to eat.

Rolly Joe Mountain reaching for the sky
Such majesty to behold as time comes to die
A thousand wonders if the mountain will endure
One more term or just one more year.

Chapter 1

W ind blew from the north moving leaves on the beech, hickory, oak and poplar trees. The leaves waved wildly from side to side, wrapping around the limbs before settling back in form as they waited for the next gust. The sound of a rain crow could be heard from a distant mountainside down Troublesome, about where Nathan's place was. Only it didn't belong to Nathan anymore. Nathan and his wife died over a year ago, leaving the parcel of land to the county to sell for the taxes. Hiram almost bought the property but thought better of it, figuring he really didn't need any more land. Mattie would never be able to marry and work the land that he owned now, and Cullen wasn't stable enough for the time being for Hiram to even think about leaving him the fine farm he'd built here on Troublesome Creek.

The dog days of July had set in dry with hardly any rain to speak of. The corn blades curled in the hot sun on hazy afternoon days. The sun's rays beat down on Troublesome, cracking the ground in the bottoms and making the hillside soil loose. Hiram's pasture land was overgrown with briars, thickets and sagebrush. He planted only a portion of the hillside and bottom land that he used to. He didn't have time to farm like he once did, because all his free time was taken up caring for Mattie, though this was time he enjoyed. He never regretted waiting on her. To do so, to him, would have been a sin. Cooking and cleaning were a full time job, and he missed Alice Marie more as each day passed. He really didn't know what he would do; his mind was stuck remembering his late wife.

Hiram stood staring at the fresh dug grave where Alice Marie rested. Mattie sat in a cane bottom chair that Hiram carried from the house. She watched her father as he grieved over her mother. Mattie's chin dropped every so often as her hands tried to stay still. Her head and neck lurched backwards from the unsteady position she sat in. Tears ran down her cheeks and dropped to the young girl's lap wetting the throw Hiram had covered her spindly, bent legs with. Now and then the throw moved as her knees bobbed upward before it fell back in place again. She didn't try to speak but low moans of sadness came from her lips as she sat there. Hiram wondered what was to become of his Mattie. "Who will take care of her? Who will wait on her personal needs since Alice Marie is gone? Mattie didn't speak, but she wanted to. Her lips trembled as she sat sobbing. Hiram's memories flooded his mind and heart as one by one they paraded past him, faster than he could keep up. The fox barks, along with the red cardinal's chirps splattered the silence. At first Hiram didn't know whether their sounds were from within or without, until he felt the swift gust of warm air whispering through the yellow popular leaves. He sighed slowly, then continued his moment of grieving.

Alice Marie had died of rabies, some three weeks ago. Hiram had no idea she'd been bitten by anything that carried the rabies virus. If he'd known, he would have gotten help for his wife. Hiram knew that foxes went mad during the summer months, but he had never heard that bats carried the disease. He remembered killing a rabid fox one time in the pasture while ginseng hunting. The fox came at him like a drunk man staggering and foaming at the mouth, barking crazy. He threw every bit of the cow's milk out for two weeks, waiting to see if Susie was going to show symptoms or not. He wouldn't even feed the milk to the pigs and when Alice Marie showed symptoms of being sick, he was afraid that she had gotten rabies from the milk, only to learn later that a bat had bitten her.

Hiram wiped the tears from his eyes as he stood there, thinking. He was tired of death. He knew he couldn't do anything about it. He remembered Mommy reading out of the Bible to him and the rest of the family as they sat by the fireplace in the wintertime. She read all the time to them. She read about life and death when she could. But that didn't keep him from thinking this way. He knew he shouldn't, but he couldn't help himself. He'd barely gotten over Ballard's death, and now it was Alice Marie.

As he remembered, he could almost hear his mother. She would read a verse here and there, reading aloud passages that seemed important before looking at her family to see if they were paying attention. "Man hath no power over death," She'd say, then raise her eyes to see if anyone had anything to say. Most of the time no one spoke. Everyone figured Mommy knew what she was talking about. Her being such a devout Christian and church goer that she was.

Alice Marie told Hiram about being bitten by a bat two weeks before she died. He asked her, "Why didn't you tell me? Maybe Cassie could have done something for you." Alice Marie cried as she watched Hiram struggle with the sadness and loneliness she knew that would consume him over after something happened to her.

"I regret not telling you about it, Hiram. But who would have thought about a bat carrying rabies? I hate leaving you, honey. I've loved you all these years since the first day I laid eyes on you when we played under the shade of the sycamore tree, there at the one room schoolhouse. I would have given my life for you then, and I would for you even today."

As the couple hugged, Hiram knew in his heart he would lose her. He held her with the loving grip he always used with Mary Liz. The love he shared for his wife was not a small thing. It went far beyond his life, beyond his strength, beyond his sense of understanding. It was beyond anything he could comprehend, but as he held her, he tried to. She fell asleep in his arms.

The day Alice Marie died, Hiram tried to forget, but couldn't. The rolling of her eyes as spittle formed at the corners of her mouth, body convulsing. Hiram used a tie rope from the barn to tie her to the bed so she would not hurt herself or anyone else. He wondered in his mind if she knew him or what was happening to her. Hiram would not let Mattie see her unless Alice Marie was in a calm state. The day she died, she was not. Hiram wet her lips with a cloth, making sure none of Alice Marie's saliva touched his skin. She was this way for four hours, then death came quickly. Alice Marie's body went limp as breath left her wretched being. In a sense, Hiram was glad it was over. He hated to see her suffer so.

Hiram came to himself as Mattie pulled at his pants leg while he still stared at the grave. Hiram turned to Mattie and placed his hand on the soft black hair that hung down in a ponytail. The same way her mother fixed it every day. Hiram used to sit for the whole hour it took Alice Marie to comb and twist Mattie's hair into place. Except for her disability, Mattie looked like her grandma, especially in her hair. It was long and black, full and free flowing, and blew in the breeze as she sat on the porch. After Alice Marie fixed her hair she would ask either her father or mother to rock her for an hour or two as she listened to the evening sounds of lazy days coming to an end. Days that seemed to end too soon, but Hiram knew they had to. Time could not stand still. Time was like a river that flowed. Never ceasing, going to wherever it goes. Not ever coming back but always flowing forward. Never stopping until it reaches the sea of life. Taking whatever it could pick up along the way, to be gone forever. Hiram felt so lonesome as he picked Mattie up, along with the chair. He must get her home; it was supper time. He looked to the grave one more time. Then he glanced to the left where Mary Liz rested. Then back to the middle where his final resting place would be.

"Planted in the heart of the earth is as normal as being born," He thought out loud. One day he would rest from his labors gently placed between his two wives. Yes, he was tired of death.

He packed-walked Mattie down the hill to the framed house, setting her down on the porch in a cane bottom chair. He turned around as he held to one of the poplar posts that held the porch roof up, glancing toward the dogwood point another time. Then he picked Mattie up again and carried her to the sofa.

"What do you want for supper?" he asked as he washed his face and hands in the wash basin while staring into the looking glass. Most people now days called it a mirror, but not Hiram. Not yet anyway. When he spoke of his mother and father, it was always "Mommy" or "Poppy," and he couldn't get away from that. Neither did he want too. That was the old way that he wanted to hold on to. Hiram was very reluctant to change the way he talked or did anything in his life. Even though he had hooked his house to electricity, he didn't like it. He was never afraid of hard work and had endured a lot of things to keep his way. His daughter Cassie said his way was plain stubbornness.

Mattie smiled her crooked smile at Hiram and said, "Anything will do, Poppy."

Mattie had never gone to school and, her being younger then Cullen, she had never had anyone outside the family that influenced her in any way. This pleased Hiram. He loved the soft voice she used when she talked to him. He remembered how much pleasure she brought to him and Alice Marie when she first began speaking. Her mother loved and made over Mattie something awful, but she was worthy of the praise. Hiram did the same when he could.

Cullen walked through the front door and flopped down on the sofa, spraddling his legs over the settee's arm. This always made Alice Marie angry. Hiram watched him as he lay there. He wondered what would become of Cullen. He wasn't like any of his other three children. Cullen was more like a young Reldon, quiet, but sulky at times. He never payed anyone's feelings a second thought. When he was in one of his moods, he was almost too much to figure out. Hiram had to speak to the school master at the one room school on more than one occasion because of him, but it didn't seem to help. He fought with about every boy that attended there sometime or other. Hiram quarreled with Cullen when he got in trouble at school, but it didn't seem to help. Just made him bitter at his father.

Hiram began supper by peeling new taters he'd graveled out of the tater patch. Some were big as ripe paw-paws. He peeled the taters and washed them off, then sliced them before dumping into the iron skillet filled with hot, sizzling grease. The taters hissed when the flesh of the tater met with the hot grease, sending hot splatters of the popping liquid over onto the stove top. The taters stopped splattering grease when Hiram placed a cooker lid over the iron skillet, letting the lid sat cock-eyed so the heat could escape the corner where the lid rested. He didn't have time to make a lot, so he stirred water and flour together to make a hoe-dab. Before long, the frying taters and frying biscuits made the kitchen smell good. He finished the supper off by scrambling a half dozen eggs and frying pieces of salted ham. Hiram loved the smell of salted ham. He placed the remaining slices of meat back inside the Frigidaire's freezer box.

Hiram set the table with a glass of sweet milk at each plate. Then he set a bowl of fresh cow butter in the middle of the breakfast table. He hollered for Cullen to come and eat. He picked Mattie up in his arms and carried her to her place and gently sat her in the chair. He raked taters out of the platter into Mattie's plate, making sure they were cool enough for her. He tested the golden brown soft strips of spuds with his tongue and blew air from his mouth on the ones that were too hot for her. "Come on, Cullen, and eat," He yelled a little louder. Cullen had disappeared into his bedroom.

Cullen came out of the bedroom and pulled the door shut. He yawned as he walked to the table and knocked the chair against the table's leg. He reached for the tater plate and raked a good portion of the fried taters, along with grease that filled the bottom of the platter. Hiram had sprinkled a small amount of meal over the frying taters just before taking out of the iron skillet. That is the way Mattie liked them.

Hiram broke a piece of the hoe-dab for Mattie and gave Cullen the other piece. Cullen began to eat.

Hiram stopped him and said, "We'll ask a blessing for the food first, young man."

Cullen stopped and held his fork in his left hand. He could use either hand to write or eat with, but most of the time he chose the left hand. He waited impatiently for his father to finish. Then Cullen began eating again, gulping it down. Hiram watched him and wondered what would ever become of him. After prayer, Hiram thought about the crops, and he figured Cullen would just argue with him and fuss all the time if he asked him to help. To leave Mattie by herself was out of the question, and he wouldn't ask Cullen to sit with her. He would figure something out before crop gathering time, which was approaching fast. Fall would be here before long.

After supper, Mattie hummed a song. Hiram could understand his daughter when she talked, but most people couldn't. Her father watched as she sat on the sofa. He knew she was missing her mother, and he could feel Mattie's pain, but he said nothing. Cullen had already went to bed. Cullen did say 'good night' to his father and sister, but nothing extra. Hiram washed the dishes and sat down beside Mattie and hugged her close to his side saying, "My little girl," while looking down at the smiling face that greeted him. He loved her. She rested against his side, sobbing. He patted her shoulder, gently. He held her for at least an hour, maybe a little more. Finally, she snored lightly, and Hiram picked Mattie up in his arms and laid her down on the feather tick mattress. He covered the girl's small body with a sheet, pulling it up to Mattie's underarms. He pressed the quilt in under her arm pits. She was sound asleep.

Hiram walked out on the porch and listened to the sounds of late summer. Crickets sang, and tree frogs were asking for a drink of water. Swamp frogs were hollering as the last of the lightning bugs filled the air. It would soon be too cool for them once the weather changed for the fall and then winter. Hiram sat quietly in the swing. Off in the distance, on Rolly Joe Mountain, fox hounds barked as they ran the race. Hiram could see the dim light of a wood fire, where he knew men sat and told tales as the hounds ran. These sounds took him back to happier times, when things were better for him. He wondered what the future might hold. "Who knows," He thought as he sat there in the darkness. An owl hooted down the holler, then moved to the northern side. He thought, "This is a sure sign of rain." A little past midnight, Hiram thought about the owl when he heard rain drops on his roof top. He slept good but dreamed most of the night. When morning came, he had forgotten all the dreams he had during the night, but he was refreshed and ready to work.

Rain splattered on the roof of the house and beat against the four windows. Hiram had drifted off to sleep again before waking from his dream. Something brought him wide awake as he turned over to see the 'Big Ben' alarm clock staring him in the face. "Six o'clock," He said out loud. He closed his eyes for a few more seconds, then climbed out of his bed and walked to the kitchen. He stopped at Mattie's bed. She was sleeping peacefully, drawing in her breaths so effortlessly. He started a fire in the cook stove, trying to be as quiet as he could. After the fire caught, he opened the door and walked to the far end of the front porch. Fog was rising in the swags and mountain tops, drifting skyward, mixing with the low lying clouds. Rolly Joe Mountain could not be seen this morning. Troublesome Creek was running about half full but was still clear as the rushing water pushed down the creek bed heading toward Slonetown. It was too early for a tide this time of year, so he wasn't worried. This much rain in October would worry him. After relieving himself, he walked back inside to the wash basin and washed his hands before starting breakfast.

He dried his hands and face and combed his graying hair, parting it down the middle and combing the sides backward over his ears. "For a man of seventy-five years, I haven't aged too bad," He said as he gazed at his slim waist. A Vshaped rib cage ran under his arms to his shoulders. "I've done as much hard work as any man in River County." He finished drying his hands and began frying eggs and salted ham, stirring flour for biscuits to bake in the oven. Then he fried some of the August Start apples he picked last week. He finished frying the meat and put two tablespoons of Little Princess flour into the hot grease to make brown gravy. He liked Snow Goose flour better, but that flour company must have gone out of business because no stores carried it anymore.

He stirred the flour with the gravy spoon his mother used when she was alive. After a minute or two, the greased flour turned a dark brown. Then he added the cream out of the gravy bowl. Not the bowl Mommy used, it had been dropped and broken long ago. But he bought Alice Marie a new gravy bowl from Sissy's store in Slonetown. It was a white bowl with a gold colored design that ran around the top of the bowl, just below the rim. He stirred the gravy until it became the right thickness. Then emptied it into the bowl and set on the table to cool.

Hiram woke his daughter, by kissing her cheek. Then he carried Mattie to the slop jar and sat her down. Hiram disliked having to shame her this way, seeing Mattie's nakedness, as she sat there. But who else was going to do it. No way would he ask Cullen. He wouldn't do it any way, and Hiram didn't expect him to. Cullen did empty the slop jar now and then, if Hiram asked him to. He left his daughter so

she could have as much privacy as possible. When she hollered that she was through, he picked her up and helped Mattie to the wash basin and poured in new water and washed
her hands with soap. Then he washed Mattie's face trying to
get all the matter out of her eyes. She was wide awake now.
Hiram helped his daughter to the table and sat her in a chair,
then walked to the bedroom door and hollered for Cullen to
come and eat.

Hiram had set the breakfast table with clean plates, along
with a fork and spoon for Mattie and ones for Cullen and
himself. He poured a glass of sweet milk for each plate. He
got a bowl of cow butter out of the refrigerator and waited
for Cullen to finish washing off. Hiram told him to take the
biscuits out of the oven and bring them with him. The brown
topped biscuits were warm and soft. Hiram could feel the
warmth from the plate of bread as Cullen sat it down. Cullen
took his place as Hiram offered prayer. It wasn't the fervent
prayers his mother prayed long ago, but he figured it was
better than nothing. Hiram had not joined the Old Regular
Baptist church, but he attended regular and deep down inside
he hoped to join someday.

Hiram passed the eggs and meat to Cullen, then he fixed a
plate for Mattie. He tore her ham piece apart in small pieces,
then broke one of the soft biscuits into her plate before pouring gravy over it. He mashed two fried, over easy eggs into
her plate before adding a spoon full of apples. A chunk of
cow butter was placed on top of them. The butter melted

down into the apples, making the top of them a creamy yellow.

Cullen finished off the gravy bowl by mixing the last fried egg and another biscuit into his plate. Then he drank the last glass of milk from the mason jar. Hiram watched him as he ate.

"I'm going to town today if you want to come with me and your sister. I need to pick up a few things, and Mattie needs to see Cassie and have a check-up before winter sets in."

Hiram waited for Cullen's answer. Cullen didn't look at his father, but kept eating his breakfast.

Finally, Cullen spoke. "I'm going to Ben's Fork today to see Ruby. I've been seeing her for over eight months, and I'm not going back to school this fall. I guess we'll get married. She's in a family way, and I don't want people saying my child is a base-born baby," he said, cleaning his mouth as he rose from his chair and pushed it back under the table.

Hiram said, "I expect you to get an education so you can get a good job. There is not much work here in these mountains except hard work for a person without some higher schooling. If Ruby is with child then you need to marry all right, so people will not call the baby a bastard, but you still need an education. You can live with us here and still go to school in Slonetown."

Cullen reached for his hat and walked toward the front door without saying another word. Hiram knew it was helpless trying to convince Cullen about his future. Hiram thought, "Making a go at raising a family here in these rugged hills will be a hard life. There are two small coal mines operating down in Perry County, but the coal business has not caught on here in River County yet." Hiram had been digging a little candle coal from the coal bank to burn in the stove. He thought, "It burns too hot for the fireplace. Can't use the candle coal in the grate because it flakes off and scatters over the floor, making it dangerous about burning the house down." Cullen didn't pay Hiram any mind as he turned and walked out the door. Hiram shook his head.

Hiram asked Mattie if she would be all right while he milked Old Susie. She gave him that crooked smile and said, "I will, Poppy."

He picked up the milk bucket and walked to the barn and milked the cow as fast as he could, not wanting to leave Mattie alone for too long. He then walked to the well and drew a bucket of fresh water and carried the water and milk into the kitchen, carrying a bucket in each hand. He sat the water on the wash basin. Then strained the milk and poured it into two half-gallon mason jars and put the warm milk into the refrigerator. He dressed Mattie then locked the front door and walk-carried her to his pick-up truck and sat her down in the passenger side. Hiram started his '57 Chevrolet stepside pick-up so the engine would warm up. He was thinking as he looked the truck over. It had taken him over ten years to get the money he was promised when Ballard was killed. The federal government seemed hard to get anything out of. He had to hire a lawyer to get as much as he did. At first he felt guilty about spending the money. But finally, he thought, "That is what Ballard would have wanted."

Halfway to town, it stopped raining. The wet road was slick as Hiram drove toward Slonetown. The pick-up fish-tailed as he navigated the curves near Turner Branch. Hiram was glad he learned to drive four years ago. After learning to drive, he did a little work for the government, building roads and the one bridge over Troublesome. The low water bridge near Turner Branch was covered with water, but Hiram had driven over it so much he knew where the sides were. Water splashed on the tires as he drove across the bridge into town. No more plank sidewalks followed the street through town. They had been replaced by concrete and stone. Hiram marveled how the rock masons had cut and chiseled stone from the hill side on the southern end of town. Immigrants from Italy located in these mountains to make Eastern Kentucky their home. The Romeo brothers had built five new buildings out of cobbled stone. Sissy and Grant had a new store building built beside their new clothing store and a new general store that only carried food items. There was also a new hardware store owned by Samuel Slone. Samuel moved from Rolly Joe Creek to Slonetown. People here thought he might have found some of Tivis's buried silver dollars.

Cassie had the rock masons build a new building that

housed her office and living quarters. It was a fancy house, with stone posts that held the porch roof. Not the poplar posts Hiram was used on his farm. Windows were on each side of the cobble-stone house, and the doctor's office had three windows in front and back. Cassie had made a good living doctoring the people of River and surrounding counties. She delivered so many babies that she had lost count. She could tell you most of the names of every baby born by her, but she'd lost count of how many a long time ago. Hiram's truck rode easy on Slonetown's street that had been paved for a mile in and out of town. But a lot of the roads in River County were still rough paved and patched. Streetlights were installed near the courthouse, to give light in case Judge Carrol was holding a late court for a murder trial or someone that had been charged for stealing. There hadn't been a murder trial here since Joe Greasley was found murdered by his house on Lem Wilson Road. Greasley had been shot three times in the chest area and died instantly. Cassie testified to this in court. Lone Gibson was the culprit who way-laid Greasley and, after killing him, took his wallet and burned his house down. Lone was caught spending money over in Catlettsburg. When he opened Greasley's wallet, someone noticed the letters 'J G' in bold print. Lone had made that mistake, after getting dog drunk and flashing the wallet around for everyone to see. The jury gave Gibson the fate of hanging in the courthouse yard for the crime. People came from miles to watch the hanging. Hiram did not attend but listened intently to all the tales told by different men that were there. The way they described the scene, he was glad he didn't attend.

Hiram parked in front of Sissy and Grant's store. He opened the door and picked Mattie up in his right arm and walk-carried her and the cane bottom chair with his left hand. He walked up the steps and opened the front door that led into the large open room that held dresses and blouses for women on one side and slacks and shirts and wide brimmed hats for men on the other. Belts for both sexes hung from racks that stood in the middle, separating the men apparel from the women's gallantry of colors that only a woman would wear. Bonnets of any shape and size hang from the ceiling where the windows lined the outside walls. Mattie looked all around as Hiram turned his body so she could see. He didn't want her to miss a thing. She smiled her crooked smile. Mattie's mouth was open smiling from ear to ear, exposing teeth that were not straight. Her smile showed some of her gum line. Hiram could tell she was excited. When she got excited her gums got exposed from smiling so wide. She made little moans of excitement as she looked. Hiram wished so many times that she had been born normal, but it wasn't to be. Only God knew why.

Sissy ran to greet Hiram and Mattie, throwing her arms around them both, hugging him and kissing Mattie's cheek. Sissy rubbed Mattie's arm as she made over her like she was something special. Mattie was special. The young girl reached her arms to receive Sissy's embrace, turning her head so it would rest on her aunt's shoulder. Mattie made little moans, her mouth drooling saliva onto Sissy's dress. Hiram dressed Mattie in one of her mother's favorite dresses. Alice Marie picked out the dress two months before she died. It was a red dress with white embroidery that encased the entire neckline and darted down the breast area to her waist, where a line of white buttons appeared. Then the dress flowed into a complete bottom skirt that never separated from the upper material. The sleeves were long, like Mattie always wanted. She did not want to show her crippled arms or legs to the public.

Sissy said, "My, Mattie, you look so beautiful this morning. You're prettier than the morning sun that shines in the noon sky, with the blue heavens as a background."

Sissy hugged Mattie again before turning to gaze into her brother's eyes. She stared at his brown tan, tight skin where a small patch of wrinkles were starting at each corner of his outer eye socket.

"How've you been Hiram?"

Hiram felt his face flush up from her intense stare. Sissy had always been able to make a person feel as if she could see right down inside of their soul.

Hiram spoke, "I've been doing all right. I'm not bragging, but I'm still able to do a honest days' work, and I don't have any pain to speak of, just a joint ache now and then." He placed his hand on her hair and ran his hand down the flowing heap that hung down to Sissy's waist, in the same way Mommy carried hers. Sissy was not a church member, but she never laid a pair of scissors to her hair as far as he knew. Hiram said, "Where's Grant? Is he here?"

"No, he is running the hardware store. We're trying to get down to just carrying food items for the general store and household goods, instead of carrying everything together. Easier to keep up with that way. Slonetown is beginning to grow a little. Why we've got two barber shops now and two places to eat supper if we've a mind too," She said.

Someone called out from the tables of women wares that was still in the store.'Out of date stuff', Sissy called them. It was Claire Polly, Rell's wife. Sissy turned her attention to the plump customer as she threw her hand that looked like half a wave and walked over to where the woman stood. Sissy smiled as she took a dress from the table and holding it up to her body, then she held the dress to Claire's stomach. Sissy was smiling all the time. Sissy made a good salesperson, and she and Grant had money saved up. The way they were expanding, it brought more business to the little town.

"Oh yes, we've also got a new shoe cobbler now too. I wish we had one when we were growing up, Hiram," she said as she walked away from the satisfied customer. The contented Claire Polly continued to do the rest of her shopping. "Remember that pair of high topped leather boots you wore so long? They were the best looking boots I'd ever seen. You kept them shined and instead of going back to your old brogans, you wired them together with a piece of fence wire. If we'd had a shoe cobbler then it is untelling how long them boots would have lasted," She said, laughing while she turned her head to see if Claire needed any more help. Hiram shook his head to agree with his sister.

The front door opened, and three children walked into the store, followed by a woman. Hiram would guess the woman's age to be in her twenties. She was tall and big boned. If she'd been shorter, one would think she was fat. The woman motioned for the children to get in line as she walked to the counter. Her clothes covered her nakedness but were tarnished with dirt and grime from working. But the two girls and one boy were tidy as could be. Their hair was in place and their faces and hands were washed and clean. So clean that their cheeks shined in the store light. The store's light came from double chandeliers with twisted plaid electric cords that hang from the ceiling. Sissy had two more high standing shade lamps in the darker corners of the store.

The homely looking woman marched the children up to the counter, lined up in order of their height. The boy, being the tallest, led the rear. The children stopped and spread out, facing straight ahead waiting for the next command from this new person. Sissy asked the woman if she could help her while reaching out her small hand for the familiar shaking of hands when a new customer came into the store. The new stranger took hold of Sissy's hand and it disappeared in the woman's larger palm.

"My name is Dora, and these are my two sisters and brother," She said, naming them as she pointed to each: Jo-anna, Ceora and Lundy. Lundy was a little hair-lipped. Hi-ram watched as the stranger looked around at everything and everybody in the store, while the children stood perfectly still.

"I'm here to buy school clothes. These two will be attend-ing grade school near Cody, while Lundy will be going to the high school here in Slonetown. He's in his second year."

Hiram watched as the unknown woman stared at Sissy as she stood behind the counter. Sissy stared back at the chil-dren, then showed the stranger where the dresses were for the girls and the trousers and shirts for the boy. Hiram told his sister he would be back later, not thinking much about the stranger. He picked his daughter up and carried Mattie outside to the pick-up truck, setting her in the passenger seat. He climbed in and headed for home.

He asked Mattie if she wanted to go for a longer drive as they approached the turn that led to Troublesome. "We'll go this way for a little piece," He said as he turned up the mountain that led to Betty's Troublesome and Ben's Fork. Mattie was so excited she could hardly stand it. She asked if she could roll her window down.

"You can about half-way," Hiram said, watching to see if she could manage the window crank. Mattie struggled some but soon had it a little over half-way. She sat back in her seat as the wind blew. The light wind moved her hair sideways, as it engulfed around her ear that faced the window. She smiled her crooked smile. Hiram loved to please her when he could.

Hiram drove up the curvy Brinkly mountain road and crossed the top and down the other side. Hiram geared the truck back into high gear and the pick-up rolled along. The V-eight engine hummed in perfect tune as Hiram drove along the Betty's Troublesome road. After four miles they came to the mouth of Ben's Fork. He thought about going on but decided against it. He turned around and headed back to Troublesome Creek. He and Mattie arrived home an half hour later. As he picked Mattie up to carry her to the house, he thought about Cullen and wondered if he was all right. He worried about him, but he soon brought his attention back to Mattie.

"We'd better fix supper," he said and closed the door behind them.

The next morning, Hiram was up early. It was Sunday. He fixed breakfast, fed Mattie, milked Old Susie and laid corn out for Mingo and the chickens. Back inside the house, he asked his daughter if she wanted to go to church. She was all for it. He washed the dishes and heated the water on the wood cook stove and picked out her favorite dress to wear. After he had washed her off, he dressed her and combed her hair. She could do very well with it but sometimes he had to comb the tangles out. Finally, she was ready.

He walk-carried her to the truck and they drove to Sandgap Church. He had many memories in this old church. He pondered how the old church had grown into two extra churches. Sandgap Church members had armed off to form another church at Ben's Fork, and then Ben's Fork had armed off to form a church at Turner Branch. Each church had two male members, along with ever how many sisters to receive an arm. The new church had to have working power. The sisters could not make moves and seconds, only the male members could do that. Then the three churches decided they needed an association. So, they formed the Rolling Springs Association and picked Clinton as their first moderator. Brother Lonzo was the assistant. Harvey Jennings was the association clerk. He was educated and could keep books like no other. The association met once a year to iron out any problems they encountered during the winter and summer. Hiram always enjoyed association time. Plenty of preaching and the most wonderful food a person could want: chicken and dumplings, pies, cornbread, fried chicken, green beans, tater cakes and pies. His thoughts were interrupted by a handshake and a hug from one of the sisters.

The house was quickly filling up with the new converts. The older members souls had gone to their reward and their bodies were sleeping peacefully on the hillside graveyards that dotted the landscapes. Seems like every family had their own graveyard. The families would meet in May and have church over the dead and then everyone would go to one member's house and have dinner, usually the one that lived the closest. Hiram wondered many times, "Why preach over the dead?" Preacher Silas preached all the time that "The dead knoweth nothing, but the living know they must die." He'd pondered on that thought quite a few times before.

Hiram sat Mattie down near the middle of the pews and waited for all the sisters to come by and make over her. Sister Rainy Sparrows was the first to come by. She was about Hiram's age, and he wondered if it was Mattie she wanted to make over, or him. She always hugged him frontwards and this made him feel uncomfortable. She was such a big breasted woman. Rainy patted Hiram's shoulder then caressed Mattie's cheeks, but she never took her eyes off of him. She was a pretty woman for her age. She still had a somewhat small waistline. Her eyes were a dark brown with auburn long hair. Her movements would make one think she was in her forties instead of sixty-seven, but Hiram wasn't interested in her. When she was married to her late husband Melvin, he told everyone she was bossy, making him do what she wanted, nagging until he gave in to her. Melvin was a humble man. He died over five years ago of pneumonia. Sister Rainy has been looking for a man ever since. She started just a few days after they put Melvin away. Rainy had to make way for the other sisters, though she didn't want to give up her space. Sisters Callie, Mavis and Rory wanted their time and when they were finished Mattie was tired and flushed. Hiram was afraid she would take the weak trembles and began shaking uncontrollable. He reached into his pocket and gave her a piece of candy to eat.

Hiram looked over the crowd and two rows back, on the third row of pews, sat the strange woman from Sissy's store. She wore the white and blue laced dress well, as it filled out the curves of her waist. Her ample bosom lifted up in place. Her long sleeves swallowed her muscled arms as her tanned and rough hands protruded out the dress sleeves and rested in her lap. Her hair hung loose around her shoulders flowing across her stiff back, reaching down behind the pew where she sat. A small boy watched her hair move and when it did, he tried to catch it lightly with a small hand. Hiram could tell the boy wanted to grab her hair but was afraid of what his mother would say, so he pecked at it.

Clinton came in about that time, hugging all the sisters as Susanna followed closely behind. Hiram thought, "That's the way of a preacher's wife. They were always kept kind of apart, while the man of God was showered with every one's attention. A preacher's wife had to be the helpmate and pertained to his wishes as far as the church goes, and Susanna didn't give it another thought. She was willing for her husband to be made over by the congregation. She took pride in being a good and faithful companion to him, and supported him in every way. That's how the Bible reads: a bishop must rule his own household and keep order in his house."

Sisters Mavis, Callie and Rory hugged and kissed Clinton's cheek, patting his back to where he could hardly turn around. Hiram thought, "It's a thousand wonders Susanna would be jealous of these women, but she wasn't." Susanna was thankful that Clinton stayed with her and babied her. A lot of men would have left their wives because of what happened to her. Clinton had a hard time with it, and Hiram always wondered if he killed the old vagrant, Baskum. But Clinton always insisted he didn't, and Hiram had no reason to doubt his brother's word.

The church house filled to capacity. Brother Lonzo set out cane bottom chairs for the visiting preachers after all the minister seats were all taken. The brothers and sisters were getting reacquainted. This happened every meeting time at all three churches, just like they hadn't seen each other in over a year.

Brother Lonzo started the singing, lining out Amazing Grace, and picking up higher on the second verse. Some brothers couldn't reach as high as he did, but when they could, the singing made the bell ring. The singing was filled with the Spirit as the sisters shouted for some time before becoming quiet. Mavis and Callie whimpered quietly as they had reached their Spiritual height as the Spirit slowly faded from them. Then they settled back into their natural state again. Hiram could now tell the difference between the Spirit and the natural man. He wanted the Spirit but wasn't quite ready for it.

Clinton stood and sang, *Mommy Can't You See That Angel Band*, singing it straight through. The rafters rang as his voice carried all around the room. He was filled with the

Holy Ghost as he approached each convert that was seated on the church pews. Chill bumps covered Hiram's arms and the back of his neck, as tears flowed freely from his eyes this morning. He was not sure whether it was from being in church or whether it was the closeness of Alice Marie's death. But he cried a fountain. Mattie was crying too. Hiram felt so sorry for his little girl. He knew she missed her mother's caring ways because she always babied her. He took every pain to make sure his daughter was comfortable and well as could possibly be. Tears dripped down her nose and cheeks as she tried to wipe them away. Hiram removed his handkerchief from his back pocket and wiped them for her. He was so glad he came to church this morning.

He hadn't noticed before, but he caught a glimpse of the strange woman staring at him. She smiled at Hiram as he glanced away then back again. She scolded one of the smaller children that sat next to her. She pointed her finger at the red-faced almost crying girl. Even the young girls many freckles seemed to glow red as she stubbed up and folded her arms together, staring at the floor. By this time Clinton had gotten wound-up, preaching on the Hebrew children and their faith in God. That even when they were thrown into the fiery furnace, God delivered them. The church brothers would say a loud, "Amen!" The sisters wanted to shout but this kind of preaching was what the Bible calls 'Meat.' Meat was for the full-grown brothers and sisters that had been in the church for a while and had been seasoned.

Clinton changed direction of his sermon into a softer tone. The sisters loved this tone, and they began to shout again, bringing the meeting time for prayer. Clinton asked one of the visiting brothers to hold prayer for him, and this brother lifted the Spirit to a higher pitch as it filled the church house. Hiram had never heard a person pray like this since Mommy. Even Clinton couldn't get hold of the Spirit like this brother did. By the time he was halfway through his prayer, he was pray-crying. The preacher closed with whispering, "Amen."

Another visiting brother closed the meeting out and dismission was called. Everyone slowly walked outside. Hiram watched the strange woman as she marched her brood out the door and down the steps. She turned and spoke to Hiram as he walked Mattie in his arms. "Nice to see you again," she said, then continued on down the path to the lot where cars and pick-ups were parked side by side. Some were parked along the roadway near ditch lines. Hiram figured she must have walked to church because she walked past the parked vehicles. Hiram thought maybe he would give her a ride home. He thought he knew where she lived over on Ben's Fork.

After getting Mattie adjusted in her seat, he asked the stranger if he could give her and her siblings a ride. It was too early for him to think about talking to another woman, but he could be polite to one. "That wouldn't be against the law," he reckoned. The woman hesitated a minute as she looked down at the children. Hiram watched her as she hesi-

tated about making a quick decision. Her face shined in the
sun's rays as she stood there. Her skin, a light tan from working outside during the summer months, was smooth and soft.
Not a blemish anywhere, except where she probably had
been scratched while picking black berries. Hiram felt a little
flushed in his face, but it soon left him as he waited for her
answer.

She finally said, "I guess it will be all right." She put her
two older siblings in the bed of the truck, then climbed in
beside Mattie and nussed the younger Ceora in her lap.

Hiram let out on the clutch and the truck lurched forward.
The boy in the back was laughing and talking out loud. He
changed gears into third and the pick-up drove smoothly up
the road towards Betty's Troublesome. He figured he might
get a glimpse of Cullen if he watched really close. He hadn't
seen his son for two months. Cullen was living with his in-
laws, working what jobs he could pick up. Hiram knew his
wife, Ruby, was going to have a baby but wasn't sure about
the due date. Hiram shifted the truck into second as he drove
up the small hill that led down into the valley. River County
had picked up four new communities: Ben's Fork, Betty's
Troublesome, Cody and Smithboro from Bolster County.
The annexation of these communities helped River County
because of the revenue these communities produced .

Slonetown was growing because of the annexation. Gro-
ver Butrum built a movie theater in town. Three new clothing

stores quickly went up, along with another hardware store and two new grocery stores. Grocery stores were popping up in every community, but most went out of business the first year. Hiram thought about going into business, but he would need someone to help run it while he farmed and took care of Mattie. He had been thinking about that a lot lately. Getting someone to help with Mattie. He turned right onto Ben's Fork road and slowed down as he watched for Cullen. He passed the house where he was living but saw no one was to be seen. He soon arrived at the stranger's house and pulled into the dirt driveway and stopped the truck. He looked over at her as she pulled up on the door handle and slowly scooted out. She sat the young girl down to run into the house after her older brother. The lad had exited the truck bed as soon as Hiram stopped. She looked bashful as she turned around to thank Hiram for bringing her home. She raised her head and finally looked at Hiram and Mattie as they waited to see what she would say.

"My name is Dora, and I'm thankful Mr. Daniels. The walk home would have taken me at least an hour, while tugging my brother and two sisters along. Hope to see you at church again."

She turned and walked into the boxed house. Hiram watched her go, then put the truck into first gear and he and Mattie enjoyed the trip back to Troublesome. He hummed as they drove along the mountain road. He watched the creek as it flowed along lazily. Hiram was thinking. He arrived home about two o'clock. He carried Mattie into the house and sat her down on the sofa while he stretched out on the settee to rest.

The next morning, Hiram was up early fixing breakfast, humming as he went about his work. He missed Alice Marie, but he knew she couldn't come back. After setting the table, he walked to Mattie's room and waited a minute before he woke her, thinking as he looked at her "Who will watch over her if I'm not here?" He made up his mind right then and there that he was going to ask Dora if he could see her again. Maybe take her to church some Sunday morning. Mattie needed a woman to help her. She needed help with personal things in life because the things she needed were just too private for him. He would have to do it until he found someone to help.

He woke Mattie and she tried to sit up in bed. She tried her best to roll over and then get up, but she wasn't stout enough. Hiram placed his arms under her armpits and raised his daughter to a standing position. Hiram put his left arm under her thighs and his right arm around Mattie's waist and sat her down on the slop-jar. He walked back to the kitchen. He waited for her to holler, "I'm through Poppy." He then walked back into the room and cleaned her as best as he could. He hated this. Not that he didn't love his daughter. It was just so private, and he felt like he was embarrassing

Mattie as he invaded her privacy. He knew she felt as uncomfortable as he did. But someone had to do it.

He carried Mattie to the table and wetted a washcloth. He
washed her hands and face. He combed her hair for a minute. After breakfast he would brush it all out and style it the
best he could. Hiram sat down beside her, fixed his plate and
begin to feed Mattie and himself. Mattie said, "Breakfast is
good, Poppy," still unable to look her father in the eyes because of the encounter with the matter of privacy.

Hiram smiled at Mattie and she raised her eyes to look at
him.

"I'm sorry, Mattie," Hiram said. "I will find someone to
help with you and everything will be better. I promise."

They ate the rest of their breakfast in silence.

After breakfast he milked the cow and turned her out to
pick the rest of the day. He watched the cow wobble along
picking grass. He picked up the bucket of milk and carried
it to the house. He hollered to Mattie then set the milk on
the table to strain. He looked for a clean rag and placed it
over the mason jar. He poured the milk through the rag into
the jar, then set the jar in the refrigerator to keep cool. "Not
like the old days when Mommy kept the milk in the bottom
of the well," he thought. He asked Mattie if she would like
to sit on the porch for a while and wait for the mail man to
run. She smiled. She loved to see Dar Higgins when he came
in view. She was always hoping for a letter to read or some
kind of catalog to look through. Mattie was a good reader.

Mattie's mother taught her when she was seven, and she was a quick learner. She sat still, looking down Troublesome. Hiram watched the creek as it ran by his place. The water was still clear, even though it had rained pretty hard two days ago. It was awful peaceful this morning.

Hiram drifted off to sleep as he sat in his rocking chair, rocking. He was awakened by Mattie's cough. She was staring toward the road as Dar approached the house. He had replaced his mule for a pick-up truck to carry the mail. Made it a lot easier on him. He could stay a lot drier and warmer. He pulled up to the mailbox and started to deposit mail, but then he saw Hiram and Mattie sitting on the porch. He opened the truck door and walked up to the porch singing *Poor Wayfaring Stranger*. Dar was good at this song. He probably sang it a million times as he traveled along.

"Howdy, Miss Mattie and Master Hiram. Shore is a nice sunny day out here this morning," he said as he reached Mattie the mail.

Dar made sure the mail pieces were steady in her hand before he turned loose of them. She smiled as she went through the mail. She picked out a catalog and reached the rest to her father. Hiram twisted his body until he could reach the letters. Mattie began to thumb through the latest issue of a Sears Roebuck wish book. She awkwardly and carefully turned each page so as not to tear any, smiling as she looked up and down each section of pages.

"How you doing Dar? Is everything all right in Slonetown this morning?"

Hiram waited for the answer from the black man. Dar had gained twenty pounds or more over the years and it made him look better. He used to be so skinny, skinny as a poke stalk. His clothes always looked to be two sizes too big for him. His face shined in the morning sun; his forehead wet with perspiration. His forehead seemed to bead with sweat making the rest of his face seem smooth without a wrinkle anywhere. A patch of a mustache grew under his nose that had turned gray. His lips were a blueish black. When he smiled his teeth were white as cotton. His gums and tongue were red like an Alberta peach's skin. He had round white eyes with streaks of small red blood veins streaking across his eyeballs. The blood veins looked like lightning streaking the sky on a stormy night. His pupils were as black as his skin.

"Why, I's as good as a black man can be, Master Hiram. People has been good to me on this holler, and I's been good to them. People can get along if theys want to, can't they Master Daniels?"

Hiram agreed with Dar and offered him a drink of water, but he declined saying, "Nope I's got to go, mo mail to deliver."

He stepped down off the porch steps and walked back to his truck and drove off to his next stop. Hiram helped Mattie up and guided her inside to the sofa so she could continue looking over the catalog.

Next morning, Hiram was up early. It was Sunday, and he planned to take Mattie to church. He drove over to Ben's Fork to pick up Dora and her three siblings. He was glad the sun was out and it was not raining. Church was at Sandgap today, his favorite place to go. So many memories he had of this church. On his way, he stopped at a little country store run by Maxwell Taylor. He bought Mattie a pop and candy bar, and candy bars for Dora's brother and sisters. He bought Dora a brown paper poke full of pink coconut strips. He planned to ask her to marry him soon. He knew it was kind of fast. Alice Marie had only been dead six months, but he needed someone to help with Mattie. Dora seemed to like Mattie and he knew Mattie would take to her after a while. He didn't love Dora, and the marriage would only be one of convenience. He would be good to her and treat her right, and the lonely cold nights of winter would be more comfortable with Dora being around.

Hiram slipped the truck into second gear to climb the small, paved road. He shifted gears down Betty's Troublesome hill that led into the valley of Ben's Fork. He didn't give the engine any gas, until it reached the bottom, then with a quick foot he double clutched into third gear. Then gave the engine fuel to keep it running smoothly. The gears raked slightly as Hiram moved the clutch in then let it back out.

He blew his horn at Dora's place. Her brother with the slight hair lip came running out of the rundown, slabbed, boxed house and climbed into the back of the pick-up. Mattie scooted over near her father and asked, "Poppy, can I ride in the back with the children? I'll sit down and I'll hang on tight."

He looked down at her and smiled, "I guess it will be all right."

He put the truck in first gear then opened the door and helped her out. He helped Mattie climb onto the rear bumper to get in. The truck bed planks were clean, and Mattie sat down in one of the corners and held on to the side. Hiram left the tailgate down and secured it by the chains that latched the gate. He opened the door for Dora and looked one more time to make sure Mattie and the children were safe and began the trip to Sandgap Church.

Hiram parked the truck along the creek bank and walked around to the other side and opened the truck door for Dora. She let him take her hand while she climbed out of the truck. She held on to Hiram's still steady hand and grabbed the door handle with the other one. Hiram unchained the tailgate and let it hang down. Dora's brother was the first one out and ran toward the church building. Then her two sisters did the same. Mattie, with Hiram's help, climbed out of the truck bed. Mattie was a little wobbly trying to gain her balance. Hiram steadied her, and he and Dora led Mattie to the church building. Together they walked up the steps and sat her down in the fourth pew from the back. The small girls slid in beside her, then Dora, and finally Hiram. The singing hadn't started, and the crowd was still talking and laughing. Hiram watched as the sisters and brothers filed in. After shaking hands with everyone, each took their usual seats. Church was good that morning, and so was the rest of the day.

Chapter 2

It rained on and off for the next two weeks. Troublesome Creek filled to capacity as the raging waters flowed down towards Slonetown, taking loose soil and debris as she moved with force. There was no stopping her. The water was a little muddy this morning, probably from silt upstream where road work had recently been done and new deep mines had been opened. Companies were mining the number four coal seam that outcropped middle way the mountain side. Just small operations. Nothing like the bigger mining companies from Perry and Breathitt counties where coal was mined and shipped away to other states to power large generators for producing electricity.

The first frosts of fall were nearly every morning. After the rain let up, the Indian days of summer warmed to an unusually high temperature for over two weeks. The warm days and hazy air coated the heavens and mountainsides, making the valley look like a fire had been burning for days on end. The smoke was thick, and it clung to Hiram's lungs. He dug his taters and gathered fodder and corn shocks, fighting the stings of the pack-saddles. He tried to stay away from the black widow spiders that loved the dried brown corn blades. He'd got sick from spider bites before. His skin, where the bite occurred, turned a dark blue and lasted for a week or more. But Hiram couldn't let a little thing like a spider bite get him down.

He hauled all his field corn in his truck bed to the barn and unloaded it into the crib. Mingo had grown old and was unable do a lot of work. Hiram sold his ox to a man at the stock sale that took place a mile east of Slonetown. Mingo was all he needed now. Hiram wasn't able to work like he used to. He was letting his pasture grow up because Susie couldn't pick all the grass. Small saplings grew where Bay, Sweetie and Polly used to clean the pasture and keep it clear of blackberry briars and vines. If Cullen had taken interest in farming like Hiram had when he was Cullen's age, the farm would have produced crops right on. But that was another thing that brought change to these mountains. People would not work like the older generation did, and Hiram didn't care for that.

Hiram was done for the day. He fed Mingo and Susie and, after milking the cow, he carried the milk to the house and took care of it. Mattie watched him. He'd hired Lizzie to watch Mattie while he worked. Lizzie was a kind soul that lived in Nathan's old farmhouse. She and her husband, Curly, had bought the place from the county and worked it for a few years before Curly died of a heart attack. Lizzie sold her land and kept just the homeplace to live in and a garden spot to tend. She got enough money from the land to live comfortably the rest of her life. In the summertime, she worked nearly every day in her garden doing something. She took care of a flock of chickens that kept her busy. She'd work in the hot sun in the middle of the day as the sun's rays beat down on her. She always wore a long dress that clung to her ankles and often drug the ground as she hoed her beans and sweet corn. A bonnet provided shade for her face as she worked along no matter how hot the sun got. The sleeves of her dress covered her arms completely leaving only part of her hands exposed. She was a devout Old Regular Baptist.

Hiram walked through the front door and glanced toward the sitting room. Mattie raised her eyes to glance at Hiram. Her lips moved into the famous crooked smile. She looked at Hiram as he went straight to the kitchen. She awkwardly held a small, knitted cloth in her raised, wobbly hand to show Hiram. Lizzie taught Mattie to sew. Smiling, she tried to move closer to the edge of the sofa but was unable to. She finally settled back against the back of the seat to rest from the attempt she'd made. Hiram sat down beside his daughter and hugged her close and bragged on the new knitted potholder.

He kissed her jaw and asked, "What do you want me to fix you for supper?"

Lizzie had already left the father and daughter to be alone together. Times like this is what Hiram loved. Mattie loved these times also. To him, there was nothing that compared to life just sitting and enjoying his little angel's company. He knew life was too short to not take pleasure in the little things, and it didn't take much to please Mattie. Just having her father there was all the joy she could stand in one day, anyway.

Hiram nudged her aside and rose from the sofa. He headed for the kitchen to build a fire in the cook stove. He loaded the firebox inside the iron stove with a piece of paper that he wrinkled up into a pile. He put an arm load of kindling on top of the paper and placed two split pieces of oak wood on the kindling, then lit the paper with a match. Before long, a roaring fire was burning in the firebox making the stove top hot. Then he went into the sitting room and helped Mattie walk to the breakfast table and sat her down. He greased the iron skillet to fry eggs. Then mixed flour with water and greased the other iron skillet to make a hoe-dab. Hiram warmed over left over dinner apples. In ten minutes, supper was ready. Hiram poured Mattie and himself a glass of milk and set out the cow butter. After putting a good helping of butter on top of Mattie's fried apples, he watched her eat. Hiram loved to watch her. He stopped only to help his daughter when she needed him too. He wanted her to be independent as much as possible. Supper was good.

The nights were cool, and good to take Mattie out on the porch to sit and listen to the night sounds that permeated from the mountainsides. This time of year, swamp frogs and

crickets were already gone, leaving only the sound of a barking fox. Sometimes the scream of a bob-cat could be heard.
Other times, the occasional hoot of an owl. Hiram carried
Mattie to the sofa, chunked the fire in the fireplace and threw
a large block of coal along with a shovel of slack to bank
the fire before retiring to bed. He heated water on the cook-
stove to later wash off with. He would wash Mattie off in the
morning.

He sat down on the sofa and began to tell her a story
about the early days of Troublesome Creek. How the land
was settled and the hardships his folks encountered when
they first moved here. She listened intently as she watched
the flames of fire dance around the grate, ashes falling to the
chimney floor. The burning embers looking like little stars
in the darkened room. Hiram covered her with a small blanket so she would be cozy. Mattie's eyes were wide as the
fire burned higher. Her eyes got wider, only to squint when
the flames died down. Hiram picked Mattie up and walked
into the bedroom so she could have privacy to use the slop-
jar. When she was through, she hollered for her father. He
helped her to the bed and covered Mattie with a quilt and
blanket before covering her body all the way to the neckline.
Hiram would always kiss his daughter good night.

He banked the fireplace with slack coal again and went to
bed. He was worn out in more ways than one. Mattie was
so sweet, but he yearned for an adult to talk to and spend
time with. He stared at the ceiling for hours thinking about

the past and the present and pondered about the future. He wondered if he had a future, and what it might bring. He dropped off to sleep and dreamed the rest of the night. He first dreamed about Mary Liz, then Alice Marie. He woke from his deep sleep with Mattie crying out, waking from a bad dream. She missed her mother so much. It worried Hiram of how this might affect his daughter's mental state. He always reassured her the best he could. He held Mattie until she went back to sleep. Then he slipped back under his covers to sleep the rest of the night.

Sunday morning came, and Hiram was glad it was church time. He wanted to see Dora again and be around her and the rest of the church brothers and sisters. He fixed an early breakfast, got Mattie ready, and they headed for Ben's Fork. Hiram watched Mattie as she glanced out the truck window. the air was too cold for the window to be rolled down. Hiram's truck heater didn't put out too much heat, so he threw a small blanket over Mattie to keep her warm. She was happy, even though her disability slowed her down. She caught her father looking at her. Mattie's head bobbled from the rough ride of the truck.

At Dora's, Mattie's face lit up as she became anxious to see the children. Hiram pulled into the small dirt lane and blew his horn, alerting Dora that they had arrived. The door of the house flew open and Lundy, as usual, was the first one out, followed by his smaller sister Ceroa. Joanna was always the last to come out the door. Dora held the door open for Joanna. Hiram helped Mattie out and squeezed the two younger children in the truck seat. He let Mattie nuss Ceora and Dora nussed Joanna. Lundy sat near the window. They were in close quarters, but Mattie wouldn't have it any other way. Hiram watched his daughter. She was so happy while in the presence of Dora and her siblings.

Hiram pulled into the church parking lot, parked against the side of the road and unloaded everybody. He and Dora helped Mattie inside the church house and set her down in the middle pew. Her brother, Lundy, sat with two of his classmates, while Ceora sat with Mattie. Joanna sat next to her boyfriend, Gaberal. There was a large crowd out this morning even though the weather was cold and frosty.

Clinton and Susanna walked through the door and down the aisles, greeting the crowd. He hugged the sisters and brothers. Both Clinton and his wife laughed as they met each one of the couples, not shunning any. Hiram watched his younger brother and said to himself, "Clinton would have been a perfect politician." But Hiram was glad that he hadn't entered any county races. Politics had become so crooked, and it was hard to believe anyone who ran for office anymore. Because of politics though, Slonetown got more paved roads, and the Kentucky government had built a state garage near the one room school. The highway department built more roads as the county expanded. The WPA had marked out roads throughout the county. In Slonetown, stone masons cut stone out of the native rock cliffs to build more houses of cobblestone, complete with windows and doors. The hardware store and the jail were still wooden planks, but the rest of town was built from cobblestone and brick. The jail was so weak, it was a thousand wonders they didn't have a jailbreak every week.

He watched Brother Lonzo walk down the aisle and the old preacher stopped to talk to Hiram for a minute. He told Hiram, "Dora's a good woman, and she would make some fine man a good wife."

Hiram blushed as he shook hands with the preacher. Hiram was really old enough to be Dora's father, but being older might be an advantage for the couple. Dora seemed to like Hiram, and she was just crazy over Mattie.

The service was filled with the anointing of the Holy Ghost as both Brother Lonzo and Clinton preached a short, but wonderful sermon. The sisters shouted while brothers sang toward the wind-up. Two converts came forth and told their experience and church carried on a little longer than usual. Both were baptized that day.

Hiram held Dora's hand as he led her back to the truck. Every car was still parked the same way as when they arrived. On the road, Hiram sang a church song as they drove along, with Mattie and Dora joining in as they went. At her house, Dora let Hiram walk her to the door and the children hollered goodbye before they went inside. Mattie was still seated in the truck cab.

Hiram spoke to Dora. "I enjoyed the outing today." He asked her if it would be all right to come to see her now and then.

Dora said, "Anytime, Hiram, will be okay with me." She let him bend over and kiss her cheek, then he walked back to the truck where Mattie waited on him.

This was the beginning of their courtship, which lasted only two months. The third Friday of March, Hiram picked Dora up at her place and they drove to Slonetown to get marriage licenses. At the courthouse Hiram asked for the licenses, and he and Dora drove by Clinton's place to see if he would perform the wedding. Clinton had been ordained to preach and perform the Gospel duties of the church for over a year now. Hiram had attended Clinton's ordination, and he thought it strange the way the church deacons questioned him as he sat in a chair. The chair had been placed in the middle of the room, with each brother asking Clinton questions on how he would handle himself under different situations. The sisters are not allowed to take a part in the ordination, but Hiram figured a few would have liked too. Some sisters thought they knew more about the Bible than the preachers did, but the Old Regular Baptists went by the scriptures and said the sisters are to remain silent in church work.

Clinton was sitting on his porch swing with Susanna by his side. They were talking to a couple from the church that had stopped by on their way home. Hiram figured that would work out fine, since he and Dora needed two witnesses to sign their license. Clinton was eager to perform the marriage. He used Susanna and the other woman to sign the marriage document after he had Hiram and Dora to say their vows. Hiram kissed Dora then offered to pay Clinton, but he refused to take any money. The newlyweds said goodbye and were on their way to Hiram's house to cook supper. Hiram thought as he drove along, "I really don't feel I'm married. Nothing like the first two times." But he was happy, and the rest didn't matter.

As he pulled into the lane, Lizzie was sitting on the porch. Mattie sat in a chair as she turned to see Hiram get out of his truck and help Dora out her side. Mattie eyed both as they walked to the porch steps and sat down in separate cane bottom chairs.

Lizzie congratulated the couple and rose from the chair saying, "I must go. Joanna is inside primping in front of the looking glass. Ceora is in her room and Lundy is over at the barn."

Then she left for her house, congratulating Dora again as she walked by, smiling.

Mattie looked up at her father as he walked by. He was showing Dora the bedroom where she placed her clothes and personal belongings on the bed and walked back to the sitting room. She sat down by Mattie and took her hand. Dora thought the world of Mattie and made over her every time she got the chance. She smiled as she took both of Mattie's hands and rubbed her palms. Mattie loved the attention she was receiving as she smiled her crooked smile, her lips trembling from the excitement. She was glad her father had married again. She'd been missing a woman's touch in her life. She would welcome the certain personal care that could only be handled by another woman.

Hiram built a fire in the cook stove and asked Mattie and Dora what they wanted for supper.

Dora quickly said, "Now, Hiram, that is my job. I'll take care of the cooking, cleaning and taking care of the children."

She walked to the kitchen, looked around to make sure where everything was located and went right to work. She was used to hard work. Before long, the kitchen smelled of frying food and cornbread. The familiar smell drifted into the sitting room where Hiram sat with Mattie. Ceora and Lundy came into the room, and Joanna watched from the bedroom as the two younger children sat down beside Mattie and joyfully played with her. Mattie squealed with delight. Hiram had never seen her happier, and he was glad.

Hiram had suffered through so much. Enough suffering that would do for two lifetimes. Death had robbed him of so many of his loved ones, and he wanted a little comfort for a while. He rose from the sofa and joined Dora in the kitchen, asking her if there was anything he could help with. He didn't carry on with her the same way he did with his first two wives. In fact, he hadn't ever even kissed or tried to kiss her, except at the wedding and one time when he brought her home from church. Everything had moved so fast. Hiram was true to treat his wife right. He would help raise her siblings and furnish a home for all of them. In return the only thing he expected was for Dora to help with all of Mattie's personal needs.

Hiram spent his time working at the barn and taking care of his garden and some corn he'd planted. Nothing like he used to tend. Dora waited on him hand and foot all the time whether he was inside or on the porch. Hiram felt guilty, really, because she did so much for him and Mattie too. He furnished her with the money she needed to keep the house going and to raise the children. He bought all their clothes and things they needed for school. Joanna was old enough to help out in the kitchen and help with the house cleaning. That helped Dora a lot.

Every Sunday they went to church somewhere, either Sandgap, Ben's Fork, Pointing Fork or Beach Creek. The children rode in the back of Hiram's pick-up if the weather permitted. If not, all rode in the cab. Clinton and all of the other churchgoers were so happy to see them. All the sisters made over Mattie so much that she begged her father to let her go home with some of them, but Hiram wouldn't hear of it. He figured she would do better to stay at home.

Clinton preached, followed by Brother Lonzo. A younger brother from Bolster County came next. Hiram had never heard this young brother before. Hiram liked him. He couldn't have been more than twenty years old, but he could touch Hiram with his loud voice and humble nature. When he began singing, Hiram noticed a familiarity about him. He had actions that were similar to Preacher Silas, a sure man of God whom Hiram had all the respect in the world for. Hiram's heart melted as quick as the young brother started, and when it was time for him to quit, Hiram didn't want him too.

After church broke. Hiram made his way to where he could shake hands with the young preacher. Hiram asked him his name. The young brother's eyes penetrated Hiram's waiting stare the same way Preacher Silas' always did. Hiram could feel the same warm stirring in his heart that had been there in earlier years.

"I'm John Belcher from the Little Jewel church over in Bolster County. My daddy was a preaching man, and I followed in his footsteps. Only been in the church three years," the young man boasted.

Hiram talked on for a minute and invited him to come back anytime. He talked to a couple of other visitors, then loaded his family into the pick-up and headed for Troublesome Creek. He stopped at the small store at the mouth of Ben's Fork and bought everyone a pop and bag of peanuts, except Mattie. He was afraid she might get choked on peanuts, so he bought her a moon pie. At the house, everyone laid around and rested while drinking their pop and eating their peanuts. Hiram and Dora poured their peanuts down into their pop.

Monday brought rain, so Hiram told Dora that he wanted to go to town for supplies. After milking, he helped Mattie into the truck beside Dora and told her to roll her window down a little. Mattie let her left arm rest on the truck door as her hair blew partly out the open window. She smiled from the side of her mouth as she watched the landscape go by. She was having a ball. It didn't take much to please her.

Dora's leg brushed up against Hiram's when the pick-up swerved on the stiff curve. Hiram didn't mind, but he wondered what Dora was thinking. He'd never touched her intimately yet, but he'd had thought about it few times while he lay on his bed at night. They slept in separate beds up to this point, and he figured she would make the move if their marriage ever came to being full.

In Slonetown, Hiram noticed how clean the streets were. A good crowd roamed the streets, back and forth, shopping from store to store. Slonetown had grown over the last five years, ever since the new communities came to be part of River County.

Slonetown had added two more grocery stores beside the two they already had. Another hardware store was in business now, competing with Grant and Sissy. There were two service stations to do mechanic work on automobiles and trucks, a new car dealership, a new barber shop, an additional shoe cobbler and a new modern jail house made of bricks. The jail was complete with bars and locks. Three clothing stores, a dime store, a pool hall, several law offices, two doctor offices and two church houses – one Baptist and the other Methodist – had also sprung up. Slonetown had grown into a bustling little town.

Men sat on benches jawing with one another while some whittled and others dropped swapped their knives. Some were trading guns and just visiting, telling about whatever had happened since the last time they were together. A new courthouse had been constructed of cut cobble stone, replacing the old wooden one. The new courthouse was complete with offices for the sheriff, clerks, prosecuting attorney and tax collector. Two hotels made up of the rest of the town, with new dwelling houses here and there.

Hiram took Dora and Mattie to Sissy's store. Claire Polly met Hiram as he walked through the door. He stepped out of her way to let her pass. She gave him a frowning look as she passed by, gazing at Dora. She did grin at Mattie though. She'd been mad ever since Hiram and Dora married. She wanted Hiram for herself, and she put in against Hiram wherever she could, even at church. Claire thought Dora was too young for Hiram and that she would eventually cause him trouble. Hiram tipped his hat at Claire, and this made her madder than before. Swishing her dress tail, she turned swiftly and walked down the steps to the sidewalk and swayed toward Madden's Five and Dime. Hiram knew she was mad, but he figured she would get over it.

Sissy came running to hug Mattie and greet Hiram and

Dora. She embraced all three and spun Mattie around while she held her close so she wouldn't fall. Sissy adored Mattie, and Hiram had in his mind if something happened to him, Sissy would take Mattie in and care for her as long as she lived.

Mattie felt the same about her aunt and uncle Grant. Mattie smiled her crooked smile as air escaped from her lips in a whistling sound. She had trouble breathing fast because her breath was a little late being exhaled. It made her feel lightheaded, but she enjoyed every minute of the close attention she received. Immediately, Sissy gave Mattie a piece of coconut candy. Mattie bit a piece of it off, chewing until the candy made her mouth water. Candy and saliva ran down her chin. Mattie liked coconut candy better than any other kind.

Grant was working the post office this morning. Grant had expanded it twice, and he had plans to build somewhere in town just for doing post office business only. Dar Higgins had gotten too old, so a new mail carrier worked the mail toward Troublesome Creek now. He was a white man from Breeding's Creek. His name was Buford Collier. Hiram liked Buford, and he always was good to the new mail man. Hiram liked and respected him. He even gave him vegetables from his garden.

There was a post office in every community just a few miles apart now. Mason owned a small store and kept the post office in it. Bundy was what the post office was called, and it was just below Hiram's house. Hiram wanted to put in a country store but had waited, fearing it would interfere with Mason's business. Hiram traded with him when he needed small things like flour and sugar or just household things and such. If he needed larger items he traded in Slonetown.

Hiram gave Dora money to buy whatever she needed for the house and for Mattie. He bought a new pair of boots and a new hat. The hat was a black wide brimmed hat with a fancy ring just above the brim. Hiram tried the hat on and looked at himself in the looking glass hanging on the wall beside the counter. Dora was paying attention to him and so were two other young ladies. She didn't like the stares they were giving Hiram a bit. She walked up to Hiram and took his arm and looked at Hiram's reflection in the mirror, smiling up at him as she claimed her territory then and there. She wasn't about to let any other woman enjoy or even entertain the notion that Hiram wasn't already taken. Mattie was watching everything, not missing a thing. She had a disability that held her body down but nothing escaped her eyes and mind. She smiled her crooked smile and looked upward at Sissy, who still held to the young girl's body to keep Mattie from falling.

Hiram helped Sissy put the goods they bought in brown paper bags. He told Dora to load the things onto the pick-up. He wanted to see Cassie. The last time they talked, Cassie had told him she might be able to help Mattie. "With the help of leg braces, she might do well." Hiram had thought about this and even dreamed about seeing Mattie walk as others did. He'd made his mind up. He would get whatever she needed if it helped her. Sissy would keep Mattie until he and Dora returned.

Cassie was seeing a patient as Hiram walked into her office. The little girl was being held by the child's mother. She squirmed in her mother's lap, trying to get away from Cassie. Cassie was examining her ears and throat, but the young girl was not having it. She cried every breath. The little girl's mouth was wide open as she turned red in the face from losing her breath. Finally, she caught it and screamed at the top of her lungs. Hiram had seen things like this before when Dora's sister Ceora got mad about something and took a fit. Ceora would jump up and down and cry just as loud as she could. Hiram would laugh at her. She would then run to the bedroom and stay there for an hour or longer. But she came out when supper was ready. The young girl would sit down at the table and eat like nothing had ever happened.

After the woman and girl left, Cassie asked Hiram how he was doing.

"Fine as a frog hair and ready to work my fields for another year." Cassie hugged him, smiled and sat back down in her swivel chair turning to Hiram.

She said, "I see more white hair on that top; more than there used to be. You need to take it easy instead of planning to plow all day in the hot sun. If you have to work at something, do something light."

He watched his daughter as her face showed concern for him. His lungs had gotten worse, and he'd had walking pneumonia twice last year. But Hiram wasn't ready to give up and do nothing. He rather be dead than to be housed up all winter and summer.

"What kind of life would that be?" He said to her when the subject came up. Hiram didn't look sick, but looks are deceiving.

Hiram changed his tune and asked if she'd inquired about the foot and leg braces for Mattie. Cassie walked over to the window and looked outside, then turned back to her father and said, "Yal, they have them down in Louisville, but they are expensive. Each brace is fifteen hundred dollars apiece. That's three thousand dollars beside the expense of traveling to Louisville and back. Quite a bit of money."

She watched her father's face grimace when she told him the price of the braces.

He thought a minute and looked out the window toward the courthouse. "I'll get the money somehow," he said as he rose from his seat and hugged his daughter. He left for the pick-up and opened the door for Dora. Then he drove to Sissy's store to pick up Mattie. Dora helped Mattie in her side and grinned at Hiram as he slid in beside his wife. Hiram started the engine and headed for Troublesome Creek and home. He didn't speak much as they drove along. Dora figured he was thinking, so she left him alone. After supper, everyone sat on the porch until bedtime. Hiram was tired. He retired early.

Sunday morning was cool but a good day for church going. Hiram had all the chores done before eight o'clock. The
door to the corn crib had fallen halfway down. Only one
steel hinge still held the door on the entrance. The wooden
door swung from the crib cock-eyed. Hiram had meant to
buy new hinges but had put it off. Seems like he forgot about
them every time he was in Slonetown. "No matter," He
thought." He didn't raise corn like he used to. His pastureland was growing up with young saplings and blackberry
briars. It was not clean like it used to be when he had a cow,
horse and mule.

Hiram did not like to work on Sunday, but the crib door
needed to close to keep the chickens out. He found an old
pair of brogan shoes, cut out the tongue, and nailed the leather tongue to the door. This would work as a hinge until he
could buy one from the hardware store in Slonetown.

Hiram washed his face in the wash basin near the sink
and was ready to sit down to breakfast. Dora cooked well.
No wonder she'd kept house since she was a young girl. She
set a good table, and Hiram was delighted. He helped Mattie
to the table and set her in a chair. She claimed this particular
part of the table and wouldn't let anyone else use it, not even
her father. Hiram was happy this morning as he watched
Mattie eat. Mattie was watching Lundy and Ceora. Ceora
was mad at Lundy from last night. Hiram asked her why she

was so mad.

Ceora replied, "Lundy let a biggin after we went to bed last night. I'm still mad at him."

Her face turned a bright pink as Lundy snickered at her. Hiram just smiled, not wanting to hurt Ceora's feelings. If he'd been outside somewhere he would had had himself a good laugh, but he held it in.

Dora was ready, and she loaded the children in the pick-up. Hiram started the engine and let out on the clutch and drove toward Sandgap Church. A large crowd had gathered. Almost every parking place was taken. Hiram pulled the truck across the creek to the flat bottom and parked. As they walked toward the church, Clinton stopped him.

He said, "Well we don't have to worry about who killed Baskam Owens. When I was in Bolster County for church last Sunday, brother Lige Greely told me. Baskam's widow, Martha, owned up to killing her long dead husband. She'd been sick and joined the church. While giving her testimony, she owned up to killing Baskam. So that solves that mystery for good."

Hiram said, "Can't imagine her doing that. She was always so timid. But you can never tell," He shook his head in disbelief. They all walked into the church and sat down.

Claire Polly stared a hole through Hiram and Dora both. Hiram just shrugged it off and told Dora to do the same. "You have to look over her," He said, "Her mind is not right, and she's always been jealous. She couldn't stand the sight of Alice Marie and Alice Marie felt the same way about her."

Hiram watched the gossiper as she walked toward the stage, shaking hands and throwing her arms every which a way. She stopped to glance at the back pews where Hiram and Dora sat before finally taking a seat. Hiram thought, "If Preacher Silas was still alive, she wouldn't act this way. She'd be dealt with by the full authority of the church." The church had changed just like everything else. Nothing stayed the same, and Hiram felt sad.

When the church began singing, Hiram's mind was raised to a place of peacefulness. He couldn't and didn't want to let anything take away from his joy, and he wasn't about to let someone like Claire Polly interfere.

Before church started, children played. Men and women talked. Babies cried. But when the singing started, everything and everyone became quiet, even the babies. Hiram watched the full operation of the church. After the singing was complete, Brother Lonzo came forth and opened church with a roaring sermon. He preached on the wily ways of Satan and how cunning he was. He ended his sermon with a shout and called for a brother to start the song *Amazing Grace.*' As quick as the song was finished, he offered prayer to the only God of the universe and of the world the same God that ruled the seas and the heavens all over the world and even in a lowly place like River County and Troublesome Creek. Hiram marveled at Brother Lonzo's knowledge of the scriptures.

There were several 'amens' as the preacher rose to his feet and looked the congregation over before he took his seat. Claire Polly crouched in her seat from his intense stare, trying to hide from him. She felt guilty as sin. He didn't have to point fingers at anyone; his stare did the job every time.

Clinton followed next with a heartfelt song. His mellow voice blended with the soft noises of the church-goers as the sisters wept and the brothers moaned. Hiram watched as his brother's countenance changed when the Spirit took over. The Spirit sent Clinton into another realm that would almost be unbelievable, had Hiram not experienced the revelations himself. Dora cried as she sat next to Mattie. Mattie's trembling hand wiped tears from her face with the handkerchief her father had given her.

Clinton's sermon changed into the softest words that Hiram had ever heard as they flowed from his mouth just as fast as they were formed. The sisters began shouting from their seats. Mavis moved about the church house as she shook hands with everyone there. When she was through, she slowly sank into her seat. She waved the handkerchief in front of her face, trying to cool off. She blew air past quivering lips, trying to clear her nasal passages at the same time. Hiram felt a new sense of wanting salvation, but it left after the church came to an end and dismission was called. He knew he needed to be stronger, but he just couldn't help it. He knew he had to hold on to the Spirit with both hands and he promised he would the next time.

Outside, Hiram greeted as many of the crowd as he could. He shook hands with the men as the sisters hugged him and told him how much they loved him. He welcomed each handshake and hug as he introduced Dora to the ones she didn't know. Everyone seemed to like her, except Claire. Claire snubbed her nose and entered her car and drove in the direction of Betty's Troublesome.

Hiram, Dora and her siblings, and Mattie got into the pick-up truck and headed for Troublesome. Hiram clutched the truck and it lurched forward with a quick jolt, as Hiram let the truck ease out onto the highway in bull-dog gear. Immediately, he shifted the standard transmission into first gear, making the pick-up speed up. By the time Hiram hit third gear, the truck moved on the road smooth and easy. The only time the truck bounced was when the road had a pothole in it. Mattie enjoyed the ride so much with her window rolled down. The brisk air caused Mattie's eyes to water. Dark black hair blew around her face and neck and it was all Mattie could do to keep it straight and in place. Lundy, Ceora and Joanna rode in the back. Hiram let Lundy ride the tailgate sometimes if they were only going a short distance. The young lad would let his feet hang down from the lowered gate, as he held on to the chained latches that supported the tail-gate that kept it level.

At home, they all went inside the boxed house. Hiram and Dora fixed dinner. Dora told Lundy to take the woven basket and gather the eggs. Dora had a good flock of chickens and raised them all for eggs and for frying and cooking. She had a little Banty hen the color of blue. Its feathers were slick in nature and when they had moisture on them their color was a tinted grayish blue. She loved that little Banty and watched it like a hawk to make sure the little hen would not come to any demise. She knew her flock just like the back of her hand. When Hiram asked her about a certain pullet, she'd always tell him, "That's the blue hen's chicken." Dora never let her set on any Banty eggs, it always had to be big stock hen eggs. The Banty was a perfect mother hen. She didn't ever lose a ditler. She'd fight anything twice her size when it came to her brood.

After dinner, Hiram laid around the rest of the afternoon. He wanted to rest all he could before next week when the planting season came. He had his garden and bottom plowed last week by his friend, Theodore. Theodore lived two miles up the road, towards Rolly Joe Mountain. He'd made decent money, working the small truck mines on Defeated Creek. He received twenty dollars a shift for eight hours of work. He saved his money and bought a new Ford tractor and a set of plows and disks. Hiram loved to watch that tractor turn ground. When Theodore plowed, Hiram would sit and watch until he was finished. Hiram had a new white barked woven chair he packed to the shade of the August Start apple tree. His thoughts were about what he could have accomplished if he'd owned a tractor when he farmed his bottom land. Cattle grazed most of them now. Hiram only planted enough of his bottoms to raise enough corn to feed the livestock.

Supper came early that evening, and after he and Dora sat on the porch with Mattie, swinging in the porch swing. Hiram wanted to buy braces for Mattie's legs to help her walk. He didn't know where he was going to get the money, but those were his plans. He had some money saved up but knew what the cost of the braces would be a lot more then he had. Bedtime came early so he laid down and dreamed all night.

A stranger came to Hiram's door on a Monday morning. The sun had burned away a huge April fog as the sounds of roosters crowed from neighbors' chicken flocks. A rain crow called from the backside pasture, promising a future rainstorm. The stranger was dressed in a two piece suit that was a thin gray. His white shirt and tie made him look neat to the appearance, and he was very polite. He was young, probably in his mid-twenties, sporting a short black mustache. His eyes were hazel, and his complexion was a light tan. He stood tall. Hiram figured six foot three. He held a pen and notebook in his left hand and offered Hiram his right hand to shake.

Hiram shook hands with the young man and welcomed him to a seat on the porch. Hiram offered him a dipper of water from the aluminum bucket. He always kept a fresh bucket of water sitting on the basin near the door. He kept the water cold with ice cubes from the Frigidaire's ice box. He never let the water get hot. If it did, he drew a fresh bucket from the dug well.

The young man drank a dipper full of the water and reached the dipper back to Hiram.

He said, "My name is Canton Miller, and I represent Black Panther Coal Company. I want to make you an offer on leasing your coal minerals. The Black Panther Coal Company is prepared to offer you twenty-five cents a ton for every ton of coal that we extract from your land. We will have to build a road across your pasture to get to the number four seam though." The young man took another breath and began again. "We will not disturb no more of your land than we have too."

He watched as Hiram looked towards the hillside, directly behind the barn. So many memories he had of that hillside. "They were mostly good," he thought. He waited a few more minutes before he spoke. Hiram knew he could use the money, but he didn't know if he was ready to let a dozer gouge around his property, tearing up his fertile farmland.

He leaned back in the chair and said, "Let me sleep on your offer. Come back to see me next week on Thursday. I'll have an answer for you."

The young man shook hands with Hiram, sealing the future appointment. Then he stepped off the porch and drove his automobile down Troublesome Creek. Hiram watched the car as it drove out of sight, leaving a cloud of smoke behind. He sat there in his chair for a few more minutes then walked into the house and closed the door behind him.

The next morning, Hiram was up early. He ate breakfast in silence. He guessed Dora wondered what was on his mind this morning, but he didn't offer her any explanation. He kept his thoughts to himself and just as soon as breakfast was finished, he walked toward the barn. Fog covered Troublesome Creek. At the barn, he fed Mingo and wished he had a cow to milk. He'd been buying his milk from his neighbor or from the store down the road. Hiram was glad because he didn't have to drive all the way to Slonetown to buy something when he needed it. He leaned against the new fence post that stood near the draw-bars. His mind was remembering the days gone by when he and Poppy plowed and grubbed these new grounds to raise food for the table and for the livestock. It hurt his feelings to even think about giving in to anything that would change his life or his livelihood, but he knew he needed the money. Money that might give Mattie a chance to walk or do better then what she could do right now. His sleep was troubled that night, and dreams filled his head most of the night. He dreamed of Mattie being able to walk and take steps from inside the house to the porch and sat in the porch swing. Her crooked smile radiated across her face as her eyes sparkled. She was happy. Hiram almost cried as he thought about his dreams. "That's all I want is for her to be happy. I've had my happiness," He said. He yearned for hers. He looked toward the pasture one more time before walking back to the barn.

As he passed the dogwood point he couldn't help noticing how peaceful Troublesome Creek was. He could see how the white blooms matched the color of the clouds as they floated the sky. As they drifted along lazily, the clouds looked like the cotton gauze Cassie used in her doctor's office. The ground where the sassafras saplings stood held a variety of white blooms from the puccoon and wild trilliums. Lady Slippers grew in abundance throughout the sapling thicket. Hiram used the roots of the sassafras tree to boil tea and make the house have a sweet aroma. As he stood gazing at the dogwood point he made his mind up saying to himself,"I can't think only of myself. I have to think of Mattie and her well being." He walked into the house and sat down on the sofa, satisfied that he was doing the right thing.

Chapter 3

Thursday came, and Hiram was up early. He sat on the porch waiting for the mine representative to come by. It was a warm morning with a hint of rain. Dark clouds passing over the mountains stirred the east winds. Rain was needed for his garden and the only bottom he tended to raise corn. He thought of Cullen and wondered how he was getting along. Cullen hadn't been by to see him in over six months, and Hiram figured he was working too much for him to visit. Cullen and his wife Ruby already had two children, one girl and one boy. The girl's name was Alice Marie, after her grandma. The boy's name was Jimmy. Hiram loved his grandchildren and wished to see them more often.

He heard a car driving toward his house. The vehicle drove up to his yard and the car door opened. It was Mr. Miller. He carried an arm full of papers as he walked toward the porch. He climbed the steps and sat down beside Hiram, reaching his hand out for Hiram to shake. After they shook hands, Mr. Miller spread the paper forms in front of him. The young Miller rattled off words to him as Hiram listened intently, his mind trying to take hold of all the terms and conditions the young man mentioned. After five minutes of talking Hiram asked the man if it would be all right for him to take the papers to let his lawyer look them over.

"Why sure, Mr. Daniels. Take these and I will be back here next Monday, at noon." He thanked Hiram and rose from his chair and left.

Hiram told Dora to get Mattie ready, "We are going to town."

Dora got Mattie ready while Ceora and Joanna rushed to catch the school bus. Lundy had stayed with a friend in Slonetown.

Hiram helped Mattie down the steps and opened the truck door for her. Dora had already slipped into the middle of the truck seat so Mattie could sit by the window. Mattie loved the wind blowing in her face as the truck rolled down the road toward Slonetown. Hiram could hardly reach the gear shift as he fumbled for control to change gears. He managed when Dora moved her body over toward where Mattie sat. Mattie sat with her eyes glued to the countryside as the pickup bounced along. Hiram turned onto the better paved road and the truck rode smoother.

Hiram's mind was on the leasing of his coal minerals and wondering if he should sign the papers that rested on the truck's dashboard. He noticed two new mine openings as he drove by Lem Wilson Road and Turners Branch. A loaded truck was inching off the meandering haul road that led out of the holler. The red cab, ten wheel tandem truck was over-loaded with the black mineral. The truck's mudflaps drug on the blacktop as the driver slowly pulled onto the high-way. The truck swayed under the weight of the coal. Hiram thought as he followed the truck for a while, "That coal will end up at a power plant to generate electricity." So much change had come to Troublesome Creek, and Hiram did not like it. He wanted more than anything to have the money for his little girl's braces, but he did not like the thought of making scars on his mountainsides. Mine openings where there used to be pastureland and fields of fresh grubbed new grounds plagued his mind. He passed planted corn plants that waved in the blowing wind as waves on the oceans. Waves of water moving with force then eddying back out into the vast sea. He mumbled to himself, "Now soon there will be gouged out dirt for roads and level spots where the coal company's tipple would be built." He did not like it and he was having cold feet whether he would allow his land, land that had provided him a livelihood and his people be-fore, to be mined. "I've always protected it from whatever tried to destroy or take it away." He wasn't happy thinking about it.

As he drove by the country store where the one-room school stood. He thought about the larger schools that the county board had constructed. The new grade schools housed all eight grades under one roof and two new high schools across River County besides the one in Slonetown.

The board had built one near Cody they named Ben's Fork and one on the lower end of the county to serve the community of Ross's creek, called Ross's Creek.

Even the churches had changed. Church buildings were built in several hollers and even in Slonetown. And they weren't all Old Regular Baptists either. Slonetown had two new churches, one Missionary and one Methodist. There was even a United Baptists. "There is religion everywhere "He thought. In each community there had sprang up a post office, calling each after someone or someplace. Spider, on Ben's Fork was where Cullen and his wife lived, just beyond Joe Romeo's bridge. Hiram hoped he could see him before long, but he wouldn't let his mind linger there for now. Too many other things to attend too.

Hiram guided his pick-up into the concrete parking lot and parked. He told Dora to buy the supplies they needed and shop for clothes for her and her siblings. "I'll take Mattie with me. Be sure and get Mattie a candy bar from the store. We'll meet back here."

He helped Mattie out and walked her to the law office and found a seat for her to sit in. He walked to the open window and told the attendant he wished to speak to Mr. Johnson. Ralph Johnson was from Rolly Joe Creek, a distant descendant of Tivis Slone, and was supposed to be one of the smartest lawyers to set up a practice since Ballard. The attendant told him to come back into a separate room. Hiram told Mattie to sit still and he would be back in a moment.

Hiram opened the door of the office and entered into the dark room. He could never figure out why law offices were dark and dimly lit. Shelves of books lined the walls behind where the lawyer sat. A large light fixture hung from the ceiling with a cluster of light bulbs under round globes. The light fixture broke the darkness as much as they could but not accomplishing what Hiram wanted. Mr. Johnson stared out his window. When Hiram walked in, he reached out his hand to the waiting lawyer. The lawyer turned in his swinging chair and shook hands with Hiram's right hand and with his left hand motioned Hiram to a cushioned seat. Hiram thought to himself, "This lawyer must be pretty good to afford furnishings like these." Hiram sat down and stared around the room and then stared at the lawyer. Mr. Johnson was young, maybe twenty-five. He was clean shaven and had a brand new haircut. His features were plain, except for his slightly flat nose that ended abruptly at the top of his lips. He dressed in a two piece suit that was blue suede with light stripes. Hiram had never seen a cleaner person anywhere. Even his fingernails were clean. Cleaner than any lady's nails he'd seen before. Hiram immediately took a liking to Mr. Johnson as soon as he smiled. When he smiled, his lips reached into the corners of his mouth, where they ended with deep dimples on each side of his cheeks.

Hiram introduced himself. "I'm Hiram Daniels, and I need some legal advice on a matter," he said as he reached the papers to the young lawyer. Mr. Johnson quickly took the papers and opened them and scoured the pages one by one. His eyes roamed the forms as his eyebrows danced up and down while he read. When the lawyer was finished, he sat back in his seat and held the mining papers extended high in his left hand, rubbing his jaw with his right palm.

He said, "The papers are in correct order, except for the price that they are giving you for each ton mined. Over in Perry and Breathitt Counties, companies are paying two dollars a ton. I hear in Pike County, they are paying two-fifty a ton. That beats the karn out of twenty-five cents." He smiled his dimpled smile and twisted his swiveled plush chair as he placed the papers in front of him on his desk.

Hiram didn't like what the lawyer told him. He didn't like anyone trying to take advantage of him and short-changing him. His face flushed a bright red as he sat there in the dark office.

Mr. Johnson finally broke the silence saying, "When you get ready to draw up a mining lease, come by here, and I'll make sure that you are compensated right and I won't charge you an arm and a leg." He could tell Hiram wasn't pleased with the mining company's offer.

Hiram rose from his seat and shook hands with the lawyer and said, "I will."

He turned and opened the door to where an anxious Mattie awaited. Mattie's crooked smile advanced across her face, telling Hiram she was glad he didn't keep her waiting any longer. He helped Mattie to her feet, and they walked out to the pick-up, where Dora awaited in the front seat.

Hiram helped Mattie in his side and slid in under the steering wheel, started the truck and drove back to Troublesome. It was dinner time when they arrived home. Hiram had made a decision. No mining on his property at this time. He really didn't want to tear up his land anyway and when the lawyer explained the drawn up papers were not right, he made his mind up. He was sure there would be another route to Mattie's happiness.

Chapter 4

The May's sun light bounced off the mountains and hill-sides under a clear blue sky. Troublesome Creek's clear waters splashed along peaceful as it flowed over rocks and boulders. Bubbles and foam formed at the drop-offs under the stream bed where the boulders' sides submerged under the flowing water. Hiram sat on his porch enjoying the beauty of the bloomed hillsides and listening to the sounds of the singing birds. Dora's Banty rooster crowed right along with her Silver Laced Wyandott trying to out match him but he was too little to compete with the larger breed. Dora's blue hen, Banty clucked as she pawed and scratched the ground for edible worms and bugs that the plowed ground had to offer. A Red Tail hawk circled the sky but was soon scared away when a flock of crows irritated it. It was Monday morning, and Hiram awaited the promised arrival of the mining representative.

He watched the car pull into his yard, stop, and the young man rolled his window down. He opened his door and walked up the steps to the porch and greeted Hiram as he sat in his porch swing. Mattie looked out through the screen door at the stranger. She held to the screen door handle for support. Hiram helped her out to sit with him on the swing.

The stranger shook hands with Hiram and nodded to Mattie. Mattie glanced up at her father as the stranger opened his large envelope of papers and said, "Did you show your papers to your lawyer, and did he tell you everything was in order?"

Hiram nodded his head and told the stranger he did.

"But everything was not in order, and I've decided not to lease my coal at this time."

The mining representative looked at Hiram, puzzled, and asked, "Why not?"

Hiram stopped the swing and moved his hips to the swing's edge and said, "I don't want my land tore apart for a dollar or two. It has made a living for me all my life, so I'm going to leave it the way it is for the time being. My remaining timber will bring enough money to get braces for my Mattie here."

After trying to persuade Hiram to let his company mine Hiram's mineral, the mine representative gave up and left. Hiram figured that would be the last time he saw him.

Hiram helped Mattie to the table and sat her down in her place. Dora was finishing putting dinner out. She cooked Hiram's favorite, strawberry dumpling with cornbread. Hiram grinned at Dora as she patted his back. Hiram and Dora still didn't sleep together, and their relationship was still on business terms only. It really didn't bother Hiram because he had other worries to keep his mind full. He did think about it at times, especially when he caught a glimpse of her nakedness as she sponged herself clean. He didn't make it a habit catching her bathing, it just happened. It had been a year and a half now since Alice Marie died. There were many lonely nights he spent tossing and turning, sometimes until daylight. There was too much pride in Hiram to take advantage of Dora in any way. He felt himself lucky to have her. She took care of Mattie's personal needs. Mattie attached herself to Dora and to Dora's two sisters and brother, adopting them as her own family.

Hiram spent a lot of time at his barn busying himself in his work. He did a lot of thinking while there. Lee John died a year ago now, and that affected Hiram in a way far from anything that had happened in his life lately. Lee John died of heart dropsy just like Mommy. He was the first one of the Daniels that was embalmed by the undertaker in Slonetown. He was kept up for three nights and buried on the dogwood point on a sunny day. Mommy had always told him, "If it rains during a wake, it means a soul has went to heaven. The rain falling is the angels crying." Hiram didn't know about such, and he figured no one else does either.

All of Lee John's children came in, and Russel stayed until Sarah sold her place and she moved to the state of Washington with him. Russell told Hiram, "There is plenty of work out there, and logging companies beg people to work."

Astor Campbell bought Lee John's place and started building boxed houses for renters.

Ebbie died a year before Lee John did. They buried her beside Reldon. Neither one of her girls came in for the wake. Hiram didn't like the word funeral. He still called it a wake. He thought calling it a funeral seemed so final. There was a big crowd at Ebbie's wake. People came from all over River County to pay their respects to her, and to no wonder. She prepared just about every corpse around, far and near. She would be missed.

Hiram held dear to Clinton and Sissy. They were the only remaining siblings left, and the feeling left Hiram wanting. Wanting it to be the way it was when everyone was young, enjoying life here on Troublesome Creek. But he knew it could never be. But he could dream.

Hiram heard a car pull into the yard and heard the car door open. He glanced a look toward the house and watched a woman figure get out, tagging two young'uns behind her. Then the car drove away. The woman walked up the steps onto the porch and knocked on the front door. Hiram quickly walked to the house and asked her if he could help her.

The woman spun around, startled like, and said, "Why Hiram you don't recognize us, do you? I'm Ruby Daniels, and these are my two young'uns, your grandchildren."

Hiram's face blushed with embarrassment. "The law sent Cullen to the federal pen for a year. My daddy too. They got caught for making moonshine. Daddy is spending his time in

Georgia, and Cullen was sent to Catlettsburg."

She hesitated a minute, then said on, "Mommy can't keep us. I'm wondering if you might put us up for a while." She was about to cry, her lips shaking, her eyes a bloodshot red. Hiram looked at the children as they hoovered around their mother's skirt tails, trying to hide their faces from the stranger that stared at them. The oldest boy stood directly behind his mother, and he was the spitting image of Cullen when Cullen was that age, blonde hair and blue eyes with dimpled cheeks, his whole face covered with freckles.

Dora opened the door and stepped out on the porch, watching the visitors that had appeared on the Daniels porch. Hiram told Dora to get a drink of milk for the children and offered coffee for Ruby. Hiram didn't know what to think. His thoughts whirled in his head as fast as they could without stepping on top of each other. Finally, he said, "When did they send Cullen off?"

Ruby quickly answered him, "Day before yesterday. A bus picked him, Daddy and two other prisoners up behind the Slonetown jail and hauled them away. I don't know if he'll have to stay the whole year they gave him or not."

Her eyes had a hopeful glance that the government would be lenient to him.

Hiram said, "All of you sit here on the porch." Hiram told Dora to follow him out to the barn.

Hiram told his wife, "I'll have to build an extra room for them if they stay. Ruby will have to do her part of work, taking care of her children and help with the cooking and cleaning. Maybe I can talk to the governor, and maybe he will pardon Cullen early. I want you to be willing to take on the new responsibilities if you will. I'm not going to try to force anything on you."

Dora looked at Hiram, her eyes softly saying before she ever spoke, "We can't have them out with nowhere to stay, Hiram."

Hiram hugged his wife. It was the first time since that day they were married. It felt almost sinful to Hiram, but he felt a surge of passion stir in him. A passion that had been absent for so long now. "Too long," He thought. He and Dora walked back to the house, walking closer together.

Hiram told Ruby they could stay. "Dora will show you where to put your belongings."

Hiram watched as Ruby picked up a large paper poke and crowded the two children inside the front door. Hiram sat down in his favorite rocking chair looking down the holler toward his bottom of corn thinking to himself, "I'll have to raise more food to feed everyone." He looked toward the barn and figured it was time to buy another milk cow. He'd run to Slonetown tomorrow to buy supplies and inquire if anyone might have a good Gursney for sale.

June set in dry, and his extra crops were doing good. Hiram bought a large Gursney milk cow that gave enough milk to feed his family, and there was even extra to sell. He'd sold all of his timber. He saved the money planning to spend the money on braces for Mattie, but now he would have to use some of it to build more room for Ruby and his grandchildren. That way they could have a little privacy. Hiram soon adjusted to having the little ones around the house, and Mattie was thrilled to death. She had more fun out of them than a little. Hiram figured it was worth seeing her happy and smiling.

Clinton helped him build the rooms, and Susanna took up with Ruby right away. They talked and talked about how hard it is to be separated from your husband. Susanna and Ruby worked alongside Dora doing the housework, cleaning and washing. Dora watched Hiram work on the extra room that would be Ruby's and her children's home until Cullen was released from the penitentiary. Dora left Susanna and Ruby to do the washing, while she helped Hiram hold planks for him to nail. Secretly, Dora loved Hiram but wasn't about to let on, afraid he'd reject her. Dora seemed pleased to be allowed to help as they went about building the room. She lifted as Hiram nailed the boards Clinton sawed for him. In four days, the room was completed, roofed and ready to move in.

Ruby thanked Hiram just every chance she got, saying, "I just don't know what I was going to do. I'm in a family way again already, and it is due this fall."

She sat down on the bed that Hiram moved into the room, looking around nervously. Her and the children would all have to sleep in the same bed, but at least they would be fed and dry. Hiram grinned at his oldest grandchild, Jimmy. Jimmy grinned back at his grandfather and hurriedly took his place on the bed beside his mother. He reached for his younger sister, eight-year-old Alice Marie. Ruby rose from the bed and walked out on the porch where Susanna and Clinton were. Clinton held Susanna's hand as they swung in the porch swing. Hiram could tell Ruby was jealous of the closeness the couple were enjoying. Ruby's face showed a smile, but Hiram could see a longing in her eyes that she had never experienced before but she wanted too. Cullen was never close to his wife or children. Hiram and Dora were enjoying the rest with them when Alice Marie ran out on the porch crying and jumped into Ruby's lap. Jimmy followed closely, hugging his mother's knees. Ruby asked the girl, "What's the matter?"

Alice Marie raised her eyes toward her mother's and said, "Jimmy let a biggin, Mommy. He's rotten!"

She made a face as she snarled her freckled nose. Everyone laughed, especially Mattie. Hiram could tell Mattie was excited, showing her gum-line. Mattie watched the girl as she sat in her mother's lap. Hiram told Mattie to come to him. She walked with the help of Dora and stood in front of her father. He turned his daughter around and pulled her into his lap. Mattie was happy as she watched Alice Marie look at her. Mattie loved to be petted by her father. They had been through so much together.

The women cooked a large meal for supper, and Clinton asked a blessing for the food as they all sat down to eat. Hiram watched his grandchildren eat. They were hungry, and Hiram was glad he could provide for them. He was hoping this would draw him and Cullen closer. He couldn't help but worry about him and all the things he was doing and getting himself into. Clinton and Susanna went home as the sun set in the bright orange western sky. Hiram sat and viewed the colored sky and wondered how dry this spell would be. He was ready for bed. He'd worked hard all day, and his body was paining some from arthritis. He laid down in his bed and waited for Dora to slip under the covers with him. They would have to sleep together for a while because of the company. Hiram felt shy at first as he first turned his back to Dora but for some reason he turned to face her. Their eyes met in the semi-darkness. She was studying his features as they lay there. Hiram reached for her and she didn't resist as she wilted in his strong arms. Hiram kissed Dora's willing and hungry lips. They were moist as ripe strawberries fresh from the vine, wet and soft. He kissed her long and wanting, burning with a desire that had been missing from his life for a long time. Dora cried out low moans from his sweet touches as the couple became one in nature, branching together. Dora was fresh as a white daisy, blooming early in the midsummer's July heat as they both clung together. Hiram held Dora until her breathing smoothed. He slipped out of her arms and laid on his back.

The white man had quit carrying the mail, and Dar Higgins' son, Lawson, had taken over the route. Lawson wasn't as easy to get along with as Dar was. He was more independent with his ways and feelings. Proud as a peacock he was. He still lived on Colored Holler. Lawson had finished high school and talked about going to college, but for some reason he didn't. Talk around town was he'd gotten a white girl big with child and she left River County. If she hadn't it is untelling what the people would have done with Lawson. People weren't ready to accept a colored and white person marrying or living together in River County. Hiram figured as long as Lawson quit running after white women, the county would soon forget. Hiram remembered Poppy telling him about a hanging on what now is Clifford's Hill. A colored man was only accused of talking to a white girl, back in the early part of the nineteenth century and a group of men hung him in a drunken rage one night. Left his body hanging for all to see for half of a week. Poppy said one of his brothers was in on the hanging, but no one was ever charged. It was several years before River County could live the incident down.

Lawson drove his pick-up truck up to Hiram's mailbox. The mailman stopped and put letters in and closed the box lid, then sped down Troublesome. Hiram watched Lawson's truck as it vanished around a curve. Hiram walked to the box and retrieved several letters, then walked back to the porch and sat down in his rocker. He thumbed through the mail, resting his eyes on a white envelope addressed to him. It was from the courthouse in Slonetown. Hiram gazed at the letter, then opened it. It was a summons to appear in court. As he read it, his skin turned a bright red. He looked the letter over, then rose from the rocker and walked into the house. He stopped at the table. He hollered for Dora, "Come in here for a minute."

Dora and Ruby both came to the doorway and peeped into the kitchen. Hiram reached the letter to Dora. "What exactly does this mean?"

Dora received the letter from his hand and unfolded it, reading it silently until she reached the place where the summons part started. Her right hand flew to her mouth as she exclaimed, "Hiram, they're taking you to court. The coal company says they own the mineral rights beneath your land and are going to mine it." She gave Hiram the document back as a worried look grimaced her face.

Hiram sat down at his table place and leaned his chair back.

"Get Mattie ready. We are going to town to see the young lawyer I talked to the other day."

He walked back outside and glanced down the creek, thinking about all the work his father, mother and grandpa put in this place. Hiram didn't like the way he felt.

Mattie and Dora walked out the front door and waited on Hiram. Dora asked Ruby if she cared to look after things while she was gone. Then she climbed into the pick-up next to Hiram and helped Mattie in the seat beside the window, making sure Mattie's door was closed. Hiram started the motor and let out on the clutch, switching gears as the truck rolled along Troublesome. He didn't speak until they were almost in town.

He said, "Dora, go by the bank and draw out fifteen hundred dollars. I'm going to buy a car. We'll need it to haul Ruby and my grandchildren around. Meet me at Sissy's store."

The lawyer sat in his plush chair as Hiram walked into his office. Hiram laid the letter down on the desk and slid it toward the young man. His eyes were stern. The lawyer picked up the letter and began to read. After a few minutes he turned to Hiram and said, "Do you have the deed to your property with you?"

Hiram leaned forward and poked at the table.

"No, the deed is on record in the courthouse. I used to keep it at home, but I've had it recorded ever since the new clerk started keeping records."

The lawyer spoke. "I'll take a look at it tomorrow and see how it reads. Come back to see me Friday, and we'll figure this out. I really can't tell you anything until I study the deed."

The two men shook hands and Hiram left for Sissy's store.

Sissy was glad to see Hiram. It'd been over three weeks since Hiram had been in Slonetown. She hugged him and smiled at Mattie. Mattie watched Sissy as she hugged her father. Mattie's crooked smile stretched across her face as her head bobbled slightly. Hiram told Sissy the situation. She gave him a reassuring pat and said, "They can't do that can they? That land has been in our family for years. Poppy inherited it from Grandpa Jennings, and you bought it from Poppy. I don't believe they can do a thing." Hiram didn't want to show any alarm but the obvious showed in his face. Sissy gave Mattie a candy bar. Hiram knew Sissy would help if he needed her. As Dora walked in, Hiram asked her if she got the money out of the bank. Dora nodded her head.

Hiram said, "You buy what things we need. I'm going to walk down to the car lot for a minute." He walked out the front door.

The car lot had both new cars and used ones. Hiram searched the lot to see if he might be interested in what they had to offer. He knew he didn't need a new one, so his eyes settled on a gray Buick. The salesman watched Hiram open the doors and look at the tires, before asking, "What's the price?"

The car salesman grinned and told Hiram the Buick was a good buy. "It don't have a lot of miles and has been taken care of."

He started to say something else, but Hiram cut him off. "How much is the price?"

The salesman told Hiram the price. "Fifteen hundred and fifty dollars. It's a sixty-four model. A dyna-flow push button drive, automatic," the salesman exclaimed proudly.

Hiram examined the car again and thought it would be better than his pick-up to haul everyone around in. He told the salesman to write up the papers and walked to the office and sat down. The salesman filled out the bill of sale and reached Hiram the keys. Hiram counted out fifteen hundred and fifty dollars in greenback, then reached it to the salesman.

Hiram said, "I'll need someone to drive my truck home. My wife doesn't drive."

The salesman hollered out back. "We'll take care of that. My mechanic will drive your truck home."

Hiram pulled the gray Buick in front of the grocery store and blew the horn. He opened the door and looked it over again as he walked to the porch. It was a pretty car, he thought. Dora and Mattie loved it. Dora helped Mattie into the back seat, then she slid into the passenger's side, opposite Hiram. Hiram pushed D for drive and the car slowly began to move forward. The car was so heavy it did not sway and bounce around like Hiram's truck.

Hiram pulled the heavy car into the yard, cut the motor off, and rolled the window down. Dora could tell Hiram was upset as he walked into the house, carrying groceries. She set her arm load down on the table and helped Mattie to the table chair. Mattie didn't know the seriousness of the matter, and Dora wasn't going to tell her either. She figured her father would if he wanted Mattie to know. Hiram helped place everything and walked to the barn. He wanted to be alone.

Hiram sat, milking. He could hear a loud sound coming from down Troublesome. The noise was getting louder by the minute. Hiram rose from his milk stool and peered in the direction from which the noise was coming. He could just barely see a large truck, pulling a trailer, with a bulldozer resting on the low boy. He watched as the truck struggled to pull the small hill that was just beyond his house. Dust raised from the pavement where dried mud lingered waiting to be washed off when the next heavy rain came. The trailer squatted from the weight of the bulldozer. The truck stopped in front of the barn and the driver opened his door and swung out. He walked down the steps to the ground, looked around and walked to the back of the trailer. Hiram watched him as he began to fidget with the chains that held the dozer in place. Hiram was done milking, so he asked the man what he was about to do.

"I am trying to figure out the best way to unload this dozer here," the man said as he unhooked the metal chains.

Hiram said, "I didn't hire anyone to unload a dozer on my property. I think you need to tell me what is going on."

The driver stopped and turned to Hiram.

"The Black Panther Coal Company hired me to make a road to the number four coal seam and look for the outcrop and face up the coal."

Hiram cleared his voice and replied, "Panther Coal does not own my minerals, and they are not going to mine any of it." Hiram's voice was loud and stern as he spoke.

The truck driver looked at him and asked, "Didn't the coal company even tell you what their plans were?"

Hiram said, "No. I did get a summons to appear in court, but that was all. I've got a lawyer looking at the deed for me."

Hiram stared at the man's red face. He thought about going to the house and getting his pistol, but he figured he might get to upset. Hiram was glad when the truck driver climbed back into the truck and rolled down the window, looked to the back of the truck and started the engine. He pulled the heavy load onto the highway and slowly geared the truck up Troublesome. Hiram watched him go out of sight. He picked up the milk bucket and carried it to the kitchen, set it down on the table, then walked back out on the porch and sat down in his rocker. He was upset.

He could hear the truck turn and start back toward his place. The driver geared the truck down into low gear, lugging the heavy piece of equipment as the truck passed by. Dora, Mattie and Ruby came out on the porch and Dora sat beside Hiram. Ruby helped Mattie to the swing.

Dora said, "What's going on Hiram?"

Hiram was fuming mad, and she knew it. He didn't want to speak about the matter. When he was angry, his voice quivered. He was trying to settle his nerves first.

Finally, he said, "Black Panther Coal Company is trying to move onto my property without my say so. I need to drive to town tomorrow and get this business straightened out."

Supper that evening was silent, except for Mattie asking questions about why coal was mined anyway. Hiram told her, "People away from here use the coal in factories to make electricity with."

That seemed to satisfy her for the time being. Hiram told her everything was all right. But everything wasn't all right. Hiram had an uneasy feeling about the whole situation. He figured this trouble would take all the money he had saved for Mattie's braces. Untelling how much the lawyer would charge for his fee. He was worried.

Hiram was up early. After milking and feeding Mingo, he drove to Slonetown. The lawyer wasn't in his office when he knocked on the door. Hiram waited for a few minutes, then he walked to the courthouse and found Mr. Johnson in the county clerk's office, searching the deed records. Hiram watched the lawyer as he maneuvered around the room, searching book after book. Finally, he opened the one he wanted and ran his finger down each page. He stopped about the middle of a page and glanced at Hiram. He smiled as he carried the heavy book over to the table and laid it open for Hiram to see.

"This is it right here. I've already looked at your deed, but this is the one that will tell me what we need to do."

He read as his finger moved from word to word. He stopped and his eyes and countenance glowed as he read the deed.

"This is the deed back before your grandpa Jennings bought your property."

He read further and stopped again, his eyes squinting, his eyebrows moved upward. He was mumbling and half talking under his breath.

He looked up and turned to Hiram and said, "Manford Collins owned your tract of land before your grandpa bought it. It says right here." He took his finger and placed it in the middle of the page and continued "It says here that Collins sold the mineral rights to a coal man named Red Potter. And it mentions Mountain Coal Company was the company Potter was representing."

The lawyer read on and then closed the huge deed book. He then turned to Hiram, looking worried. He walked over to the clerk and said something Hiram couldn't hear, then came back to Hiram.

"I have to research something in my law books. Give me two days and come back to see me." The two men shook hands and Hiram left for home.

Hiram arrived at his house at dinner time. Dora had a large meal fixed, but he wasn't hungry. Hiram still managed to eat some.

Dora said, "Ruby has been sick all morning. I'm worried about her. She needs to see the doctor."

Hiram pushed his plate back and noticed Mattie watching him. She studied his every move. He smiled at her as she chewed. She ate slow because of her inability to swallow well.

Hiram knew he should be planting his garden and bottom, but he felt it important to see to Ruby's needs. His future grandchild meant something to him. He wished that Cullen could be home at this time.

He told Dora to get ready. "Lundy can watch Ceora, Joanna and Cullen's children while we are gone."

Hiram carried his plate to the dishpan and poured water over the plate. He went outside to wait for the rest to get ready.

Ruby looked pale as she walked down the steps of the porch to the car. Dora opened the door for her. Hiram helped Mattie sat down in the front seat. Dora rode in the back with Ruby. Hiram listened to Ruby moan as he drove down Troublesome. He remembered those groans from days passed when Mary Liz and Alice Marie had his children. Even having a baby was different now. A lot of women drove all the way to the hospital in Hazard to give birth. Cassie still made house calls and gave deliveries in her office, whatever the mother wanted.

Hiram parked in front of Cassie's clinic. He opened the door for Ruby, and Dora helped her out of the car. Dora held Ruby's arm as she walked gingerly toward the doctor's office. Hiram stayed with Mattie while Dora and Ruby were gone. After thirty minutes, Dora and Ruby appeared in the doorway, followed by Cassie. Cassie helped Dora lead Ruby to the car and helped her in the seat. Then Cassie turned to her father and hugged him and showered Mattie with a kiss and hugs, which Mattie liked.

"Cassie is my best friend," She always told her father. Her crooked smile raced across her face as her eyes widened with the affections from her half-sister.

Cassie said to her father, "It's a false alarm this time, but she's getting close, Poppy. You'll be a grandpa again."

Cassie smiled as she watched her father's face. Hiram grinned at her but didn't say a word. Hiram's insides were happy of the news he received. The only thing he worried about now was Cullen. He wanted his son to be a responsible father to his children. If he would only work and take care of Ruby and them. After several 'good-byes' were said, Hiram drove everyone back home. Sleep came early.

Hiram stayed busy with his chores. His thoughts were about how things were changing so fast. There wasn't any talk of witches except water witches. Several neighbors around Hiram had drilled wells now. They all got Denver Mullins to come by their place before they drilled for water. He would take a forked willow branch and would walk over a spot of their land until the willow branch would bend toward the ground. Denver would mark the spot. When the drill rig pulled into the farm, the landowner showed the operator the spot Denver marked. That's where the drill rig was set up. Hiram watched one day as Clive Adams rolled his rig into his neighbor's yard, stopped, and backed the truck into place. The driver raised the drill hoist. He jacked the front end of the rig upon wooden blocks, to make the rig level before drilling. Hiram watched as the drill bit bore into the ground, making a hole. After several feet, a gray liquid mud like paste came out of the hole and ran down hill. The drill rig continued on into the evening. 'Thump, thump, thump,' the noise echoed across the creek and over the mountainside until quitting time when the driver shut the rig down for the night.

Hiram was up early the next day. He wanted to see how long it would take to drill a water well this way. It always took Garner a whole week to dig a well, rock it up and finish it off after building the well drum.

Hiram talked to the rig operator before he started the engine to commence drilling. The rig fired up. The drill began drilling, 'thump, thump, thump.' All day and into the afternoon the rig worked. Toward the evening, the operator changed the drill bit to a bailer and bailed muddy water from the dug well. After a few bails, the water turned clear. It was finished. The drill operator put two twenty foot pieces of casing into the drilled well to hold the sides and to case off any sulfur water from running into it. The well was complete and ready for use. The rig operator told his neighbor, "Your well is producing two to three gallons of water per minute. It is a good well." Hiram helped his neighbor dig a hole on each side of the well, put a post into the newly dug holes and nailed a cross member to hold the bailer. He'd ordered the bailer and chain from Grants hardware store. Hiram nailed a metal wheel hook to the cross member and attached one end of the chain to the bailer and hung the bailer on a nail driven into one of the posts. The bailer was lowered into the fresh drilled well. When it touched water, a splash could be heard bouncing off the well's walls. Hiram watched close as his neighbor pulled the chain bringing the bailer to the surface. Hiram could tell when the bailer neared the surface. His neighbor held the bailer over the aluminum water bucket and pulled the latch at the top, releasing the cool water into the bucket. One bailer full filled the bucket to the top. Hiram was amazed that the thing worked so easy, but he wasn't ready to give up his dug well just yet.

Hiram told Dora and Ruby about the new way for drilling water wells.

"Things are sure changing and changing fast."

A few families in Slonetown had televisions and telephones too. Hiram didn't like these changes, but he did have a radio that he listened to sometimes.

Chapter 5

Monday came, and Hiram drove into town to talk to his lawyer. Mr. Johnson was happy this morning as Hiram greeted him in his office. The young lawyer leaned back in his chair and said, "I think we can win this case. Your farm has been in your family's possession all these years. Your grandpa, your father and now you own it."

He smiled. "We are going to claim back your mineral on the grounds of adverse possession. You've occupied this property and made enormous improvements and paid taxes all these years."

He leaned forward and his dimpled smile grew even bigger. "I found a case just like this on court records where your son, Ballard, had a similar case. He argued the same evidence and won."

Ralph Johnson studied Hiram's face at the mention of his son's name. He, like everyone else in River County, had heard about the ship named in honor of Ballard Daniels.

"You know, Hiram, I marveled at all of your son's legal abilities and his accomplishments. He must have been a smart lawyer."

Pride swelled in Hiram's throat, and his heart beat a little faster from discussing his late son.

Hiram said in his mind, not wanting to brag in front of the lawyer, "Yes, he was a smart lawyer and a good person. I miss him so much." Tears ran down Hiram's face as he turned from the lawyer's stare. Hiram wiped the tears with his handkerchief, rose from his chair and walked out to his car. He started the engine and drove home. He wanted time to think.

Dora had a large super fixed. The daylight was slowly coming to an end for the day as the shadows crept across the valley. The May weather was warm and semi-hazy, and the bug filled air was full of flying creatures, floating dust and spring pollen. The early spring tree blooms had shed, and the tender buds and leaves were greening fast, making way for seed pods and berried fruit. The raspberries and blackberries were hanging full. That's what Hiram loved to see. Wild strawberries were turning ripe under the Troublesome Creek sunlight. The sun's rays made the berries sweet and delicious. He'd picked a dishpan full last Saturday. Dora made dumplings and filled small bowls of what was left over and froze them in the Frigidaire's ice box.

Every evening, Mattie always sat on the porch with her father until late. Mattie watched and listened to the sounds of late spring as Hiram thought on his law case. So much was going on in his life, and changes were taking place faster than he could keep up with everything. Two country stores were running between Troublesome Creek and Slonetown. A drive-in movie theater was open near town. Slonetown was full of people every time Hiram went there. Cars were parked along paved streets. Sidewalks ran along in front of each business. A few parking meters were erected around the courthouse and on main street. Changes Hiram could not embrace. He told Mattie it was bedtime. He helped her inside, and Dora put her to bed. She still slept by herself. Joanna and Ceroa slept in the same bed, and Lundy slept in the room upstairs.

By Wednesday evening, Mattie was bad off with allergies. Her cough was raspy and mucus filled. Hiram placed his palm on her forehead. Mattie felt hot to the touch, but she did not have a fever. Her head drooped as she sat on one end of the sofa. Tears fell unto her chest and wet her blue blouse.

Hiram asked her, "Are you feeling bad, baby?"

He cuddled her head in his arms. She raised her eyes toward him. Hiram felt so sorry for his daughter but thought she would be all right. Dora fixed a cup of chicken soup and set the bowl in front of Mattie.

Mattie smiled weakly and turned to her father saying, "Poppy will you feed me?"

Hiram answered her as he took hold of the spoon.

"I will do anything for you, my sweet daughter."

He smiled as he held the spoon full of soup to her lips. Mattie slurped each spoon full until the bowl was empty. Everything seemed to be fine as Hiram tucked his daughter in. He turned out the living room light and retired to bed.

 Hiram was awakened by Mattie's groans from her bedroom. He jumped to his feet and rushed to the darkened room and opened the door. Mattie was crying as if she'd been scared of something. Hiram turned the light switch on. Mattie lay in a crumpled heap. She held her stomach as tears fell down her cheek. Hiram took hold of her thigh and turned Mattie over.

"What's wrong child?" He said as he looked at her frail frame. Hiram was about to cry too. Dora came into the room and stood beside Hiram. He quickly said, "Get ready, we're taking Mattie to Cassie's clinic."

He dressed, as did Dora, then held Mattie in his arms until his wife was ready. She told Ruby to watch her brother and sisters. Hiram carried his daughter to the car and laid her in the backseat. He covered Mattie with a blanket Dora had fetched. Then he drove to Slonetown.

Dora banged on the clinic door until a light came on in the back room. After a few minutes, the front door opened to Cassie tightening her housecoat. She looked startled as Hiram brushed past her and laid Mattie on one of the clinic beds. Cassie quickly began examining her sister. Cassie pulled open Mattie's blouse and touched her lower stomach. Mattie cried out in pain when Cassie touched the tender spot above her gallbladder was. Cassie stepped back and glanced up at Hiram.

"She needs to be in the hospital. Her gallbladder will have to be removed!"

Hiram felt a rush of weakness rush over his body. He would rather be sick himself than to see Mattie in all the pain she was in.

Cassie said, "I'll go with her. You take Dora back home then come to the hospital."

Hiram said goodbye to Mattie and rushed Dora back to Troublesome Creek.

He drove like crazy until he reached the Hazard hospital at Combs. He ran to the front desk and asked where his Mattie was. The nurse directed him to the lower wing and pointed to the open door to the left of the hallway. Hiram found Mattie laying on a bed covered with a blanket. Cassie told the doctor on call about Mattie's symptoms. The doctor had sedated Mattie to ease her pain. Hiram was worried. Cassie told her father to settle down and stay calm. Hiram wanted to, but it was not easy. Cassie got a chair for her father to sit in because she knew he would not leave Mattie. As Hiram leaned back in the chair, he fell asleep. He was worn out. Cassie covered him with a blanket as she sat down to wait on the hospital doctor.

A loud noise down the hall from another room awakened

Hiram. He stretched as best he could and glanced at Cassie. She was covered with a hospital blanket. Then he rose to check on Mattie. She was asleep. Hiram noticed how frail she appeared. He rested his palm on her forehead. Without realizing it, he was praying out loud, begging God to help his little girl. He must have cried out, because his voice aroused Cassie and she quickly rose from her chair. Cassie grabbed her father by the arm. Hiram finished praying with an "Amen."

The door opened and a young male doctor walked in and smiled at Cassie. Cassie smiled back and began talking to the young doctor. Hiram listened as the two conversed. He could barely hear his daughter, and he wondered what they were talking about.

He turned from Mattie long enough to ask, "What is wrong?" Cassie grabbed his hand and introduced him to her friend.

"This is Doctor Porter. He will be attending to Mattie and he's one of the best doctors here. Tests will have to be run, and it will take a little time to find out the results. Poppy, please go home and rest for a while."

Hiram walked to the window and gazed outside to the breaking of day. He remembered he had a court date this morning, but he didn't want to leave Mattie. It took more of Cassie's convincing words for him to decide to leave her in Cassie's care.

"I'll take good care of her, Poppy" Cassie said, as she

gently pushed her father toward the door.

Hiram felt helpless as he walked outside to his car. He drove straight to Troublesome Creek to get ready.

Chapter 6

Hiram was ready in minutes. It was time for the trial. The circuit judge had set the trial for 9:00 AM sharp, so Hiram rushed dressing so he would be on time. Hiram was a bit nervous, and his plans were to meet with his lawyer before court took up. Dora fixed breakfast for him, then she got herself ready, and they both got into the truck and headed for Slonetown. Ruby promised to look after the house for them, and she would get word to him if any news came about Mattie.

He and Dora talked as Hiram drove down Troublesome Creek. As the couple drove by the Narrows, Hiram was surprised. He could see where the county road department channeled the creek bed and took away the landmark that had been there as long as he could remember. He lost interest in the creek when his wife moved over to sit next to him. She took hold of his hand. Smiling she said to him, "Hiram, I've got something to tell you. I believe I'm going to have your child. I've been having morning sickness. I've not told anybody about it, but I think I may be pregnant."

Hiram felt his face flush as he turned abruptly to her. He glanced toward her stomach and back to the road again.

Finally, he grinned and said, "I don't reckon. Why, I'm an old man. I figured I was past my prime."

He drove another mile, then looked over at his wife again in disbelief.

Dora squeezed his hand and said, "I believe it's true. First chance I get, I'll see Cassie. "

Hiram thought to himself, "So many things happening all at once." On one hand, he was worried about his dear Mattie, and now his wife springs news of him being a father for the sixth time. His emotions didn't know which way to go. Hiram didn't know what to think about him being a father in his old age.

Hiram parked beside the courthouse and fed the parking meter a dime. He took hold of Dora's hand and led her up the steps and opened the double white doors to the first floor. Then they walked up the flight of stairs to the second floor, where the judge held his court. Hiram gazed around the room, trying to locate a seat for his wife. The courtroom was almost full. Finally, he spotted a seat near the middle of the room. He led Dora to it.

Hiram said, "I have to sit with my lawyer."

Mr. Johnson sat at a table just opposite the lawyers for the Black Panther Coal Company of Pittsburg, Pennsylvania. Their two lawyers wore two piece suits that were made with the finest quality that Hiram had ever seen. One lawyer was slim with a balding head of hair, had a well-trimmed mustache, and he wore glasses that hung loosely on his beaked nose. Hiram could tell right off that he wasn't from around these parts. He was accompanied by Slonetown's other practicing attorney, George Hamilton. Mr. Hamilton had made a name for himself handling civil cases while representing energy companies. That's how he had made his living for the last thirty years. He started practicing law back around the time World War II ended. No one in River County liked him. He was a huge man who spoke with a gruff voice. His eyebrows bushed up the front of his forehead to a receding hair line, but he wasn't bald like the foreign lawyer. Mr. Hamilton watched the crowd of people as they talked back and forth with each other. It was like a social gathering in a way, Hiram thought.

Hiram walked over to join his lawyer and sat down in a chair beside him. He bid him a nervous, "Good morning."

Hiram had never been in a law case of any kind. He hadn't even been in a courtroom since long ago when the inquiry about the death of Pharoah and Perry. How the new courtroom had changed. The whole courthouse building had changed. Hiram had only done business in the clerk's room downstairs. Getting his truck licensed or paying his property tax in the tax commissioner's office happened only once a year. Hiram didn't get involved in politics. He did make it a point to vote in the county's elections, as he felt it necessary to vote for county judge's race and for sheriff.

Mr. Johnson greeted Hiram with his dimpled smile. He showed Hiram a stack of legal papers he wanted the judge to rule on before the trial would start.

"This is the day we take back your mineral rights that somehow were sneaked away from your grandfather. Deeds and records have been known to be changed to suit a company's case, for money crooked clerks would change records and deeds. But I think we'll be all right."

The lawyer eased back in his chair and swung around to look at his competition. Hiram waited anxiously for the judge to appear. He could hardly hear himself think with all the noise coming from the crowd. He did glance back at Dora, and she gave him a reassuring smile and a half wave. He wondered how the county gossipers would talk about him when the news got out about being a father in his old age. What about Claire Polly at the Sandgap Church? No doubt she would have a field day with the news. But Hiram really wasn't worried about that. He was most worried about Mattie and the safety of his land. He planned to fight for what was his. He worried about the braces for Mattie, but he figured her health came first. He could hardly contain himself. Thoughts of becoming a father again made him want to scream.

Then the court room became quite as the bailiff announced the entrance of Judge Alford Jacobs. He was the truly sworn in circuit judge of the ninety-fifth district of River and Bolster counties, and he ruled his court room with a fair and impartial, but stern, rule. Everyone that Hiram had ever heard mention Judge Jacobs said, "He's a tough judge. He has no foolishness in his court."

Hiram studied the judge after everyone was seated. Hiram figured him to be sixty years old, at least, with a full head of hair. The judge kept his hair combed back toward the back of his head and slicked down with some kind of hair tonic. The tonic gave his hair a wet and shiny look. The judge's long black robe dragged to his feet when he stood up. His eyes were a deep sky blue. His skin on his face was a light pink and smooth as a baby's skin. His skin was soft and fluffy around his eye sockets with bags hanging down under his eyelids. Hiram figured the judge didn't venture outside in the sunlight much.

The judge beat his gavel against the podium and scanned the crowd, demanding their attention. He glanced at the lawyer benches and said, "Are we ready to proceed with this case? Ahh, ahh Black Panther Coal versus Hiram Daniels."

Hearing the very mention of his name in this court proceeding hurt Hiram. Hearing his named out loud in the same chambers where people were tried for murder, raped and all kinds of illegal crimes made him feel like a criminal. It hurt his pride, and he slumped down in his chair, slightly. The silence was deafening as the judge asked the clerk and the bailiff if they were ready. They gestured they were.

He turned to the lawyers for the plaintiff. "Are you ready to give opening arguments for the plaintiff?"

Mr. Hamilton rose from his seat and said loudly in his gruff voice, "We are, Your Honor." Judge Jacobs looked at Hiram's lawyer and asked if he was ready.

Mr. Johnson rose from his chair and said, "Your honor, I need for you to rule on this legal document first, if you will."

Hiram's lawyer walked to the front of the podium and handed the judge the paper forms. The judge read the forms and asked the plaintiff's lawyer to approach the bench. After some discussions, Hiram's lawyer took his seat beside him, mumbling something under his breath that Hiram could not make out but figured wasn't good.

The judge asked again if both sides were ready. The coal company presented their case first. The company lawyers, especially the city lawyer, used long word terms to describe their case, terms that Hiram had never heard before. He felt lost in the proceedings and found himself hoping that his lawyer knew what he was doing. Hiram leaned forward in his chair and tried to keep up with what the lawyers were talking about. After an hour, they said they rested their case without presenting a single witness.

The judged turned toward where Hiram and his lawyer sat.

"Are you ready?"

Mr. Johnson answered by rising to his feet and addressed the court.

"Your Honor, we are," he said confidently.

Hiram noticed a slight quake in Ralph's voice, but he

soon settled down as he talked on. Sweat formed on his fore-head. He wiped it off with his handkerchief.

He said, "Your Honor, my client's family has owned the property that is in question here today for three generations now. I have searched the deeds where each time ownership of the said property has changed hands from when my client's grandfather bought it from a Mr. Collins. No mention of a transfer of mineral rights were ever mentioned in the writing of any deed. My client bought the said property from his father, and his father had inherited the property from his father, Mr. Jennings Daniels, a Civil War veteran. No mention of transfer of mineral rights."

Mr. Johnson waited a minute then started again. "Furthermore, my client has lived and worked this property ever since he was a young boy. He's made all sorts of improvements on said property and has paid taxes on this land all this time, and I'd like him to take the stand and explain in his own words what this land means to him."

The judge glanced at his watch and said, "We'll take a brief recess and meet back here in ten minutes."

He rapped the podium with his wooden gavel, rose from his chair and walked through the doors into his chambers. Everyone rose at the bailiff's order. Hiram walked back to where Dora sat. She rose from her seat and hugged Hiram. The couple quickly exited the courthouse to call and inquire about Mattie's condition. Cassie assured her father that Mattie was still resting. He and his wife returned to the court room and waited for the judge to enter.

The judge took his seat and got everyone's attention by rapping his gavel. After a few minutes, Hiram walked toward the witness chair and turned to the bailiff as he was sworn in. "Raise your right hand and place your left hand on the Bible. Do you swear to tell the truth and nothing but the truth, so help you God?" Hiram didn't like this. The Daniels family had always told the truth and had always been honest. No one had ever questioned the Daniels' integrity before.

He quickly said, "I do."

The bailiff said, "Be seated."

Hiram's lawyer told him to state his name. Hiram looked the crowd over. He felt all eyes on him. He said, "Hiram Daniels."

He felt like he was under investigation from all these people. Most he knew.

His lawyer said, "How long have you owned and occupied this land?"

Hiram answered, "All my life, except the two years I lived on Graves Creek, when I married my first wife. Besides that, I have lived there since I was born."

The lawyer asked Hiram several questions about all the improvements he'd made on his property. "You fenced your whole boundary, and, when clearing new grounds, you saved a few trees to help hold the land when storms and cloudbursts came so not to erode the hillsides?" His lawyer asked.

Hiram told how he farmed and let his bottoms lay out ever seven years so the nutrients in the soil would not be depleted.

"I've took the best care of my land that I could." Hiram felt so uncomfortable sitting there with everyone staring at him, but he went on. "I gave a lot to this land, and she has taken a lot from me. I've been trying to tame Troublesome Creek ever since I have owned my property. But no one can tame her! She has her own will and she makes her own way. If you try to crowd her she fights back, taking what she wants, when she wants. I have gained respect for her and for my land. You can rob the land and get by with it for a while, but if you haven't taken care of the land, then when you ask something from it the land will refuse to give you what you are asking."

Hiram waited for the next question. Judge Jacobs was listening to Hiram as he told about his property. He could sense the respect Hiram had for his land and surroundings.

Mr. Johnson asked Hiram about his family and their standing in River County. Hiram said, "My family settled here a long time ago and made their home here in these mountains. We've all lived and died here, making a living the best we could. A honest living! My grandpa Jennings fought in the Civil War, my brother Clinton fought in World War I and I lost a son in World War II, Ballard Daniels. Ballard was honored by the government. They presented to him a medal and named a battleship after him."

Hiram wept at the mention of Ballard's name. The judge sat up in his chair and cleared his throat. The jury consisted of eight men and four women. Two of the women were crying as they listened to Hiram tell his life's story. He'd never talked in front of this many people before. But after he started, it was easy for him. It was always easy for him to talk about his family. He had never been ashamed of any of them, especially his twins. Most everyone knew Cassie; she had doctored almost everyone in the Troublesome Creek valley in everything from delivering babies to treating snake bites.

Hiram wiped his eyes and began again. "Ballard was killed in action. In Guadalcanal it was. The only time I have been out of this state was when I traveled to New Jersey to christen the battleship in his honor. I have been to Jackson and Hazard and Pikeville, but most of my life has been right here on Troublesome, and I've never wanted to leave. I was born here, and I want to be buried here beside my family when my time comes."

He waited for the lawyer to ask him another question, but he didn't.

The company lawyer rose to his feet. He turned pages of paper in front of him. He stopped and picked a certain one up and held it in his hand and said, "This form holds the mark of Mr. Collins dated 1867, two years after the Civil war was over. Pilgrim Energy paid the said Collins fifty dollars in cash money for that signature. His mark is the same as him handwriting his name. Can you write, Mr. Daniels?"

The lawyer asked Hiram and looked at the jury box.

Hiram spoke up, "Yes, I can write my name, and I can read some too. I quit school in the fifth grade to help Poppy with his farm work. That is one reason I wanted my children to get an education; so they wouldn't have to work as hard as I have. Ballard made a good lawyer, and the people of River County can judge if Cassie is a good doctor. She has made a name for herself here."

The company lawyer soon saw it was no good to try to compete with Hiram's likeable nature, so he closed his case by saying, "Your Honor, I have no more questions."

He picked up the loose papers from his table, tapped them together and sat back down.

Judge Jacobs looked at Hiram and his lawyer and said, "We'll recess for dinner then come back, and we'll listen to your closing arguments."

The bailiff said, "All rise" as the judge walked back to his chambers and closed the door behind him.

Hiram asked Dora if she wanted something to eat. She slipped her arm under Hiram's elbow and they walked to the little store near the courthouse and ordered a sandwich. After half eating his sandwich, he asked Dora if she would call the hospital.

Dora walked outside to the phone booth. When she returned, she was smiling,

"Mattie is awake and improving Hiram. Looks like God has answered your prayers." Tears fell from her eyes as they embraced.

Dora said to Hiram, as she caressed his hand, "I'm proud of you, Hiram. I know how much you dreaded this day, but you did well."

Dora loved Hiram, and she appreciated all he'd done for her and her family. She was thankful to him for taking in her brother and two sisters. No doubt she could have married someone else, but they wouldn't have been as caring as Hiram was. They finished eating in silence after that. Hiram waited for her to go to the bathroom, and then they walked back to the courthouse. Both took their seats and waited for court to continue.

The judge rapped his gavel, and court was in session. Hiram's lawyer addressed the court and talked about how Hiram took care of his land and the caring way he nurtured the soil.

"We ask this jury to take notice of how long this property has been in the Daniels family hands and we claim all the mineral rights under the adverse possession law and hope this court agrees with us. Think about the hardships Mr. Daniels has endured to hold on to his land and think about all he has lost. No one here can judge this case any other way."

Mr. Johnson sat down beside Hiram and touched his left hand. His eyes were hopeful but not full of confidence.

The judge gazed toward Mr. Hamilton. The lawyer looked all around the court room before he began speaking. He rose his ruffled voice higher than he did during his opening statement.

"Ladies and gentlemen of the jury, I think this is an easy case. Our company bought the disputed mineral rights and have a deed for them signed by the said Collins, owner in 1867. His mark tells the story, and we have legal right to the coal and natural gas on the Daniels property. You must find for Black Panther Coal and to honor the court system and it's integrity. I know you know Mr. Daniels and he tells a very good tale of his family and all he has encountered along the way, and we all feel for him, but the law is the law." He looked at the judge, then at the jury and glanced at the crowd before saying, "I close my case." His ruffled voice carried all over the room as he sat down in his chair. There was a hush over the courtroom.

Judge Jacobs broke the silence by saying, "The jury may go to the jury room and try to reach a verdict."

Hiram talked to his lawyer for a while, then went to Dora. Several people from Sandgap Church said 'hello' as they mingled in the crowd. Hiram and Dora walked to the front balcony and peered down to the street to watch cars drive by. Men and women walked the sidewalks going from store to store. Men sat on wooden benches talking and laughing. Slonetown was alive. Grant and Sissy were well thought of business people. Each one sat on the town's council, making ordinances for the town to grow by. Hiram heard the bailiff call court to order. He and Dora walked back inside and took their seats. Hiram waited for his lawyer to say something, but he didn't. Hiram was nervous. It was past five o'clock. Hiram wanted this over with.

The judge came in, sat down in his chair and rapped his gavel. The bailiff reached him the paper from the jury foreman. The judge read it and then scanned the crowd. He said to the foreman "You may read the verdict."

The juror rose from his seat and said, "We find for the defendant."

Hiram could have jumped for joy. His heart was racing but soon settled down as he and his lawyer shook hands. Judge Jacobs grinned at Hiram as their eyes met, and the judge congratulated him with a wink. Hiram ran to Dora and picked her up by the waist and swung her around. She smiled down at him as he sat her back down. She was happy for him. Hiram thanked his lawyer and told Dora to pay him a hundred dollars. She opened her purse and counted out five twenty dollar bills and reached it to Mr. Johnson. The young man took the money. He folded it together and put it in his coat pocket, then he walked out of the courthouse. Hiram noticed the company lawyers. They weren't happy. He figured he'd have more trouble out of them.

He made his mind up as he stood there thinking, "I'll go ahead and mine my coal before someone else tries to take it." Several landowners had already lost their coal to outside companies. The companies moved onto the owner's property and mined coal under a new law called a 'Broad Form Deed.' The coal companies damaged the land and only paid a small fee in royalties. Hiram had mixed emotions – happiness for winning the court battle, but he was still feeling worry for his sick daughter.

Hiram told Grant and Sissy about the verdict as they traded for groceries. Dora paid Sissy. She and Hiram drove home. Hiram sang *Amazing Grace* as he drove along. The trip home seemed short.

After supper, Hiram drove to the hospital. He stayed with Mattie the rest of the night. The next morning, Mattie was smiling and alert, but still sick in her chest.

The doctor told Hiram, "I don't know what is wrong with her. Her tests show an infection. She probably will be here for a few weeks. But I think she will be fine, if I can get her body to respond to the medication I have been giving. I gave her a double shot of penicillin last night, and she has been on an IV drip since she arrived. Her gallbladder will wait a while longer."

His daughter did not know what Hiram knew. Hiram knew of a higher power. A healing power that a lot of people don't believe in, but he did. Hiram sat in his chair all day except to visit the bathroom. He hadn't eaten anything to account for much since last evening and was becoming hungry. He wasn't about to leave Mattie's side. He dozed off to sleep.

He was awakened by Cassie. She convinced him to go home to rest.

"I'll sit with Mattie."

After a few minutes he drove home and went to bed.

Chapter 7

It was raining hard and thundering early in the morning of July 10th. Ruby woke Dora complaining of labor pains. By the time Hiram got out of bed, she was screaming.

Dora said, "She needs Cassie bad. Cullen is in the pen, so you'll have to run the 'granny race.'"

Dora was grinning from ear to ear at Hiram. She knew he didn't want to. He would rather Cassie came here and delivered the baby. But Dora knew Ruby would be better taken care of in Cassie's office in Slonetown. She put a few clothes into a bag then helped Ruby into the car and laid her down in the back seat. Hiram started the car's engine and sped off toward town with Ruby moaning. Hiram hurried as fast as he could. He made it to Slonetown and stopped in front of Cassie's office. He half carried Ruby to the door and knocked hard, hollering for help. The rain had soaked both of them. Rain drops dripped from Hiram's hat as he stood pounding on the door. Finally, Cassie opened the door and let them in. She told Hiram to bring Ruby to her examining room. Hiram helped Ruby into a bed and watched Cassie take over. She knew exactly what to do. Cassie talked to the soon to be delivered mother to calm her. Even though Ruby had been through this two times already, she still was scared. Cassie told Hiram to holler for the midwife in the back room. He pounded the door until it opened. The new midwife was no older than Dora. Bertha had died, and this new midwife was a new learner, but Cassie had confidence in her. Hiram figured he wasn't needed, so he walked out on the sidewalk. The rain had let up a little. He could stay dry by standing under the overhang on the porch roof. It wasn't long before he heard Ruby scream, and he could hear a baby cry. He opened the door a little. The miracle of birth always touched him; it didn't matter whose baby was being born. He knew the ordeal was over when he heard the same scream come from the birthing room again. But he didn't hear another baby cry. It was silent, and Hiram wondered what was wrong.

Twins ran in his generation, and it wasn't unusual for twin babies to be born in his family. He waited for Cassie to come out of her office and when she did, Hiram inquired what was wrong. She touched her father's chest.

"The second baby didn't make it. It was a little boy. I don't know what happened. The first baby is healthy as can be, and it's a bouncing boy, with a chest full of lungs. Daniels lungs."

She grinned and opened the door to her office and disappeared.

Hiram's feelings were a mixture of happiness and sadness. He thought of his mother at that moment. He remembered the scripture, "One shall be taken, and one shall be left." He knew another grave would be dug on the dogwood point. He wanted to be home at his place. He felt more secure there. Ruby would have to stay here a couple of days, so he drove home in the pouring rain. Dora was excited when she heard about a new baby boy. Hiram told her that he would dig the grave for the dead baby as soon as the rain quit and the ground dried some.

Hiram slept until after three. Talking from the living room woke him. Clinton and Susanna had arrived. They had heard about the new baby from the telephone party line. There was always something to be discussed on the party line. There were only a hand full of houses hooked to the telephone service. During the evening after supper, the gossipers of River County gossiped about a little bit of everything. Local talk. They discussed everything from the war in Vietnam to who was running in the local politics and of course who the county tramp was at the time.

Hiram shook hands with his brother and sister-in-law and said, "How have you all been? Is church doing all right? We've not been for quite some time, but as soon as the new addition to the Daniels family is able to travel, we'll be attending."

Dora asked Hiram if he was ready to eat.

"I fixed plenty, and I want you all to stay and eat with us," She said to Clinton and Susanna. The radio was on, and Dora reached over Hiram's back and turned it off.

Hiram hadn't bought a television yet, but he liked his radio. He could listen to the news bulletin and keep up with the progress of the war. Vietnam had been going on for over fifteen years now. Hiram wondered why America had to be at war with someone all the time. "A lot of turmoil in the world," he thought.

Susanna wanted to know about the new baby. "What will they name the boy, you reckon?"

She smiled, looking at Dora then at Hiram. She and Clinton could never have children, and it seemed to hurt her the most.

Clinton had come to accept the circumstances. He'd talked to Hiram about it long ago when they were logging. He always said, "Might as well let it be. Just be happy and live your life the best you can, and everything will work out."

Dora set the table and told everybody to take their places. Hiram helped set out the plates and silverware. Dora watched Susanna as she sat down next to her. Her smile spread all across her face. Her eyes sparkled. Clinton and Susanna smiled back at her. Hiram thought to himself that if anything happened to him, Clinton would keep Mattie and do by her the best he could, and who would be better to her than him and Susanna? Hiram knew Sissy would take Mattie also.

After supper, Clinton followed Hiram out on the porch. The rain had slowed to a trickle. The light raindrops hitting the metal roof patted a tune as they beaded and bounced before running and dripping onto the ground. The fog was lifting as the warm rain drops touched the moist soil. Hiram could smell the dampness. The valley would be dark in another hour with swamp frogs hollering and lightening bugs swarming the night air as they blended with the fog. No fox hounds had been heard on Rolly Joe Mountain for a long time now. Most men had turned to coon hunting. Racoons were plentiful, and a lot of coal miners used their hound dogs to run and tree the animals for sport. There were several new mines opened up towards Rolly Joe Mountain. Hiram's cousin from Graves Creek crossed the mountain every day to work. The mine owners were paying thirty dollars a shift. The miners earned what they were paid. Coal mining was a hard living and very dangerous.

Hiram brought the subject up.

"How would you like to go in business with me, Clinton? I'm planning on mining my coal before someone else tries to claim it out from under me. We've got crooked officials in Slonetown politics now, and I don't know who we can trust."

Clinton squinted his eyes at his brother as he looked toward the kitchen. Dora and Susanna were washing dishes. Joanna and Ceora were getting the house ready for the new baby. Lundy was out back chopping wood for the cook stove.

"Gas companies have drilled gas wells in a few locations. The landowners made sure when they leased the gas rights they would get free gas for their heaters. No more coal stoves for cooking and heating," Clinton said.

Hiram had been thinking about doing that too. It would make life a little easier for Dora and the children, but this was another change he didn't welcome.

"Yal, I've heard about that, but I don't know if I want that."

Clinton eased back in his chair and said, "Hiram, I don't have much money to help with the finances. I do have a little saved up. I draw a small army pension and a small Social Security check. Have you ever checked to see if you could draw something from Social Security?"

Hiram watched Dora as she moved around the kitchen. He noticed her stomach. She was gaining weight and beginning to show. He wondered what his new child would be like. Would it be a boy or girl? He could see the glow about his wife, how happy she seemed. Happiness was all he wanted in life anymore.

Hiram replied to his brother, "I will put up most of the money for our company. I can't draw anything because I never paid into Social Security."

Clinton said, "If you want me to, we'll give it a try."

Hiram grinned at his brother. The light from the open kitchen door shone through the screen and lit half the porch floor. Dora opened the door and hobbled out on the porch and sat down beside her husband. His wife rested her head on his shoulder. Hiram's thoughts were filled with Mattie. How she loved to sit on the porch. This was her favorite time, especially during the evenings. Hiram sat with her every chance he got, not wanting her to miss a thing. This was her life. This was her enjoyment. She'd never be able to experience the joy of being married or having children or making her own life. Hiram missed Mattie very bad this evening, but it would be tomorrow before he could see her. Dora walked back inside to the kitchen.

Clinton rose from his chair and proceeded to shake hands with Hiram. Hiram told him, "I'll get the papers started in the morning. We'll have to get a permit and draw up papers before we start. You be thinking who we might hire to work with us. We'll start small and work our way up. I'll get a dozer here Monday to start searching for the coal bloom. I don't want them to tear up no more of my land then they have too. We'll face the coal seam up and wait until after harvest to start mining."

Clinton agreed. He yelled for Susanna. They got into their car and drove home.

The next morning, Hiram raced to the hospital to check on Mattie. She must have responded to the penicillin, for she was sitting up in bed while being supported by pillows. Hiram was so glad that his little girl was better. He didn't give the doctors or anybody else credit. Mattie had been touched by the hand of God. That is what healed her, and Hiram thanked God every time he thought about it that day.

Hiram and Dora worked for two weeks canning corn and beans, kraut and mixed pickles. They worked a day putting up berries and apples in the icebox. Hiram had two hogs to slaughter, but most of his neighbors were taking their hogs to a slaughterhouse just across the county line in Bolster County. Hiram didn't salt his hog meat down like he used to, but he could still butcher his own hogs.

Cullen was released from the penitentiary in August. The Governor of Kentucky pardoned Cullen early. He moved his family to Indiana to find work. Hiram was glad he moved away. If Cullen stayed here, he probably would have been in more trouble. After World War Two, a lot of people moved to Ohio and Indiana, and most did good. They got jobs working in factories and mills, trying to make a new home themselves. Most never moved back to Kentucky to live, but they always came back for visits. Cullen's new baby was doing fine. Ruby didn't give the baby a name until Cullen got out. Cullen named the boy Cobert Daniels. Hiram was pleased.

Hiram and Dora were attending church more since they had more room in the house. Dora was gaining weight, and Hiram figured the baby she was carrying would arrive sometime around the first of the year. Depending, of course, if Dora's count was right. Mattie enjoyed her sits on the front porch. Hiram would sing to her as they sat swinging. Hiram often sat and thought of all the changes that were taking place. Another small grocery store sprang up on Jimbo's Nob. Hiram's cow went dry, and he was buying milk from their store. Most of the time, he'd buy four gallons a week.

He could afford the fifty-five cents a gallon now, so he didn't complain.

Hiram hired a dozer to make a road and smooth out a mine sight. He hauled cheap green lumber to build a small tipple to hold the black coal. Besides him and Clinton, he'd hired George and Herman Mosely to help with the mine. George cut mining props for the company. Hiram made sure the timbers were the right size. He didn't want to risk a roof fall and getting someone killed. Hiram spent most of the money he'd saved and thought about putting a mortgage on his farm. Clinton worked every day he could and wouldn't even charge Hiram for all the times he doubled back to work an extra shift. Hiram and Clinton did most of the inside work. He let Herman, the younger Mosley, pick slate so the coal would sell better. Herman had gob piles stacked along the walls of the mine and a slate pile beside the tipple. In a week, it had grown to twice the size. Smoke rose from the slate dump after each rain. The slate and small amounts of slack coal took heat, smoked and burned. The burned slate was used to put on coal haul roads. The miners gave it the name, 'red-dog'. Red-dog was rough on rubber tires though, causing them to wear out faster.

After two months of hard work, Hiram and Clinton began to turn a small profit. The men were back under the hill over a hundred yards. Hiram hired Joe Martin to drill and tamp the holes using the method of shooting from the 'solid.' Hiram hired a truck driver to haul the coal to the railroad tipple.

The railroad shipped it to the east coast.

Hiram named his company 'The Dora Coal Company.' Dora was getting ready to give birth any day. Hiram had Cassie examine her last week. She told her father, "Just bring her in when she is ready. I'll take care of her."

Hiram was getting anxious. He didn't know how he would handle being a father this late in life.

Dora went into labor early one morning about four o'clock. Hiram rose and told Joanna to look after Mattie for him. He didn't know if Joanna could be trusted or not, but he knew he had to get Dora to the clinic.

"Tell Mattie, I'll come for her."

The temperature was cold and freezing. Hiram warmed the car up then helped Dora to the back seat and let her lay down. Dora had a pale look that worried Hiram. He drove to Slonetown as fast as he could. A thick fog rose from Troublesome Creek making it difficult to see. Hiram knew this road like the back of his hand, but he still was careful. He arrived just before daylight. He carried Dora into the clinic and opened the door as he hollered for Cassie. Cassie was awake and preparing for the daily schedule. Hiram thought she looked tired but didn't say anything to her. He sat Dora down in a chair then turned to his daughter and said, "What do you want me to do?"

Cassie was calm. She grinned and took her father's hand. "Go to the other building and get my midwife up. Tell her it's time for another baby to be born and to bring another Daniels into this awful world."

Hiram watched Dora grimace with pain. He took off his coat and threw it around Dora's shoulders. Then he went next door to the apartment.

By the time he returned, his wife was laying down in the birthing room. The pain was so bad it made her cry. Hiram wanted to rush to her side, but Cassie stopped him at the door. She pushed him aside to let the midwife in and closed the door behind her. Hiram knew Cassie would take good care of his wife, but that didn't keep him from worrying. It was too cold for him to prance the outside porch, so he sat down in a chair, twisting his hands. He was as nervous as if this was his first baby being born. He didn't have to wait long. Cassie came to the door.

"Poppy, you might as well go home. Dora's not going to give birth this morning. I figure it will be sometime tonight."

Hiram looked worried, but he understood the baby will not come until it was ready. He kissed his daughter on the cheek then waved to his wife and slipped out the door. His trip home was consumed with his plans for his new child. Especially if the baby happened to be a man child.

Hiram found Mattie trying to wash her hands and face in the wash pan. He watched Mattie as she bent over the pan, taking water in her crumpled hand and rubbing her palms together. She lathered ivory soap on both hands. Soap suds squished between her fingers. After washing her hands, she washed her face and dried with the towel that hung from the towel rack. Dora had bought new towels from Sissy's store for the whole house. Hiram had thrown away all the home-made ones Alice Marie made from feed and flour sacks. Both products were packaged in paper bags now. Hiram still ren-dered out his lard during the winter after killing his fattening hogs. When the homemade lard was gone, he'd buy buckets of lard from the store. 'Black Hawk' and 'Fishers' were the two main brands. Most of the time, Hiram bought a twenty-five lard can full. Sometimes he would buy a four-pound or eight-pound bucket. He would use the empty lard buckets to pick blackberries or raspberries in the summer.

He quickly helped Mattie dry off and asked her, "How are you feeling this morning? Dora is at the doctor's trying to have a baby sister or brother for you. Which do you favor, a brother or sister?"

Mattie looked up at Hiram and smiled. Her head bobbled, and she said, "It don't matter with me Poppy. Just so it is healthy and not crippled like me."

Her words caught Hiram off guard. The word crippled cut him like a sharp knife. She had never mentioned being disabled before.

He put his arms around Mattie and said, "Now don't you go talking about pity for yourself. Who told you that you are crippled?"

Hiram smiled only to watch her smile vanish.

"Ceroa told me I was crippled. I know I can't walk too

good by myself and sometimes I have trouble forming my words, but I can't help that, can I Poppy?"

Hiram's face flushed as he searched for the words to say. "No, you are not crippled Mattie. You are not able to do some things, but there are a lot of things you can do that other people can't. You have a sweet singing voice, and the next time we attend church, I'm going to see if Clinton will let you sing. So, practice up. Now what do you want for breakfast?"

Hiram turned from her and built a fire in the cook stove.

After breakfast, Hiram loaded Mattie, Ceora and Joanna into the car and drove to Slonetown. He pulled up in front of the clinic and helped Mattie out and helped her walk to the door. Her words about being crippled had taken up residence in his mind, and he couldn't shake them. Hiram opened the door for her and the other girls and bragged on his daughter's effort. Ceora and Joanna asked Cassie where their sister was.

"She's in the birthing room. I look for her to have a baby by this evening. All of you can go in to see her if you want to."

Ceora bounced off her seat, followed by Joanna. Hiram helped Mattie rise to her feet and they walked through the door where Dora lay. Mattie smiled her crooked smile as soon as she saw Dora. Dora smiled back, holding her arms open for them, Hiram included.

Dora looked flushed and wet. Her hair was messed up

from where she had been pulling on it. Dora could hardly stand the labor pains. Hiram thought she was beautiful as she lay there. The lower half of her body was covered with a blue sheet.

After she hugged the girls, she stretched out her hand for Hiram and said, "Hiram, I'm afraid. The baby should have been here by now. The pain is something awful, and I've been sweating bad. Hold my hand a little while."

She closed her eyes for a minute then opened them staring at Hiram's gentle hand wrapped around hers.

"You are so gentle, Hiram. I hope to give you a child soon. Please don't leave me."

She raised her body up in the bed to try to get more comfortable. Hiram wondered if a woman could ever be comfortable having a baby, especially when it is her first one.

Hiram said, "I won't leave you. Don't worry. Just concentrate on having our baby. I'll take the children home and get Susanna and Clinton to sit with them and stay with them tonight."

That seemed to satisfy her. She closed her eyes and fell asleep. Hiram told Joanna to take Ceora to the car. He and Mattie followed them. On the way home, he stopped at Clinton's place and asked him if he and Susanna would stay with the girls until he returned home tomorrow. Then he raced back to clinic.

Hiram could hear Dora's moans when he walked through the clinic door. Cassie looked weary eyed. Hiram wondered if she'd gotten any rest today. Cassie gave herself to her patients and to River County also. Hiram recalled the same dedication that Doc Kelly had. He thought, "A doctor had to have a higher calling then most folks. That is what made them doctors." He didn't expect anything less from Cassie. She never one time mentioned marrying. She had hardly even talked to a man other than just saying 'hello'. Ever since the school days in Slonetown when she asked Hiram about the boy from Graves Creek. If she talked to anyone else he hadn't heard about it.

Cassie told Hiram she believed it was getting close. "Dora's pains are closer together now."

Hiram was still kind of worried, but he didn't want to let Cassie know it. Cassie opened the door to the birthing room and let Hiram see Dora. Cassie said, "You can watch the birth if you want to. Some city doctors are encouraging fathers to sit by while the birth takes place. But you have to stay calm."

Cassie grinned at her father as his face turned a bright red.

"No, I can't stay. I'll wait outside like all the other times. I've seen calves and foals born before, but when it comes to a live baby, that is different."

Hiram turned and walked to the porch, sat down in a chair and looked toward the courthouse. As he sat there, he thought how much the town had grown. He'd heard talk from others about the picture shows shown at the new theater, but he had no intention of going to one. He figured it a waste of time and money. He was hoping to be running his coal mine again by next week. He didn't want to wait any longer than he had to. He couldn't let the mine be idle too long. Bad air could build up inside, and it would take longer to start operating under safe conditions again. Two rock falls last fall killed three men in a mine on Turner's Branch. One of his uncle's boy was killed by a kettle head just last week. An idle mine was just an accident waiting to happen.

Hiram was interrupted by a loud moan from inside the clinic. He opened the door where he could hear clearer. After one final moan, Hiram heard the familiar sound of a slapping hand on flesh and the distinct sound of a baby crying. A wide grin spread across his face. He knew that everything was all right. He walked to the birthing door and opened it slowly. He could see Dora lying flat on her back. She looked worn out. A small bundle lay on her chest. Dora had her left arm circling the baby. Hiram inched his way forward so he could see. The baby was red faced, with rash bumps on its forehead. Its small hands wriggled as they touched each other. The baby's lips moved wanting to nurse. Cassie helped the midwife place the baby in position to, and nurse it did.

Hiram watched for a minute, then said, "It's got a Daniels appetite."

Dora grinned at him as she bonded with her newborn. It was another boy. Hiram already had a name picked out, if Dora would let him christen the child. He wanted Jesse.

Jesse Daniels. A fitting name he thought. No other Daniels carried this name that he knew of. He wanted something different. Something that people hadn't copied. A new generation; a new name; a new beginning. He was already proud of his new baby boy. No one could take the place of Mattie in his heart. He wouldn't even let anyone else try. That is where Hiram always carried his true feelings for his family, in his heart. He thought about Cullen at that time and wondered how he and his family were doing. Cullen was the only one of his children that had not turned like the others. Hiram had the strongest feeling of wishing Cullen were still on Troublesome Creek.

The baby's grunts brought his mind back to where he was. Dora was resting, holding baby Jesse. She and the baby looked like a picture lying there on the bed. Hiram was a happy man. He laid down on the bed where his wife and child lay. In a few minutes, he was sleeping and dreaming. He hadn't dreamed in a long time. But this dream was about Ballard. He was all dressed up in his Marine uniform, smiling and looking distinguished. Hiram could not recognize where he was or what they were doing. He first felt like he was in Newark, but it wasn't the same as when he was there before. After a while, Ballad vanished from view and there was open spaces where everything was beautiful. Hiram woke up to the baby's cry. He roused up to find Dora nursing Jesse again. He couldn't control his emotions. He cried tears of joy, of pride and of thankfulness. He rose from his chair and sat down on the edge of the bed, smiling at Dora. She smiled back a perfect smile, a smile of happiness and joy. Hiram thought on how the sight of a small baby can change an old person and give them hope.

Hiram touched Dora's brow. His love for her showed all over him. His smile stretched across his face. His countenance was bright with pride. Hiram rose from the bed and bent over and kissed her, then left for home. He wanted to check on Mattie. He knew she was in good hands but didn't want to stay away from her too long. He felt responsible for her care no matter what else happened. He loved all of his children, but his love for Mattie was beyond all the rest. He couldn't understand whether it was because of her condition or just because she was the last girl baby in the family. At that moment, he remembered how tiny she was at birth and how puny she was when she had the colic. He fell in love with her the first time he laid eyes on her. As he left for Troublesome there was a longing to stay with Dora and his new baby. He was torn between two options. But the further he drove along the winding road, his urge to be home grew. Mattie was waiting for him, and there would be plenty of time to spend with Jesse later on.

He pulled the pick-up truck into the 'proach,, stopped and turned off the motor. He climbed the steps to his house, opened the front door and walked in. Mattie's face lit up with her crooked smile. Her arms flung open waiting for her father's embrace as tears began to form in her eyes.

Hiram hugged his daughter and said, "Don't cry, Mattie. Everything is all right now. I'm home."

She waited for a minute, then looked up at Hiram saying, "I'm so happy, Poppy. I have to cry. That is the only way I can show my emotions. I'm happy, Poppy."

Hiram cradled her weak body and said, "My Mattie, My Mattie. You are so sweet. You will always be first in my heart, no matter what."

Hiram cried right along with her. Clinton and Susanna sat on the sofa.

Finally, Clinton said, "If you don't need us, we'll go on home." He and Susanna hugged Mattie. "Susanna has already put Ceora in bed, and Joanna is about ready. They have school tomorrow. Lundy has stayed with one of his friends in Slonetown."

Clinton turned as they were about to leave "If you need us tomorrow, let us know. Let us know about the baby too. We want to come back to see it when you bring him home."

Hiram thanked both of them as they went out the door. He turned to Mattie and said, "Well young lady, have you had supper?"

She dried the rest of the tears from her face.

"Yal, Poppy. Susanna fixed a good supper. When will the baby come home?"

Hiram said "Probably tomorrow. You'll like little Jesse. You will get a lot of pleasure out of him. Now let's you and I join Joanna and Ceroa and get to bed. A long day awaits us tomorrow."

He told Joanna and Ceora to sleep well. Hiram walked Mattie to her bed.

Hiram raised the sheet up to Mattie's armpits and said, "You sleep well now." He turned out the light and retired for the night.

Chapter 8

The slack of coal sales were over, and Hiram had received a new contract to sell his mineral. A company in Pennsylvania agreed to buy all the coal Hiram could mine. This was what he was waiting for. Dora and the baby were home and doing fine. Little Jesse grew faster than any child Hiram had ever seen. Mattie could help hold him if Dora placed him in her lap. Mattie thought she was just like any other grown up now and really doing something whenever Dora let her nuss Jesse. Mattie smiled that crooked smile until her gum line showed, making the small grunts she always did because of her excitement. Mattie loved Jesse.

Hiram and Clinton cleaned and opened the mine again. He wanted to run coal by Monday. Hiram worked all day and half the night. He was having a problem out of the mine bottom. It was nothing but mud when water seeped from the coal seam. The buggy Clinton drove would stick in the mud. Hiram worked all day sometimes hauling gob to fill the bottom, but still it sank. It seemed like the more he filled the bottom, the further it dropped. Seems like it was a bottomless pit, but Hiram didn't give up. By Monday, he was ready to shoot down a section of coal to haul out to the surface. His knees were swelled. When Hiram removed his knee pads, the puffed flesh dropped to one side. Hiram pulled his pants leg to the knee, exposing a kneecap of swelled flesh and fluid. Hiram touched the flesh and perched his finger into the swollen flesh of his knee. His finger hid itself in the soft skin.

Clinton said, as he stared at his brother's leg, "You need to let Cassie check that for you. That is the worst water on the knee I have ever seen." Clinton felt for Hiram.

Hiram pulled his pants leg down. He quickly put on the knee pads again and began work. He and Clinton drilled holes in the coal vein to load the holes with a full stick of dynamite. Joe prepared each stick of dynamite with a cap and inserted a fuse into the cap. Joe Martin had been shooting coal for years, and Hiram paid him good money in order to keep him. The man tied all the fuses together and rolled the roll of fuse to the other break and hid behind the other section and lit the fuse. Hiram and Clinton were already there.

Joe said, "Fire in the hole," just before the dynamite exploded. It made a loud boom, spraying coal dust, powder dust and slack coal flying towards the front of the drift mouth.

Hiram waited until the dust cleared, then he and Joe crawled to the fresh shot and began loading. Hiram always dreaded the smell of powder. The smell gave him a headache that was hard to get rid of.

By the evening, he and Joe loaded fifteen buggies full of

coal. Clinton figured what he hauled out would fill a tandem coal truck. Hiram had no trouble getting men to haul his coal. Lloyd pulled his ten-wheel tandem truck underneath the tipple and opened the gate and begin filling it. He loaded it just as full as he could get it. Hiram was afraid he would break an axle, but he didn't. His truck was so full that the mud flaps drug the ground as the truck pulled its load over the rough haul road. The truck rocked back and forth from side to side, spilling particles of small blocks of coal. But when the truck pulled out on the highway, the ten-wheeler rolled along pretty smoothly. Lloyd hauled coal until dark that night, then went ahead and loaded his truck for tomorrow. By the end of the week, everything was running smoothly. There were no problems, and Hiram needed the income.

The power company had sent representatives to speak to Hiram about buying some of his coal. He told the power company he would open another mine to fill their orders if need be. A coal boom was going on. The middle seventies were moving ahead, and the country was growing. Coal was needed and selling good. Coal was used to make electricity and manufacture steel for the automobile industry. Hiram was making real money. He'd worked through thin times and very few prosperous times, but it looked like the coal market was improving. Hiram opened another mine and hired a crew of men to operate it.

He worked for weeks without having a shut down. He figured he was lucky. One of the men he'd hired to work the other mine had brought his wife with him to work on a Saturday afternoon. Denzil took his wife back inside the mine one evening, riding her on the new scoop Hiram purchased.

When Hiram found out about the woman being inside the mine, he flew mad and said, "Don't you know it is bad luck for a woman to be inside a coal mine?"

He was furious as he watched the new man drive his wife back to the outside. She climbed off the scoop at the drift mouth. She was red faced and scared of Hiram. Hiram felt bad about yelling at her, but he was concerned. He figured Denzil would quit, but jobs were hard to come by. Couldn't hardly buy a good job right now that paid the wages Hiram paid.

Everything went fine for another two weeks. Then one day, early in the shift, a kettle head fell on top of the scoop while Denzil drove the machine to the outside. It caught Denzil just below the hips. The heavy rock smashed his hips and legs and snapped his thigh bone, crippling him for life. He had to be hauled out of the mines as Clinton drove the scoop to the surface. He never would be able to work again. His days of coal mining were over. Hiram hated this. He knew how he felt when he lost two men from his sawmill business years ago. He was glad the accident was no worse. The ambulance came, and two men picked Denzil up on a stretcher and took him to the Hazard hospital. Hiram shut the mine down until it could be inspected to give the okay that everything was all right. Hiram took Dora, Mattie and the baby to Slonetown for a checkup.

Slonetown was bustling. People filled the main street, talking and trading. Women shopped the stores, holding on to their small children, while older children played under the bridge that spanned Troublesome Creek. When River County annexed Ben's Fork, Cody and Smithtown, River County's taxable revenue had doubled. Ben's Fork was the rich part of the county. The creek was rich in both coal and natural gas. Several men became wealthy overnight it seemed. The richest of the group began buying up land all over the county. He built a fancy dwelling house and bought out several stores and businesses in Slonetown. He tried to buy Grant and Sissy out, but they wouldn't sell. He built a new movie theater in town. Hiram and Dora never did attend, but he let Joanna and Lundy take Mattie one time. She talked about that picture show for months. Hiram wouldn't let her go back. Joanna was talking to boys now and didn't have time for Mattie. No matter though, Hiram didn't want Mattie to go there anyway. Ceora was not stable for Hiram to let her and Mattie go alone.

Hiram helped Dora out of the car, then helped Mattie to stand. She almost fell twice. He made his mind up then and there. He was going to let Cassie take her to Louisville. Maybe the doctors can help her. He thought, "It's worth a try."

Inside Sissy's store, Hiram was greeted by his sister. She was crying. He hugged her and asked, "What is wrong?"

Sissy wiped tears from her eyes.

"The doctors in Lexington say Grant has cancer and doesn't have long to live. Lung cancer it is, and it's the fast kind."

She fell against his arms as Dora tried to console her. Finally, Sissy looked up into Hiram's face.

"I don't know what I'll do Hiram. I don't want to close our store and sell our other businesses. Marcus Wilson has offered to buy me and Grant out several times, and he's offered a more than fair price. But this is our home, our livelihood. We've been here all these years, watched this town grow and make something. We have roots here, Hiram." She broke down again.

Hiram reached Jesse to his mother and wrapped Sissy in his arms. He didn't like to see her like this.

"Grant may live for a while now. Only the Lord knows when a man's time is up. Try to be strong like you've been all these years." She quit sobbing and reached her arms to take Jesse.

The baby smiled at her then turned his head toward his father. This made Sissy forget her troubles for a minute. The eight-month-old loved attention, and he loved Mattie. Jesse never took his eyes off his sister. His eyes watched every move she made as she sat in the chair. Sissy reached Mattie her brother and let her nuss Jesse. Mattie and Jesse always had a good time together.

Hiram changed the subject.

"I am making good money now. I may buy part of your business out and help you run them. When Grant is down sick, you can take care of him and you will not have to worry about things. Dora can run the store, and I'll run the hardware store. Mattie can stay with Dora and Jesse and Ceora can help out until she gets into college or marries off."

This seemed to calm Sissy. Hiram heard Grant cough from the back bedroom. He stepped inside the door that led to their apartment and walked into the bedroom. Grant sat up in bed with two pillows underneath his head. Hiram thought Grant looked bad. He'd lost ten pounds or more since the last time he'd seen him. His face was a pale milky color. His eye sockets set inward, and his cheek bones were sharp and high. His appearance shocked Hiram so bad he had to look away. When Hiram looked at him again, he noticed Grant had lost a lot of his hair. He used to have the waviest, jet black hair. But today what was left of it was dingy and thin and graying. He looked eighty years old. Much older than his fifties.

Hiram walked over to the bed and took Grant's hand.

"How are you feeling?"

Grant stared upward with weak eyes and softly said, "Not much. Been sick, Hiram. How have you been?"

He coughed from the strain of just talking. Hiram sat down on the bedside as Sissy and Dora came in. Jesse was wanting Hiram to take him. Hiram held Jesse so Grant could see him. Grant smiled weakly at the baby.

"You've been blessed, Hiram. He's a fine looking boy."

Grant took a coughing spell, but he soon settled down. "He's a Daniels for sure. He's the spitting image of you."

He coughed again and motioned for Sissy to get him a clean handkerchief. Hiram felt so sorry or his brother-in-law.

Grant began again, "I remember the first day I saw the Daniels family. I always thought your family was as good a people as they make them. I only knew your mother for a short time, but she was one of a kind. Everyone would do well to fashion their lives after hers. I'm not going to live long, Hiram. Will you take care of Sissy for me? I love her so dearly."

Hiram dropped his head downward. He didn't want to cry in front of Grant. It was all he could do to hold his emotions in check.

"I'll try to take care of her. I might buy a part ownership in your business. That will ease part of her burden."

Grant smiled weakly again and said, "You know Hiram, I'm not afraid to die. I just hate to leave my family and friends. I made a lot of friends not only here in River County, but across several states." He turned his head and coughed until Hiram thought he might lose his breath. But he finally quit.

Hiram told him he would visit him again, then left. Hiram and Dora said their farewells and loaded Mattie and Ceora into the Buick. Jesse sat in his mother's lap. Hiram and his wife talked about a lot of things on their way home. Dora said she could help take care of Sissy's store and Mattie and Jesse could stay mostly in the backroom. Ceora would be in school.

"By the way," Dora said. "Joanna has been acting funny here lately. Have you noticed it, Hiram? She has been moody a lot."

Hiram turned to his wife and said, "You know they have been having a problem with marijuana at the Slonetown high school. Boys that went off to Vietnam came home and brought their bad habits with them. They tell me there is a lot of drugs in River county now." Dora shook her head in disbelief. Hiram said, "You know how a young man can talk a girl into doing just about anything anyway. We'll have to see the principal about her."

Dora agreed.

The weather was right for gardening. Hiram was up early and laying off his garden to get it ready to plant corn, beans and tomato plants. He'd already planted his tater patch and laid the taters by. He planted dog ticks in between the tater hills so the moles would not eat the tubers. He transplanted tomato plants. He wanted to keep the old seed alive. Seeds like red eye fall beans, mountain half runners and Big John beans. The new seeds sold in the hardware stores in Slonetown were just not the same. He also kept his salad pea seeds. Most people had already quit gardening. After the mines hired back and a few other jobs became available, his neighbors had been letting their pastures and new grounds grow up, and the weeds and saplings had taken over. A few had their bottoms enrolled in the government soil bank. For not farming their land, the government paid them to let it lay out. Every fall, Hiram mowed his hillsides with a mowing blade and plowed his bottoms, planting a cover crop.

Dora let Mattie help her cook a little. He wanted Cassie to make the appointments for Mattie to see if her disabled condition could be reversed. He didn't know if she could be helped, but he wanted to try. Mattie was born a change of life baby. He said to himself, "I'll try to do that tomorrow." Then he washed his hands and face and sat down at the table.

Mattie was already seated. She had been sitting there for a while, waiting for everyone to take their places. Dora held Jesse and smashed fried taters for the child. Jesse was sure a Daniels. His appetite was too good. After dinner, Hiram rode his truck to the mine to check on it.

Hiram made Clinton foreman of the mine operations. Hiram did all he could to protect his land, but some mine companies were trying to use new methods of mining. Auger mining was becoming an easy way of extracting the coal without putting a man underneath the ground at all.

Clinton said to Hiram, "One mine on up Troublesome just faced the coal, then used auger bits to drill into the side of the mountain, bringing out tons of coal. After the coal was pulled out, dirt was back filled into the bored out holes. It was an easy way of mining, but tons of coal was left inside the mountain. And the dirt pushed over the hillsides made for erosion problems." Hiram shook his head in disbelief.

Clinton and his crew were just finishing their shift. Hiram shook hands with his brother. Clinton did not slack in his work. He worked right along with his men. His face was covered with thick coal dust. His eyes were clear, but the rest of his face looked like he was colored, but his skin was still white from the rim up to his hairline when he took off his mining cap. When he grinned, his teeth were a pearly white.

Hiram said, "Everything go all right today?"

Clinton smiled and said, "Couldn't be better. We ran more coal today then we've run in a long time. The bottom is holding up, and my men are working good. I've got the best crew I've ever had. If we don't get blocked off, by next week we'll be ready for a new section."

Hiram listened to Clinton's assessment of the operation of the mine. Hiram was making real money now. He planned on building him and Dora a new house. A modern house made of brick and fancy rooms, with modern plumbing and water hook-ups, with a concrete driveway and a white plank fence.

Hiram talked to each of his workers telling them, "A bonus will be on your next paycheck."

The men seemed pleased with the news and they laughed with each other as they walked to their vehicles to drive home. Hiram examined the powder house and cap bin, to make sure the dynamite and shooting caps were secure. He took an inventory of what he had on hand. At the battery unit, he counted each hook-up and made sure all connections were connected. Hiram and Clinton talked to each other until the night watchman came on, then he drove off the haul road to the highway. At the foot of the hill, Hiram noticed the creek was about half black. He got out of his truck and looked towards Rolly Joe Mountain. As far as he could see, the water was being tainted by a runoff from a coal mine upstream. He decided to search where the black sludge was entering Troublesome Creek. He was mad that someone would be so careless to let their wastewater run off to the creek. He was already mad that some people threw trash into the creek or took their garbage back on the mountain sides to discharge over the mountain. Nothing made him angrier.

He hadn't traveled two miles until he saw where the black water was coming from. A new mine called 'Better Coal' was letting their ground water mix with the slate sludge, then allowing it to run down the ditch line near their haul road to the creek. He was mad but didn't want to report anyone. He drove up the haul road to the top to the mine bench and looked around but finding no one before he drove on home. He would check on the situation again tomorrow. He drove straight home.

Dora had fixed a large supper. Joanna and Ceora were watching the new television Hiram bought. He spent nearly a day hooking up a mountain line so the signal would come into the set. He didn't watch much on it. He watched the news now and then, or a western. He could only get three channels. Mattie was sitting at the table trying to nuss Jesse, and she was doing a fair job. Jesse kept wanting to get down and play on the floor. It was all Mattie could do to constrain the child.

Hiram washed his hands and dried them on the bathroom towel. He combed his hair in the new looking glass. He was the only one in his family that still called it a looking glass. Everyone else called it a mirror. Joanna spent hours at a time in front of it, primping. Then she would go off to school or go to the drive-in with a date. Hiram didn't like it because Dora didn't have enough control over her. He thought about saying something two or three times but thought better of it. It probably would just make Dora mad, and he didn't want to quarrel with her. She had been too good to him. He just didn't like it when Joanna took advantage of her sister.

He sat down in his chair and waited for Dora to set the table. He grinned at Mattie and she smiled back. He asked her what she'd been doing today.

"I've been helping Dora with the housework and taking care of my little brother." Her crooked smile raced across her face.

Hiram patted her shoulder and rubbed Jesse's head. The child reached for his father. Hiram took him and let him bang on the table with a spoon.

Dora carried the fried taters, gravy and cornbread to the table. Hiram watched her move with a young sway of her hips. Dora was about the same age that Alice Marie was when they married. He thought to himself as she moved about the kitchen, "How blessed I've been." Dora edged up against Hiram, to place the plate of fried chicken and store-bought butter on the table. Hiram loved her smell as she brushed against his side. He was in love with her. A love he didn't have for her when they first met. Now their marriage was more than a convenience. It had grown into a full blown affair that Hiram liked.

After she was through, Hiram told her of his plans to build their new house.

"I've made a lot of money for the last year. I am going to send Cassie and Mattie to Louisville next week to see about her getting braces. Maybe they can help her walk better. And I want us to start attending church every weekend some-where, starting this Sunday."

Dora passed him the plate of chicken. He gave Mattie a piece and put gravy and cornbread with it.

Dora said "That's fine with me, Hiram. I've always en-joyed going to church, ever since my mother and father died. We got a letter from Cullen and Ruby today, and you got a package from Sears. They are on the bureau."

Supper was very good that evening. He sat on the porch with Mattie until bedtime.

Cassie and Mattie were up early to make their trip to Lou-isville. Cassie stayed all night with her father so they could get an early start. By car, the trip would take anywhere from four to five hours. That is if the road was not too crowded.

Mattie sat at the breakfast table staring from person to person. She was all excited and could hardly wait to get started. She had eaten and was waiting for Cassie to get ready. Cassie was still primping in front of the looking glass. Hiram asked her if she thought they would have to stay all night or would they be back today? Hiram watched Cassie as she combed her blonde hair, flipping the ends back behind her shoulders. She grabbed bunches at a time to put into a ponytail. Cassie was a beautiful woman. Hiram wondered why she never married.

When he asked her, she would just shrug her shoulders and say, "I guess I could never find a man like you, Poppy. I've been so busy taking care of other people that I've not found time for myself, and I've missed out. But my life has been rewarding and full."

Mattie was watching as Cassie put on make-up. Hiram didn't care for the make-up but refused to say anything.

Cassie said "Poppy, why don't you trade this old mirror off and buy you a new one."

Hiram grinned at his daughter. "That old looking glass has saw about everybody in River County. If it could only talk and show you the faces that it has recorded over the years. Your grandma cherished it so much; I can't part with it."

Cassie ate a small breakfast and told Mattie, "We're ready. Let's go before the sun gets hot."

She hugged her father and Dora and said goodbye to Ceora. She helped Mattie to her feet and they both walked to the car. She started the engine and put the transmission in drive and headed toward Slonetown. Hiram watched until the car disappeared around the curve. He was hoping the doctors at the Louisville hospital could help his Mattie. He said a quick prayer for his two daughters.

Hiram walked to the barn and fed Mingo. He was thinking about sending him to the stock sale. Mingo was too old to work, and Hiram couldn't ride him like he used to. He hadn't owned a milk cow for a few years. The stores had plenty of milk, and even a dairy truck ran the neighborhood three times a week -- Monday, Wednesday and Friday. Hiram bought milk from the truck cheaper than he could keep a cow. The only thing he missed was the rich cream from the milk. Dora bought store bought butter now to take the place of cow butter. His pasture had grown up, and he received a small amount of money from the government soil bank for letting his land lay idle all year. Hiram didn't like the government paying farmers for not tending their land. He believed in raising most of his food. He watched the dairy truck pull into his driveway. He read the letters on the side of the milk truck. Southern Belle, it read. The driver honked his horn and got out of his truck and headed for the front door. He knocked and stepped back. Dora answered holding the screen door with her left hand. Dora told him something and the driver walked back to his truck. He opened the back door and took out a glass jug of sweet milk and a quart of butter milk. Dora used the butter milk to bake cornbread.

Hiram watched the truck drive on to its next stop. He missed the old, simple days of living and raising what he could on his land. He missed plowing his mule or horse instead of the tractors that plowed the bottoms and gardens. The tractor could turn over more land in a day than the mule could in a week. Hillside farming was something of the past. Most young people didn't know how to farm. A lot of young people left River County to get jobs in other states. Factories were a lot easier then farming, and they could make a lot more money. Factory jobs paid good wages and paid benefits. Hiram had never worked a public job, so he couldn't draw a government check.

The mining business was doing good. Hiram had hired two more men, one to pick slate and the other to help shoot coal. Bradford Melton had worked all his life inside a coal mine, and he loved to brag about it. Hiram didn't like a braggart, but this was different. Bradford could shoot more coal down in one shot then most shooters did in four. He was good at pulling pillars too. Hiram and Clinton worked two sections out and were finishing the new section up. Hiram told Bradford they would be pulling pillars today.

Hiram and Bradford crawled into the buggy, and Clinton drove to the main back of the section. He stopped at the coal face and turned the buggy into position to load the loose coal. Clinton did not get off the buggy. Hiram loaded from one side and Bradford loaded from the other. The section was one big room, with the roof supported by prop timbers. When the buggy was full, Clinton hauled the coal out to the tipple and dumped the load. Everything was going just fine until Hiram knocked on the last remaining timber. He hit the prop with a sledgehammer and the timber was tight. The sound of the hammer hitting the prop echoed off the darkening empty room. Hiram could tell by the sound of the timber that it held all the weight of the mountain. He said "Bradford, you get in the buggy with Clinton. Clinton back the buggy up next to me and when I knock this timber out, you take off for the entrance just as fast as you can go."

Clinton backed the buggy into position. Hiram pecked on the prop, but it didn't budge. He hit the timber with more force and the prop snapped in two. Hiram grabbed hold of the buggy as Clinton drove the machine forward. Hiram pulled himself into the machine and he watched the ceiling begin to fall toward them. Hiram watched as the roof caved in and rested on the bottom, making a pile of dust. To Hiram it looked like a wave of water coming at them, and he was glad when the buggy passed the section where the sides of the coal were still standing. He felt the force of the fall on his face and his hair. Coal dust stood in the air. Hiram looked toward the drift mouth and he could see light from the outside. He thought, "No wonder they call pulling pillars is the most dangerous part of mining."

Outside, Hiram raised from the laying position and went

to the battery house. He put his battery on charge and told Bradford and Clinton, "It's time to quit today. I don't like that kind of work. It is something to see, but there is too much force when that ceiling starts coming down."

Hiram told the slate picker to work until he was finished, and he could go home.

"Be sure and lock the gate to the haul road. We'll see you tomorrow."

Hiram thought about it a lot on his way home. He was ready to quit the mines and just lease his mineral rights to other coal companies. He could make just as much money, and he wouldn't have to work. He'd worked long enough anyway. He knew supper would be ready when he pulled into his driveway. He parked his truck and walked to the porch and opened the front door. He pulled his shirt off and threw it in the dirty box beside the Maytag washer. He washed his hands in the sink and dried them and sat down at the table. Dora kissed his cheek and continued sitting the table.

Hiram said, "Have you heard from Cassie? I thought she might be back from Louisville tonight."

Dora shook her head. "No, I've not heard from them."

Hiram's right knee was hurting bad. He pulled his pants leg up past his knee and told Dora to look at it. Hiram's kneecap was swollen and puffy. Water had built up just underneath the skin. His flesh around his knee was pink and a pale white. He wished Cassie were here. He figured it would just have to wait so he pushed his pants leg back down over his leg.

Ceora sat eating at her place. She told her sister, "Joanna was talking to a boy near the bus stop today. They were smoking. I saw her puff on a cigarette and then she reached it back to him."

Dora looked toward Hiram. "I don't know what I'm going to do. She won't listen to me, and she's failing her grades. What can I do Hiram?"

Hiram ate his ham and eggs, sopped his biscuit in the gravy and said, "I'll talk to her when she gets home. She needs to listen to you and try to study and make something out of herself."

When he finished, he walked out on the front porch and sat down in his rocker. Dora joined him and sat next to him. They held hands until Joanna came home.

A car stopped in front of the house and Joanna got out and walked toward them. As she walked up the steps to the porch, Hiram told her he wanted to talk to her for a minute.

"I don't have time, and I'm hungry," Joanna said. Her tone was hateful and sassy.

Hiram's blood began to boil. He'd never let his children talk to him this way, and he wasn't going to let anyone else start now. She took hold of the front door handle.

Hiram spoke up with a stern voice and said, "Young lady, I said I have something to say to you."

Joanna stopped and turned towards Dora as if she might tell Hiram he didn't have the right to speak to her in such a tone. Dora was mad too. She looked straight at her sister. There was no sympathy for Joanna in her stare.

Joanna let go of the door handle and turned to look at Hiram. Her head dropped, and Hiram couldn't see her eyes or hear the muffled words she said under her breath.

Hiram waited a minute, then began. "I pay the bills here, not you. I furnish you a roof over your head and provide something to eat. I buy your clothes, and your sister gives you spending money for school. So, if you stay here, you'll have to mind your sister, and you'll have to be considerate to everyone else's feelings."

Joanna's face turned red, and she blew air out her mouth. She stared at the floor and twisted her feet as if she was grinding them into the wood.

Finally, she said, "I'm seventeen, and I'm old enough to be on my own and to do what I want and with who I want."

She was fuming mad. Hiram let her stand there like that for a minute. Then he said, "No you are not old enough to tell me and your sister what you can do. You will not be seeing that boy anymore, and you'll be grounded for a week. There will be no money for buying things to take to school."

Hiram stopped and watched her stand. She shifted her weight on one foot then the other.

After what seemed like fifteen minutes, she turned and slammed the screen door shut. Dora started to rise, but Hiram stopped her. "Let her fume for a while. She needs to think about what she's doing." Dora held Hiram's hand until they went inside for bed. Hiram didn't sleep much that night. He didn't like to talk to Joanna like he did, but she was out of control. Hiram was up two times with Jesse, comforting him when he was restless. He'd never whipped his children before, but this is a new generation coming up. Different from what his generation used to be. He thought as he settled Jesse back into his bed, "So many changes since my children were young. Dope and drugs are becoming rampant. The Vietnam War has just ended. Ever since President Kennedy was assassinated along with his brother, Robert, and Martin Luther King, there had been unrest in some of this nation's larger cities. Coal mining was changing. A new kind of mining called strip mining was catching on and he hated it. "I don't like the changes that are taking place." he thought.

He woke to a pouring rain. The rain beat on the roof of his new house. He looked out his window and Troublesome Creek was muddy. The wild creek rushed by, taking loose soil and washing it down stream, filling the waterholes where all kinds of fish used to swim. Hiram hadn't seen a silver-side or shiner in the waters of Troublesome since the black water had been discharged from the new mine upstream. It slowly poisoned the creek, but the state department of government wouldn't try to stop it. The mines paid a state tax on each ton of coal produced, so the Department Of Mines and Minerals looked the other way a lot of times.

Lundy had graduated high school and somehow had avoided the draft. He was happy he didn't have to go to Vietnam. Lundy was a six-foot sharpshooter in basketball. He probably could have gotten a scholarship to a large college in a big city somewhere, but he wouldn't listen to Dora or Hiram. Hiram had tried to talk to him about trying to get an education so he could make something out of himself. He never did talk back to Hiram, but he didn't want to hear anything he had to say either. He ran with a pretty rough crowd, smoking dope when he could get it while hanging out at the pool hall. He'd visit all the dairy bars on the weekends playing the juke box and pinball machines. But the law finally caught up with him. He was picked up by the sheriff of River County. After he got out of jail, he rode a bus to Ashland to take a physical. From there, the Army shipped him to Fort Bragg North Carolina for basic training.

The next time Dora heard from him was by letter. He was stationed in Germany. Dora cried that day. Hiram read the letter. Lundy was homesick as could be, but there was no way he could come home.

Dora was sick for a few days after she received the letter from Lundy. Hiram heard her crying from time to time, and he comforted her as much as he could.

"He will have to pull at least a year over there. I think the Army will be good for him. When Ballard was lost in World War II, it was one of the worst days of my life. Our government gets us into these wars and our young men have to fight whether they want to or not."

Dora sat down beside him on the sofa. Hiram put his arms around her, and she wilted in his embrace. Hiram didn't like to see her upset. They sat for an hour holding one another.

She raised her head towards Hiram and said, "Shouldn't Joanna be home by now? It is after nine o'clock. Do you think we need to go look for her?" Dora was worried.

Hiram rose and reached for his coat, "We'll go to Slonetown and look around. Get your coat. Ceora can stay here alone. We'll take Jesse with us." Hiram walked into the bedroom and told Ceora where they were going.

Hiram started the Buick, and he and Dora headed for Slonetown. He drove down main street looking at places where some of the teenagers hang out. But they couldn't find Joanna. Hiram stopped in front of the high school, but the parking lot was empty. Slonetown High School had won a state basketball championship a few years back. That's why Hiram tried to convince Lundy to play ball, but he wouldn't. Hiram drove toward Betty's Troublesome on his way home. At the mouth of Ben's Fork, there were a few rented houses that belonged to Roscoe Cannard. One of them was used for a Jenny barn. It was a bootlegged establishment where men gathered to play poker and drink and sleep with loose women of the county. The county sheriff knew what was going on there, but Hiram figured Roscoe bought the sheriff off. He rode by there to see if he could see anyone, but no one was outside. A dim light was on in one of the backrooms, but

Hiram couldn't see inside.

He asked Dora, "Are there any other places you think we might need to look?" She started to cry again.

Hiram drove towards Little Doubles, but they still didn't see anyone. Hiram turned around and started back to Troublesome.

"I'm sorry, Dora. We'll report it to the sheriff in the morning. We'll find her." Dora cried all the way home. She'd raised her three siblings just like they were her own children. Hiram felt sorry for his wife. After they got home and retired to bed for the night, Hiram held her until she went to sleep. He drifted off to sleep and dreamed the whole night. He was restless all night long.

When he woke the next morning, fog was lifting over the mountains. He walked out on the porch and looked toward Rolly Joe Mountain, but the fog was so thick he couldn't see half mile up the road. The birds were chirping, and Dora's blue Banty hen was clucking with another brood of ditlers. Dora's rooster crowed from his roost. Hiram could barely see a form walking toward his house. Finally, he could make out the form of a girl. It was Joanna. She walked up the steps to the porch and sat down in the rocking chair. She watched Hiram with a smirk on her face, figuring he would say something to her for laying out all night. But Hiram never let on. He was going to let Dora deal with her as long as she didn't get violent. Dora must have heard her steps on the porch. She came through the front door and stood and looked at

Joanna.

Joanna began to cry. She cried and hung her head into her lap. She twisted her arms and hands around her body trying to squeeze her life out. Her face was a pale white. Her make-up had run down her cheeks, mixing with tears. A foul order of alcohol came from her blouse. A button was missing, and her pedal pushers were wrinkled where she had slept in them. A muddy patch of dirt dried on her left pocket of the white jeans.

Dora just looked at her for a minute, then motioned for her to get inside and clean up.

"I want you to take a hot bath and make sure you get clean. We'll talk about this later."

Joanna rose from her chair then bowed her head. She walked through the living room door and vanished out of sight. Dora followed her inside. Hiram sat down in the porch swing and thought about a lot of things for the next thirty minutes, then he rose to start breakfast.

After breakfast, he took his hoe and worked out the garden. His sweet corn patch was coming up, and he figured in another week he could plant beans in the corn. His tater patch was laid by for the year. He'd been eating lettuce and onions for some time now. He never got tired of his garden vegetables. He still liked his home-cooked meals. A lot of his neighbors and some of the young people were living on commodities and cheese distributed out by the government. He'd tried the powdered eggs and powdered milk, but he didn't care for them. He did like the cheese.

Men that were unemployed worked on the 'happy pappy' or 'muskrat gang' program the government provided. Hiram used to watch the men as they cleaned Troublesome Creek banks from brush and debris. They picked garbage from the creek where someone had thrown it in the creek and it washed from up-stream. This hurt Hiram. He'd always taken care of the water, keeping it as clean as he could. He never threw anything in the water to harm it or make it muddy. But mining and bulldozing and making roads and clear cutting the timber was taking its toll on Troublesome.

Hiram had all of his crops and garden laid by. July was hot and dry. Forty days of dryness was in store when dog days set in. Fog rose from Troublesome Creek as Hiram walked to the barn. He planned on walking his ridge line where chinkipins trees used to grow. It was too early to gather the fruit, but he wanted to check to see if any ginseng berry pods were full or not. It had been a long time since he'd hunted ginseng. He didn't need the money like he used to.

He took his Colt forty-five with him just in case he ran across a rattlesnake. Hiram walked to the first flat, then turned and walked the swag to the middle point. Then he started walking the difficult climb to the ridge top. He dug his heels in as the loose black dry soil moved underneath his feet. His feet would slide downhill sometimes, but he always straightened his body out and climbed upward. He finally reached the top, and he sat down to rest for a minute. He looked around to see if any kind of snake lay in the underbrush. He didn't see or hear any.

After a brief rest, he rose to his feet and looked toward Rolly Joe Mountain. The haze from the distance to the rising mountain made it hard to make out the chimney rock. He stood looking over the valley floor where Troublesome Creek flowed by lazily. The water made a roaring sound where the stream bed dropped off at the swimming hole. He wondered how many times he'd stood in the same spot when he was younger while hunting squirrels or ginseng hunting. He never got tired of this view. He loved his land and felt close to it. It was part of him. All down through the time his grandpa Jennings owned it until it was given to Poppy and then passed on down to him.

Hiram looked out on the point where the growth of chickipin trees grew. He could see the young burs maturing in the summer sun. Hiram thought, "The burs will not grow much larger. By September, the chinkipin fruit will be ready to gather." The burs were tough to open sometimes, but the nut was well worth the trouble. Chinkipins were smaller than the giant Chestnuts that used to flourish on the mountain sides. Hiram missed that great tree which could be used for just about anything, but now they had been reduced to just snags or small saplings that would not live. The blight killed even the young sprouts.

Hiram glanced back down the hill toward his home. He was ready to go. He started down the steep mountain. He slid sideways, catching himself against a tree stump. He walked through his grown-up pasture and past the swag. He followed a eroded ditch to where his barn sat. He figured Dora would have supper ready, and he was hungry. He opened the front door to the aroma of cooked ham and biscuits. He washed his hands and dried them with a towel and sat down at the supper table. Dora hugged him and continued setting the table. Joanna was sitting on the sofa. She came to the table, embarrassed from the other night. She'd been shying away from Hiram, but she had to face him sometime. Hiram grinned at her. He wasn't mad at her.

Hiram missed Mattie, and wondered when she and Cassie would be home. He was hoping to himself that braces would help his daughter walk. Mattie would always be disabled in some way or another, but to be able to walk better would be something she could accomplish for herself. His knee still gathered fluid and hurt most days. He could have gone to another doctor, but he wanted to wait on Cassie.

Chapter 9

Hiram and Clinton formed a new coal company named 'The Daniels Brothers Coal Company.' Hiram put up most of the collateral for the project. He used his savings and a bank loan against his farm. Clinton would be the foreman of the company and would oversee the workings of the mine. Hiram hired a contractor from Slonetown to build the haul road and face up the number four seam of coal. The contractor was unloading his bulldozer just after daylight and he went straight to work on the haul road. Hiram followed him up the steep terrain, watching the dozer push dirt and rock. He loved to watch the dozer work. His topsoil was black for close to a foot down into the ground. But the dozer could move and push all the topsoil off, and the brown dirt showed. The contractor was good at what he was doing, and he respected Hiram's wishes, pushing only the soil that was needed.

By that evening, the haul road and mine site were finished. The dozer operator had faced the coal seam and the outcrop of coal had a mud seam in it. It was ready to work.

Hiram showed the contractor where to make a site for the coal tipple. When he was finished, Hiram and the operator talked a few minutes, and he paid him five hundred and fifty dollars for the dozer work. Hiram thanked the operator for being patient with him.

"My family has owned this land for over a hundred and fifty years now, and I don't want to tear up no more of it than I have to."

The contractor shook his head in agreement and drove his dozer down the hill and loaded it back on the low-boy. It was nearly dark. Hiram watched the truck and dozer vanish out of sight.

Dora had a large supper ready. He washed his face and hands and sat down in his regular place. His wife yelled for Joanna and Ceora to come and eat. The food was good and filling. He was thinking of Mattie and Cassie. He asked Dora if she'd heard anything today.

"No, I haven't, but I believe we will soon. I got a letter from Lundy today. He's stationed somewhere near Berlin. I could tell by the way he worded the letter; he's not satisfied. I feel sorry for him and I've been praying for him every night."

Hiram listened to her as she described the letter.

"He writes that he is doing good," Dora said as she looked away. She seemed worried. Hiram knew how much a person can lose in just a short time. Ballard had not been in the service long at all when sad news came about him.

"It is peace time, so don't worry too much about Lundy. Clinton can tell you stories about when he was fighting in Germany."

Hiram finished his supper and turned his radio on to listen to the news before bedtime. The news reporter talked about a new president being elected. He listened as the reporter's voice boomed out of the radio speaker. Hiram turned the radio off and got ready for bed. Dora had Jesse already asleep in the room Hiram built for the lad. He spent many days sanding the wormy chestnuts planks and then varnishing them before he nailed them to the walls. Hiram bragged on that room every time someone visited. Sleep came early for Hiram.

The next day, the sun was burning off a heavy frost. After breakfast, Hiram fed his two hogs he planned to kill soon. "When the mornings get cold enough, I will get the water hot." he thought. Dora always rendered out all the lard she could. The fresh rendered lard tasted better than the store brand Hiram bought. Store bought was good, but it didn't have the same taste as the fresh rendered grease.

Hiram picked up the chainsaw, and he walked to the mine site to wait on Clinton and John Bradly Sorrels. John B. was a young man from Slonetown Hiram hired to help construct the coal tipple. He was stout and could work all day long without stopping. Hiram had heard of him through Sissy. Hiram picked out the posts he wanted to cut for the tipple. He bought planks for the sides. The bottom would have a trap door where the coal would fall through to load the trucks. Hiram heard about iron tipples being built by other coal companies, but wood tipples would do until there was more money.

Hiram stood looking down the steep hill when he caught site of Clinton and John B. John B. almost ran up the hillside as he dug his heels in. He raced over the loose dirt. Clinton walked the haul road. Hiram found himself wishing he could still work and get around like the young John B. The young man grinned at Hiram as he topped the berm near the haul road.

He said, "I'm ready and able, sir."

Not too many young people had the kind of respect to call you 'sir' anymore. It made Hiram think back to the old days when respect was expected. Hiram shook hands with the young man and greeted Clinton with a smile. Hiram grabbed the chainsaw and told John B. to grab the ax. The young man was nineteen years old. He was six foot three and weighed around two hundred and ten pounds of mostly solid muscle. His blonde hair was curly and kind of long, Hiram thought, but he would not insult the boy for wearing his hair that way. A lot of men fresh out of the army after a tour in Vietnam wore their hair long, and most of them smoked marijuana. Hiram had to keep an eye on his mountain swags to keep marijuana growers off his land. They would slip into his property and plant patches of the illegal crop to sell and smoke. John B.'s eyes were a perfect blue as a cloudless sky.

His skin was a light tan from all the work he did during the summer months.

Hiram set the saw into the one side of the oak tree and motioned for the young man to watch out. In a hour, they had the poles needed to build the tipple. Clinton dug the holes for the posts to sit in. Hiram showed John B. what to do, and he picked up the posts and placed each one into the dug holes. By dinner time, the tipple posts were set and ready for the plank. Hiram and Clinton nailed the planks while John B. reached them to Hiram. By supper, the tipple was done. Hiram stood back and studied the crude looking tipple. They were ready to run coal. He told Clinton and John B. to be back there in the morning about the same time to start. Hiram was tired and needed the rest.

Dora met him at the door.

"We heard from Mattie today. Cassie told me they would be home sometime tomorrow afternoon."

This pleased Hiram so much that he clapped his hands together and praised the Lord. He'd missed both of his daughters, but Mattie was still his special child.

Dora had supper ready and, as they ate, she said, "Cullen and Ruby will be home this weekend too. Cullen quit his job, and they are moving back to Kentucky."

Hiram didn't say anything for a while. He ate the food his wife had fixed, then he leaned back in his chair and said, "I don't know what he thinks he's going to live on. I might be able to give him some work, but probably not enough to feed and clothe his whole family. He's got seven now, three which I've not seen."

He rose from his chair and sat down in his rocker in the living room. The fire in the chimney was warm and comforting. There was a hint of frost in the cool air. He sat there rocking for half an hour, then he and Dora went to bed. He held his wife close and talked to her about his troubles. He'd been worried about Mattie so much, and now Cullen was moving back. He was worried about the coal mine operation.

"One bad move and we could lose everything we own."

Dora listened to him talk without interrupting him. Finally, when he was through, she kissed him and told him, "Everything will be all right."

They fell asleep in each other's arms.

Daylight came with Dora's rooster announcing morning to the world. It was time to get up. Hiram felt sore from the day before. He used muscles yesterday that he hadn't used in a while. But after a hour or two, he limbered up again. He fed his two hogs and walked back to the mine site. It was cool, but a good time to work. Clinton pulled his truck onto the mine site, got out and said to Hiram, "John B. won't be here today. He called me early this morning. His sister lost her two young children last night."

Hiram looked startled. He said, "What happened?"

Clinton stumped the loose dirt at his feet and replied to Hiram.

"It is an awful thing to happen. Those two little children were just eight and ten years old. Somehow, they were playing hide-n-seek and the two hid in an old chest freezer. Evidently, the door closed on them and they suffocated before anyone could find them. I have to preach their funeral tonight and tomorrow."

Hiram was speechless. His face turned pale from the news.

He said, "I hate to hear that. Little children are so innocent, and it hurts when they lose their lives at such a young age." He shook his head as he turned to stare at Rolly Joe Mountain.

He sat down on the bed of Clinton's truck, and the two men talked about the coal mine and how to go forward with it.

He said, "We'd better get to work." He put on his knee pads and walked toward the mine entrance. Clinton followed and crawled into the scoop cab. Hiram laid down in the scoop pan to ride.

Hiram picked out all the coal he could and shoveled it in a pile. They had advanced under the hill enough to start sitting prop timbers to hold the top. Hiram set the popular props in place and hammered cap wedges to make the top even. Hiram cut and sawed timbers for a week and had them stacked nearby for easy handling.

After dinner, the two men kept working and moving coal. Hiram placed four-by-fours to make the drift mouth overhead. The four-by-fours went about ten feet back inside the mines.

"Tomorrow, I'll hire Buford Wilson to shoot coal for us. I have to order new coal buggies and an electric cable to run them by. The power company is supposed to hook our juice up one day this week."

It was a slow go, but by quit time Hiram and Clinton had gone about one hundred and fifty feet under the hill. The mine was shaping up, and Hiram was pleased. He and Clinton quit, and Hiram told his brother he would be there at church tonight. Hiram wagged his mudded gum boots to the mine shed, unbuckled his mining belt and placed his battery light in the charger. Clinton did the same. Both men rode toward their homes.

At home, Hiram told his wife about the two children. He asked her if it would be all right if he went to the wake.

She hugged him and said, "Yes, it is all right. I'll be here when Cassie and Mattie get home. Don't stay in Slonetown to long though."

He kissed her and took a bath, then drove to town.

Hiram pulled his pick-up into the parking lot and parked. Inside the River County Funeral Home, there was a large crowd gathered for the children's viewing. Hiram walked through the double doors and began shaking hands with almost everyone there. He knew just about everybody. He shook hands with John Bradly. The young man introduced him to his sister and her husband.

Hiram shook their hands and said, "I'm sorry for your loss," with all the humbleness he could gather in his voice. Hiram had gone through so much death and sorrow in his own life. He knew how this young mother and father felt. He walked by the coffin and gazed down into the faces of the children. Both were laying in the same coffin, with hands joined. That's the way they found them, huddled together, holding each other's hands. They looked so peaceful, laying side by side. Cold lips had formed on each child's face. Hiram gazed at the two corpses and said an unspoken prayer. Hiram felt the loss the couple were enduring.

Flower arrangements were aligned by the walls and sitting on the floor near the coffin. Two high lamps were sitting on each end, towering over the light blue casket. A few church members were seated behind the coffin getting ready to have church. Clinton hadn't arrived yet. Hiram sat down in a folding chair to await his brother's arrival. He watched as the crowd kept coming in and mingling together. The visitors took their places in the chairs the funeral director set out. There was three rows back to back. He heard Clinton's voice, so he turned to watch him greet the crowd.

Clinton signed the guest book. He picked up one of the obituary cards and glanced at it, then he walked the aisles, greeting each person. He'd learned from one of the best – Preacher Silas. Clinton hugged most of the sisters and non-sisters. He shook hands with all the men and hugged a lot of them. Hiram could tell Clinton was well liked and respected amongst this community. When he reached the young mother and father, the young woman melted in his arms, crying uncontrollably. Clinton rubbed her shoulders as he held her up. She cried with her head buried in his chest until she finally turned and sat back down in her chair. The young father held to Clinton's hand for a long time before he let it go. Clinton hugged Hiram when he got to him. He was ready to preach. Hiram could both see that in his eyes and could tell by the sound of his voice. Hiram watched his brother walk to his seat and sit down. He bowed his head.

Hiram heard Brother Lonzo make his entrance with a booming voice. Hiram marveled how the old preacher's voice held up under years of preaching, singing and shouting. It never did waver. Instead, it seemed to get stronger as the years went by. He worked the crowd as a politician would asking for votes, but his interest in the crowd was much more important than a vote. Everyone in this county counted him a man of God, and everyone respected him, both sinner and saint alike, just like they did Preacher Silas. These men of God separated themselves from the world and kept their robes clean as they walked through temptations and the wiles of the devil while holding onto the unseen hands of a higher power, which Hiram believed in. When the preacher reached out for his hand, Hiram's lips quivered. A smile greeted Hiram as he melted under the preacher's stare. He'd felt this with Preacher Silas, and now he felt the same moving Spirit with Brother Lonzo. Hiram stared at the floor for a minute then he looked into the eyes of the man of God. Hiram felt chill bumps on his arms and neck. Hiram was sure he was looking into the face of a heavenly being. Hiram made an effort to see more then the naked eye could see, trying to look deeper than the flesh. He tried to look deep into the soul of this man, and he felt a moving deep inside his heart. Finally, the old preacher let his hand go, but he held unto Hiram with his eyes. Hiram couldn't describe the feeling completely, so he didn't try.

Brother Lonzo took his seat, and Clinton sang a song, opened services and held prayer. Then Brother Lonzo came forth and sang the song, *Gone Away with a Friend*. The sisters began to shout, and the Spirit moved about the house bringing tears to most, even Hiram. The young couple sat holding each other, crying their eyes out over their loss. They would have to start over with a family, these being their only children. Hiram's heart emptied out with all the emotions he had. Finally, church was over, and Clinton called dismission. Clinton then told the crowd the young couple did not have much money to pay for the funerals and asked for a donation to help with their debt. Two men passed a basket as people threw in what they could afford or what they felt appropriate. Hiram pitched in a hundred dollar bill. By the time Clinton had the money counted, it amounted to six hundred dollars. John B. stood and told the gathering his sister appreciated every one's help. Hiram said goodbye to all and headed for his home.

When Hiram pulled the pick-up into his driveway, he noticed Cassie's car was parked under the shade tree. He quickly exited his truck and almost ran to the front door. When he walked into the living room, he saw Mattie sitting on the sofa, smiling. He sat down beside her and hugged her for the longest time, squeezing her. She smiled her crooked smile until her gums showed as she giggled with excitement. She loved her father, and she was glad to be home. Hiram pulled himself away from her and stared at her face then glanced down at her legs and feet. Each foot had a metal brace attached to them that ran all the way to his daughter's knee. A metal ring circled each leg.

Hiram grinned at her and said, "Well, show us how they work!"

Mattie sat up on the edge of the sofa, then slowly raised her frail body to a standing, yet wobbly, position. She finally gained her balance and started walking toward her father, moving one foot at a time without the help of anyone. When she reached Hiram, he hugged her and cried tears of joy. Mattie cried too, along with Dora and Cassie. Hiram was so pleased.

Then Hiram turned to Cassie and held his arms out to her. She hugged her father, crying on his chest. Hiram gently pushed her back and looked into her eyes saying, "Ballard would have been just as proud of you as I am. You've done so well, and the people here have missed your doctoring."

Dora reached Hiram his baby boy, Jesse. She said, "I've got to prepare a snack for all of us." She disappeared into the kitchen. After eating, Hiram went to bed satisfied.

Monday morning was wet as the rain poured down upon Troublesome. Hiram fixed breakfast for himself and walked to the mine site. He sat down under the heading that helped hold the roof up. He could see inside the mine. Water was rising. He got the sump pump out of the tool shed and started the motor. He threw the hose into the water and began to pump the gallons of water from the mine. Clinton and John B. would be arriving any time, and he wanted to run all the coal he could this week. The company was behind in filling their contract, and without a contract there would be no coal company. By daylight, the water had been pumped out and the bottom was dry.

Clinton looked into the mine as Hiram pulled the pipe and put the sump pump back into the tool shed. John B. was a little late, but Hiram told him that it was all right. He really liked the young man. Hiram asked him how his sister and brother-in-law were.

"They are better. It will take a while for them to get over their loss," he said as he turned his head away.

Hiram said, "Well, let's run some coal."

Clinton drove the buggy up to the entrance and Hiram

and John B. jumped on. Clinton laid over to the left side, dodging the side of the coal as he drove the buggy deeper into the mine shaft. Hiram kept a lookout for kettle heads, which were as dangerous as a cocked gun.

"Kettle heads kill more miners then cave-ins. They are unpredictable," he told the young miner.

At the face of the coal, Hiram jumped off his side, grabbed his coal shovel and began to load the metal box. The buggy would hold over two tons of coal; heaped up they would almost hold three tons. Hiram paid by the buggy load, and nineteen buggies made a shift. John B. was young, and he could outload Hiram and Clinton both. Hiram loved to sit and watch him swing his shovel as the steam rose from the young man's back. Hiram recalled the days he could work like that, but those days were gone for him. Still, he could make a day's work count.

Soon the buggy was full, and Clinton drove to the out-side. While he was gone, Hiram piled gob-rock along the rib cage and set up a brandish cloth to seal off another heading. Hiram let John B. rest while Clinton was gone. The two men sat down and talked for a minute as they waited for Clinton's return. Hiram noticed the top of the roof was making popping sounds as water dripped from the unstable roof top. Hiram wondered how much weight the top had on it. Thousands of pounds of rock and dirt rested on the timbers.

Hiram said, "A whole mountain rests on this timbers and props you see here." Hiram tapped one and it made a tight twang as a fully tightened banjo string would.

Hiram turned to John B. and said, "You hear that? When you are pulling pillars, you watch for that sound. That sound means the weight of the mountain is on that one prop. You pull it and take off. Get out as soon as you can."

John B. was listening to Hiram because he figured Hiram was right, and he wanted to be careful as he could. Clinton pulled the buggy into position and took Hiram's place with the shovel. Clinton could almost keep up with John B. The buggy filled quickly.

Hiram said, "Let's eat."

Hiram took his dinner bucket and sat down on the mine floor and leaned back against the rib. The other two men did the same. The number four coal seam was just a tad over forty-eight inches high. The coal seam was forty-eight inches and after the draw rock came down with the coal there was plenty room to sit and eat dinner. Hiram liked working inside the mines. The hard work was just now paying off for Hiram and Clinton. They were paying for their equipment and all the mine bills. Hiram paid themselves a good wage, and each put money in the bank. Hiram told John B. that he would be in charge of night watching on Sundays. He could make extra money and save it for his future. Young John B. was tickled to have his job.

He said, "Why, thank you, Mister Daniels; I plan on marrying soon, and I'll need the money."

The day went well, no breakdowns at all. By quit time,

the three men were worn out and ready to go home.

The mining business was doing good, and Hiram and his crew were running record amounts of coal. He hired Claybern Gibson to be the shoot man after Buford quit. Claybern's reputation was known throughout the mountains, and he proved his worth in a days' time. Hiram watched him load the drilled holes with dynamite. Claybern placed a full stick of dynamite into the deep holes but only a half a stick in the shallow holes. He placed a dynamite cap inside each dynamite stick, with a fuse running to the place where the men could hide from danger. Hiram, Clinton and John B. waited for Claybern in a separate heading of the mine while the dynamite went off. Hiram watched Claybern set fire to the fuse and run-crawl to where they were.

Hiram asked him, as they waited for the shot to go off, "Did you ever get caught when the dynamite exploded?"

Claybern pulled his britch-lag up to his kneecap and showed Hiram and the other men blue patches of coal particles. "These are what was left of slack coal that embedded inside my knee cap. The doctor got what he could out, but what you see will be with me until I die, just like a tattoo. No way of removing it all."

He grinned at Hiram and yelled, "Fire in the holeeee."

Claybern watched the young man as John B.'s eyes opened wide. The blast sounded like a thud at first, then the force of the dynamite exploding could be heard as the spray

of coal and dust went by the heading where they were working minutes before. The force of the blast was deafening.

Hiram waited for five minutes to let the air clear. John B.
started to crawl back to the work heading.

Hiram said, "Wait for a few more minutes. The smell of
powder will give you a bad headache if you don't."

After five more minutes, Hiram said, "Let's go load that
coal."

Mattie was doing very well. She could walk without
crutches or a cane. Hiram knew she was pleased as she prac-
ticed slow walking, trying not to stumble. She did wobble a
bit, but she could catch her balance, then go on. She'd help
Dora sit with Jesse. Mattie learned to set the table, to cook
and to bake bread. Tickled her to death. She proudly showed
her father whenever she finished something new. Hiram gave
her all the encouragement he could, and Mattie loved it.

Hiram told her one night, "We might take you to town
this weekend. Would you like to see a show at the theater?"

Mattie's crooked smile inched across her face. Her eyes
were lit and shiny. Her cheeks were flushed.

"Would you, Poppy? Would you?"

She rose to her feet and wobbled over to where Hiram
sat. She bent over to kiss his cheek. Hiram loved to please
her. Dora smiled as she held Jesse in her lap. Hiram heard
someone at the door. He rose to answer. When he opened the
front door, there stood Cullen with his whole family. Hiram

opened the door and waited for each to enter and take a seat on the sofa and living room chairs.

Hiram was a little surprised to see them. Cullen shook hands with his father and spoke to Dora. He never did like Dora, but he could manage to hide his true feelings when he had to. Dora always treated him with respect because of Hiram. Cullen's children set looking at their grandfather, not saying a word.

Hiram asked, "Have you all had supper?"

Ruby spoke first, "No we don't have much to eat at our house right now. Cullen just got out of jail last night. The sheriff caught him for bootlegging again."

Cullen dropped his head and grinned. "One of our goody-two-shoe neighbors gave me away. I can't get nothing done sometimes because of them."

Dora rose to her feet and started setting the table for the extra company. She had washed all the dishes. She turned on the new gas stove Hiram bought her. Cleveland Gas had drilled a new gas well on his property. In the lease, Hiram made sure he received free gas for his house and a monthly royalty check. The check wasn't much, but the free gas was well worth the money. Hiram was proud of every dollar he received.

Gas heat was warmer than coal and wood, and Dora could cook faster on the new stove. Hiram missed the taste the wood stove gave the food, but he didn't complain. He kept a wood stove in the smoke house to cook beans on and bake cornbread.

Hiram invited Cullen and his family to the table. Cullen didn't even stop to wash his hands, and neither did his children. He and Ruby had eight children now, four girls and four boys. The babies were twins, Carla and Buster. The other children were Jimmy and John, the oldest boys, then Sammy, Stella Fay, Susan, and Mary Beth. Hiram thought to himself, "Looks like Ruby is with child now."

They ate mostly in silence as Hiram and Dora talked in the living room. Mattie was just fascinated with her new company. She'd never seen the twins before, but neither had Hiram or Dora. Dora said, "Hiram, I need to check on Joanna the next time we are in town. She's probably still smoking marijuana and hanging out at that jenny barn on Ben's Fork. Lundy wrote a letter. In it, he said the Army is releasing him, and he wants to work in Indiana. He'll be home for a week or two though." She asked Cullen's' children if they needed anything else. Each child held up their milk glass, wanting a refill.

Cullen came into the living room and sat down on one of the cane-back chairs. He looked around the room, examining Hiram's new house.

He asked his father, "Do you think I might borrow a hundred dollars until next month? I'll get things in order, and I'll pay you back. Every bit of it."

Hiram looked at his son and said, "When you get things straightened out, I can give you work at the mines, and I'll give Jimmy and John gin-whacking jobs on the outside. They can make them some spending money."

Cullen's face turned red at the mention of his oldest sons.

He wiggled in his chair then he turned back to his father. "I'm not asking for a handout. Me and you have never seen eye to eye. I make out fine when no one butts in my business. You'll have to ask Jimmy and John about working for you."

Cullen hollered for his wife to bring him a toothpick. She never hesitated, and she was immediately at his side handing him one. Hiram wondered why she stayed with Cullen. He guessed she had to with all the children.

Cullen said, "I bought ten acres of land from my father-in-law, and I've built a four-room house with a full basement under it. I want to finish it later. If I have too, I'll go back to Indiana to work."

Cullen looked at the television, then back to his father. Hiram sat up on the edge of his seat and fumbled for his bill-fold. He opened the billfold and took a crisp hundred dollar bill out and reached it to Cullen. Cullen took the bill in his hand and stuck it in his shirt pocket.

Hiram thought about saying. "That's no place to carry money," but he didn't. He held his tongue.

Cullen yelled for Ruby, and she gathered the children together. They all left for Ben's Fork. The car Cullen drove sounded like it was going to quit running any minute. Hiram listened until the car drove out of hearing. He sat back in his seat and watched television. Dora filled the Maytag washer with water. She loaded it with a washing of clothes and sat down beside Hiram. Mattie was washing dishes. She enjoyed whatever she could do for her father and stepmother. Dora put her arms in Hiram's and scooted as close as she could.

"Don't worry about Cullen and Ruby. They will make it fine. People that live like that always do."

Hiram turned his face to her and smiled. "Yal, they do. They seem to get by better than we do. I just worry too much I guess, but that's what I've done all my life."

Mattie came to the living room and sat down on the other end of the sofa. She had that crooked smile. Hiram could tell she was pleased.

Hiram let Mattie stay up by herself for a while. He and Dora retired to bed early. He held his wife close to him. She loved Hiram, not because he took her and her brother and sisters in, but because Hiram was a kind man. One that believed in doing the right thing by everybody. She'd never met anyone like him. Their love for each other matched the heat of the July summer night. Dora lay in Hiram's arms until she dropped off the sleep. Hiram rose from the bed and checked on Mattie. She was fighting sleep as she sat on the sofa.

He sat down beside her and said, "You about ready to go to bed young lady?"

She yawned and said, "Yal, I'm ready. Tuck me in, Poppy!"

Hiram helped her to her feet. She walked wobbly to her

bedroom. Dora had helped her dress into her night gown earlier. Hiram watched her as she got into bed and turned on her
back.

Hiram bent over her and pulled the sheet to her neck,
kissed her cheek and said, "Sleep tight Mattie. Don't let the
bed bugs bite."

She smiled.

Hiram said, "Do you want me to turn out the light?"

Mattie nodded her head. Hiram flipped the wall switch
and pulled the door halfway together. A smile was upon his
lips. Hiram was happy.

Chapter 10

Hiram was up early on the first day of August. The mine was producing more coal every day. Clinton bought a new eighteen wheeler truck and hired his neighbor's son, Tommy, to drive it. Tommy learned to drive early in life, but Clinton still had to teach him how to drive the coal truck. Tommy broke an axle the first try letting out on the clutch. But by the next day, Clinton turned him loose with it. Hiram watched Tommy back the coal truck underneath the tipple and climb up the ladder on the truck's side and open the trap door. Coal filled the middle first. Tommy pulled the truck up a little at a time as the bed filled to the brim. Small amounts of coal spilled off the sides as he rode the truck down the mountain.

At the bottom of the hill, he eased out on the clutch and drove towards Prattsburg, where the railroad had a washing bin. The coal had to be cleaned up before sending on to Cincinnati to use for generating electricity. The power companies would not buy dirty coal. Hiram had been lucky. The coal seam his company was mining was clean. He rarely used anyone to pick slate like he did in his first mine. The mine was producing so much coal Hiram hired a second shift. He couldn't keep up with the demand. His company was making money. By fall, he opened two more openings. He sold all of his good timber for thousands of dollars. It seemed that everything he touched turned to gold. The only thing that slowed him down was the cold, snowy weather. The winter of 1977 was one of the coldest and with more snow than Hiram had seen since when he was a boy.

Snow fell all through the month of January and the first two weeks of February. It wasn't anything to see temperatures below zero for most days in January. The roads didn't thaw out until the first of March. The road department tried to scrape the roads, but they couldn't keep them open enough to haul coal. Hiram and Clinton kept their crew of men busy doing gin-work inside and outside the mine. Back inside the mine, the temperature stayed the same. It never changed. Hiram saved money on his part of the wages he and Clinton split. Hiram bought Dora new furniture and a new car for her to learn to drive. Cullen's two oldest boys had quit work. Hiram begged them to stay on. He wanted to make something out of them, but they would not listen to him. Cullen was still bootlegging and doing odd job work and some farming. The government was handing out commodities. Some men got disabilities from welfare payments or working the government programs. Hiram could hardly keep enough men working to run the mines. Cullen's girl, Stella Fay, married and moved to Tennessee. She was doing well.

Nobody farmed liked they used to. Mountainsides and hillsides lay barren and overgrown with brush and briars. Hardly anybody kept a milk cow, horse or mule. Little grocery stores popped up in every neighborhood. A truck brought milk to the door about every morning. The trucks had different routes for River County. Some farmers did have pasture land, instead fencing their bottoms and planting grass for their stock to graze. Hiram had sold his cattle, and he hadn't owned a horse since Mingo died of dew poisoning. Tractors had taken the place of mules and horses. Hiram sat many times thinking about the old days and wondering how this new generation would get by. The government still played some of the farmers to lay their land out and not farm it.

By the middle of April, The Daniels Coal Company was running full blast. Hiram opened two new mines on his property and leased the neighbors' minerals. The company was driving their headings straight through the mountainside to the ridge and then turning to head either right or left. They were pulling coal from great distances from underground. He hired contractors to completely install huge fans at the mouth of the mine entrance to pump fresh air underground. Hiram worried about explosions and roof falls. He told his men to practice safe working conditions. He did not want to get a man hurt or killed, and he'd been lucky. The coal mine had only one accident where a miner was injured.

That all changed in May. John B. was taking care of the second shift and did well for a while. He started dating a different girl and stayed out late after he took off from work. One particular Sunday, on his day off, he let his girlfriend go underground with him. Hiram didn't know about it until Clinton mentioned it. Hiram was going to confront him that week after he found it out, but he never did get to talk to him about it. That night, while Clinton was doubling back, helping John B. and his crew of six men while they pulled pillows, there was a roof fall that trapped all eight of the men, including Clinton. Hiram found out about the roof fall on arrival the next morning. Hiram knew something was wrong when he first looked at the opening. The fan had quit running and the two new scoops were still inside the mine. Hiram drove the man trip back to the section where John B. and his crew were supposed to be working. When Hiram saw the enormous amount of fallen rock, his heart began to race. He could tell it was bad by the looks of things. He drove the man trip back outside to call for help.

"We'll need all the men we can get to help with this. Hurry. Their air might already be cut off."

The rescue chief knew by listening to Hiram's voice that the worst could be expected.

Hiram began to yell and peck on the fall with his shovel. He pecked as loud as he could and then would listen for a minute. He couldn't hear a word, only falling particles from the mine roof and echoes where he pecked the fallen rock. He began to think of how he could get help for his brother and his crew of men. Not a single answer came to his mind, except yell as loud as he could and bang with his shovel. Hiram heard someone's voice and the noisy sound of a buggy coming. He heard the voices of other men as they came near. Randoff jumped off the buggy and began to load the metal bed with rock and debris. The other men helped. Ben Rogers asked Hiram if he'd heard anything.

"No, not a thing. I'm afraid there's a lot of mountain between us and them." As the men rested, Hiram told about his foreman letting his girlfriend go inside the mine with him.

One of the men said, "Didn't he know it is bad luck for any female to go inside a mine?"

Hiram shook his head and said, "I guess he didn't. He knew we didn't allow him to have visitors back here after hours. But he's young and has made a big mistake. One that may cost him his life."

Hiram turned away from the man and coughed up coal dust mixed with rock dust.

After a few minutes, Hiram said, "Randoff, when you dump the rocks outside, call for additional help."

He went back to banging his shovel and yelling, but still there was no answer. He sat down to get his breath.

Ben told him to take it easy. "You're too old to work like you used to."

Hiram was nearing eighty years old and could still do

a good day's work, but all the excitement and worry were bearing on his mind. He sat resting until his breath wasn't coming in gasps. He began to pray. It had been so long since he and Dora went to church. He wondered if God would even hear him. Ben bent over the entrance to where the men were supposed to be.

"I might have heard something. That sounded like a yell for help."

Hiram came closer and listened. He couldn't hear a thing. Randoff came back with more men. The workers took turns moving rocks and busted props, making trip after trip outside to dump the loads. Hiram was exhausted, but he wasn't going to give up. By noon, a large crowd had gathered outside the mines including family members of the trapped miners. The Slonetown radio station set up a tent to broadcast from. Trapped. Hiram didn't want to use that word, but there it was on his tongue. He traveled to the outside and told everybody the situation. He stayed outside for the next three hours.

Everybody wanted to know what happened. Hiram told them a large roof fall had occurred, and they were working as fast as they could to get to the trapped men. He knew that they didn't have much time. The men's air would not last long. By that evening, the crew of men had moved a lot of falling rocks and slate. Hiram told Randoff he wanted to ride back inside with him. When Hiram got out of the buggy, he could hear digging on the other side of the roof fall. Someone was talking and yelling from the other side.

Hiram's heart raced again, not for sadness but for happiness. He could hardly believe anyone could survive such a fall. In an hour, they had broken through the rock fall and had gotten to two men, Robert and Clive.

When Hiram asked about the other five, and his brother, Clive, said, "They're all covered up with rock Hiram. Me and Robert was lucky. We were working a different section putting brandish cloth across the empty entrances when the rock fall occurred. The cave in separated us from the other six."

He cried after telling about their ordeal. Hiram looked at the other side of the fall and began to load more rock into the buggy.

Randoff spoke up.

"Hiram, you had better go on home and get some rest. I'll stay and we'll work around the clock to try and reach Clinton and the others. You'll be down yourself if you are not careful."

Hiram knew Randoff was right, but he hated to give up. But finally, after all the other men encouraged him, he left for home. He had in his mind that he'd rest at home for a while, then return to the mine. But he was just too worn out. Before Hiram drifted off to sleep, he begged God to spare the men. His prayers were long and dreadful as the sound rose up from his inward being. His true feelings rose to the point that he believed that life was not worth living as he prayed to his God, the same God his mother prayed to. It wasn't long before he was pray-crying from his heart. For some un-explained reason, his prayers were different this time. He couldn't explain what had come over him. The feeling he felt in his heart was different than anything he had felt before. All of a sudden, he felt as light as a feather, almost like he could float. Hiram didn't really know what he prayed for, but he could remember promising God he would live his life better. Before Hiram knew it, he was asleep.

Hiram rose from his bed, showered and ate quickly, then drove to the mine shouting praises to the same unseen God that his mother knew. During his sleep, God had showed him the other side of the roof fall. He knew now that his brother and the trapped men were all right. They would be found today and rescued by evening. A couple of the men were slightly hurt, but there were no severe injuries.

Hiram grabbed his mining light and cradled it with his hard hat. He picked up a shovel that lay on the ground and yelled at Randoff, who stood leaning against the tool shed. Randoff could tell that Hiram was different. Hiram hugged Randoff with a strong hold and held the younger man for some time before he let go. Tears were in Hiram's eyes. Both men cried at will, rejoicing in the Spirit, holding on to the spell each man felt from deep inside of their soul. Hiram didn't have to say anything to Randoff; everything was un-derstood between them. Randoff was a frequent church goer. He'd been in church a long time. Hiram felt a little jealous of this young man.

Hiram waded the crowd of men, followed by the rescue workers. He noticed two ambulances parked near the mine entrance, but deep down he knew that they would not be hauling dead bodies away today. He felt confident of that. Hiram and Randoff, along with two other men, rode the shuttle car into the mine to the roof fall. Other men were moving rock and dirt with shovels, bare hands and machines. One load of rock after the other was moved to the outside to dump, and then the cars were reloaded again and again. Hiram told the men to break for dinner and rest for thirty minutes.

Most of the men traveled to the outside to rest and eat, but Hiram and Randoff stayed inside. Hiram glanced at Randoff and told him he wanted to join the church. He felt the Lord had forgiven him, and he wanted his brother Clinton and Brother Lonzo to baptize him. Randoff shook Hiram's hand and embraced his older friend.

Randoff said, "We have church at Sandgap this weekend. It would be a good time to be baptized." Hiram wept.

The crew came back and began moving debris again. The hours went by fast, and the smell of sweat filled the air as the crew of men labored. Black coal dust covered them as they worked. Hiram had so much coal dust on him that he looked almost invisible in the darkness. Hiram's sweat and tears had mixed with an unshaven face full of three days of beard growth. Hiram had never let his beard go before. He always shaved as soon as he rose from his bed. It was nearing supper time, and the working men were growing weary. Some had worked through the night and all through the day. One by one, they moved out of the way to rest. Hiram's faith began to fail him as doubt crept into his mind. Could he be mistaken? Had God really forgiven him?

He knew one thing in his mind, something had happened to him. He thought he heard someone yell. He told Randoff to listen. The mine roof would not be quiet. Sounds of popping slate and small rocks falling permeated from way back inside the mine shaft.

"There!" Hiram said. "Didn't you hear that?"

He began to work more diligently, moving rock and dirt with his bare hands, crying as tears dropped from his weary eye sockets. The other rescuers moved around Hiram to get in place to do their part. The light sound of men's voices could definitely be heard behind the roof fall. A cheer went up from the crew as they began to work with a newfound energy. Word traveled outside as new crews of men arrived to spare the exhausted laborers. Hiram told the men to be quiet again. He climbed to the top of the roof fall and dug with his hands.

He yelled through the opening and yelled, "Praise God!" as he slid down the roof fall and curled into a ball. He was almost numb with emotion.

Randoff took over and commanded the men by twos. Two men to each side of the roof fall worked diligently removing rock and debris. Before long, he could see the trapped men as they bunched together as if they were praying. The work crew went into the opening of the roof fall one by one and attended to the injured miners as other crew members helped each helpless man escape the death trap that held them earlier. After all the miners were rescued, the two that were injured were loaded into the back of the waiting ambulances and driven straight to the clinic in Slonetown.

Hiram was not worried about a hair on their head. God had come through with His promise, and he meant to fulfill his this weekend. Everyone was happy and rightfully so. Eight men's lives had been spared to live on for a few more years. The crowd of men sat by a fire that was built in an empty oil barrel, talking about how dangerous coal mining was.

"When you go back inside a mine you don't know if you will see daylight again. Dangerous work indeed," one miner said, shaking his head. Nods of agreement came from the others.

Hiram sat down on a bench near the mine shed. His energy was spent. Finally, he said, "Clinton, I know you are tired and restless." He hugged his brother then said, "Please go home and rest until tomorrow. I'll take care of everything here."

Clinton bowed his head and offered a quick prayer, then left.

Hiram watched his brother drive down the hill until he was out of sight. He told his men to go home. "I'll get in touch with you after the mine inspectors inspect the roof fall and give the okay that it is safe to proceed mining again. Pick your pay up here Friday at the mine office. Everyone will get a full week's pay."

Hiram reached for a coal shovel and ditched water from the haul road as the men entered into their cars and trucks and drove home. Hiram found himself thinking of his mother. She would know the very words that needed to be uttered and what prayers to say. How he missed her at times like these.

Dora met him at the door. Hiram was exhausted. She held his arm as he walked to the sofa and sat down. Mattie saw him and came to him.

"Poppy, the news was on the radio. We were worried about you. I'm so glad that you are all right."

She sat down beside him, and they hugged. Mattie cried and held to him for a long time before finally turning him loose.

Dora asked him if he would eat anything. Hiram turned his head toward her and said, "Not right now. Let me rest a minute. Then I'll wash up and try to eat a little bit. I've not had anything since breakfast. I've been living on adrenaline all day."

He leaned back on the sofa and rested his head and closed his eyes. His puffed kneecaps hurt so bad. Hiram could hardly stand the pain, but he said nothing. Mattie sat silently watching his face. Dora prepared his bath water, making sure it was warm enough for him.

Dora helped him to his feet and led him to the bathroom. She pulled his shoes off for him while he undressed and got into the bathtub, slipping down into the hot soapy water. It felt so relaxing to Hiram. He laid there for a minute, then Dora washed his back and neck, getting the coal dust from him. He wondered why this accident had to happen at the mines.

He said, "Dora, do you believe it is bad luck for a woman to go inside a coal mine?"

Dora laughed a small laugh and said, "I don't know, Hiram. It could be. You know women are trying to take over some places in the world. 'Equal rights' they call it."

Hiram washed the coal dust off as she shut the door behind her. He dried with a towel and stood in front of the looking glass and studied his features. His hair was whiter now than it had ever been. Bags hung from under his eyes. He began to wash his face with soap and water, the wash rag turning black with coal dust. He coughed and spit into the wash basin. His saliva was mixed with dust he'd eaten earlier. He said to himself, "Coal mining is a hard way to make a dollar."

At the table, Hiram ate a few bites before he quit and told Dora and Mattie he was going to bed. After telling Dora and Mattie 'good night', he limped into the bedroom. He sat down on the edge of the bed, pulled his socks off and slipped underneath the cover. Sleep came immediately. He began to dream. His sleep was restless but satisfying. He never knew when Dora came to bed. She held him the rest of the night, but he never knew it. She knew he was devastated over the mine accident.

Hiram felt renewed the next morning. He was sore in his joints though. He had worked harder than he realized. The worry of the disaster weighed heavily on his mind, and it pushed him to the limit, straining his will power. Out on the porch, he sat down in the rocking chair and glanced up the mountainside toward the mine site. He figured the state inspector would close the mine for at least three weeks. The only work the state would allow would be clean-up work while the investigation was ongoing. He was in no hurry to be there anyway. He had Clinton, who would take care of everything. He had to worry about the families that would not be able to work.

He thought of the dreams he had last night. He thought, "Funny how when you first wake up, you can't remember what you dreamed, but they come to you later," as he began to remember his nighttime dream. He dreamed he was still young and plowing on the hillside behind the barn. It was just as real as if it were yesterday. Barrel was young and pulled the plow as easy as he ever did, turning the dirt over. The new plowed soil shined in the sunlight as if it were brand new. Hiram looked up hill toward the pasture and black berry briars were full of fruit, large and ripe, ready for picking. In his dream, he wondered how these briars were so full of berries. He had sat down beside Barrel to rest and he marveled at the size of the berried fruit. Hiram rose from the rocking chair and went inside to tell Dora he was going to the mines.

Clinton was taking care of all the details while the mine was shut down. Two inspectors rode one of the buggies back inside the mine shaft. Hiram watched as the buggy disappeared out of sight. Hiram and Clinton discussed the situation.

"I want to pay our men just like they were still working. It is too hard of times for them to go without pay. We've made a lot of money this year, and we can afford it."

He waited for Clinton to answer. The two brothers always agreed with each other, never arguing about anything.

Clinton said, "Hiram, you are a good man, fair and honest as they come. But that is the way Mommy and Poppy taught us. Never to take anything that wasn't ours. Never make fun of anyone and take up for ourselves when it is right to do it."

Clinton turned his head toward the mine entrance. He heard the buggy making a return trip to the outside.

Hiram waited for the two inspectors to get out of the buggy and walk stiff-legged over to where he and Clinton stood. After shaking hands with Hiram, the head inspector said, "Mr. Daniels, we couldn't find any violations. Everything was in order. Looks like it was just a terrible accident. That mountain top back in there weighs a lot and has very little holding it up. It's a thousand wonders one mining timber can support such a weight."

He pointed toward the tipple and said, "I do want you to support that side of your coal tipple though. You have a lot of cleaning up to do back there if you continue mining. Don't run any coal until you get that done. That will probably take close to a month. And keep fresh air back in there; never turn the fan off. There was a bad explosion last week in Bolster County that took the lives of eight men. Don't want that to happen here."

He looked the mining site over again, then shook hands with Hiram and Clinton. The two inspectors got into their state vehicle and drove away.

Hiram didn't want to work today. He told Clinton to meet him at his house around three and they would drive to Slone-town. "I want to make sure all the families are comfortable."

Clinton said," I'll be there."

Hiram picked up a piece of prop timber and carried it to the edge of the coal dump and threw it over the hill. He drove to his place and parked his truck under the shade tree. He sat there for at least fifteen minutes, thinking of how things turn out. "One day things are working just fine and the next they can be turned upside down, like they are now." He glanced to the dogwood point and cried before he exited his truck.

Mattie met him at the front door and threw her arms open for him. He walked her to the sofa and they both sat down.

Dora helped Jesse walk to his father. Hiram grinned as he picked the boy up in his arms and trotted him on his knee. Jesse's mouth slobbered as his father bounced him. He made little noises with his lips. Hiram loved his children so much and enjoyed what time he could spend with them. Jesse was growing fast. His cheeks were fat and round. His head was large for such a young child. His eyes were the same color as Hiram's, Daniels blue. Jesse's fat legs bowed as they hung over his father's knees. His hair was the color of his father's when he was a lad. Jesse had a crown in front near his forehead. Hiram reached him to his mother and turned his attention to Mattie.

"You get ready this Sunday; we're going to start attending church on a regular basis."

Mattie looked up. She smiled her crooked smile. Hiram had taken her to the dentist in Slonetown, and he had done wonders on her crooked teeth. Her teeth were white and mostly straight. The straight teeth made her look younger. Mattie could walk quite well now and didn't have to have anyone helping her like she once did. She helped with the housework and it pleased Mattie to death when Dora let her cook.

Hiram asked Dora if supper was ready.

"Yal, it is, and I'm hungry," She said as she told Mattie to come and help set the table. Hiram carried Jesse.

Chapter 11

The sun was hot when church began. Hiram and Dora sat down in the second row of seats. Clinton and Susanna sat with the church congregation. Brother Lonzo hadn't shown up yet. Hiram figured he'd be there. If not, Clinton would have to do the preaching by himself. The seats were full, and the back of the room was lined with neighbors and family members and a few strangers, making Hiram think about the old days. Clinton had already worked the crowd and had them stirred up. Clinton always talked to everyone just like he was running in an election. But most people knew that church and politics didn't mix and that was always understood.

Brother Lonzo never did show, so Clinton started the services. He had plenty of singers to help line songs, and his deacon was there. After the brothers and sisters sang three songs, he asked the deacon to offer prayer. Then Clinton came forth and sang a song straight through. By the time he was through, the sisters were all shouting, and Hiram knew the Spirit was there. He could feel it. Clinton began to preach on the troubles of Job.

"Man that is born of woman, is but few days and full of trouble. Comes forth as a flower and is cut down."

It wasn't long before God carried Clinton out in a sermon that would have matched any of Preacher Silas's. The church women took turns shouting as mothers and fathers and close kin cried and moaned. There were even cries from the congregation that could be heard. Hiram and Dora cried too. Jesse looked into his father's eyes as the tears flowed. Jesse's puckered lips quivered as he continued to watch his father cry. His young mind had never seen or heard anything like this. Mattie just bawled. Clinton preached for over an hour, then abruptly stopped just like any Regular Baptist preacher does. He talked to the congregation for another ten minutes, and he called for the church doors to be announced open to receive members by experience and baptism. Hiram rose from his chair, raced down the aisles and embraced his brother in front of the podium. His body limped in Clinton's arms. Then he came to life and told everyone in the church building that the God of Heaven had forgiven him of his many sins, and he wanted to join the church. Clinton asked the members of the Sandgap Church if any one objected. None did. A move and a second was made to put Hiram under the watch-care of the church until baptism.

Clinton said, "When do you want to be baptized?"

Hiram wiped tears from his eyes and joyfully said, "Right now!"

Everyone still continued to rejoice.

Outside, Hiram swiftly walked to the edge of Troublesome Creek and waited for the deacon to ready him for baptism. Dora proudly stood by his side, holding Jesse while holding on to him and Mattie. The deacon tied white handkerchiefs around all three of the men. Clinton and the deacon led Hiram out to the deepest part of the creek and baptized Hiram in his beloved Troublesome Creek. Rejoicing went on for an hour. Hiram felt fulfilled.

Hiram piddled around the farm for the next two days without going to the mines. He wanted a break from all that had transpired there. He hoed his small garden and helped Dora weed her flower bed. She had lost her blue Banty hen to a red fox back in the spring. Hiram asked all around River County if anyone had Banties for sale. He found some, but he couldn't' t find a blue one. He mended his barn's loft and patched the tin roof. He needed time alone to get his head straight. A large coal company up in New England had made an offer on his coal mine operation and all of his mineral rights. He didn't know if he should sell his company or not. Hiram had quite a coal empire built. The company installed all new tipples and load-outs from steel and concrete, complete with a coal washer. Belts brought the coal from deep inside the mountainside to the outside. The energy company was making a large offer of thirty million dollars. He and Clinton worked hard to get ahead, but the going had been rough. The coal mines had done well. Clinton wanted to sell, but Hiram was thinking everything over. He never did like to make a quick decision. He liked to ponder about things for days, weeks and sometimes even months. That was a big decision to make. Hiram always wanted to sleep on things, and this was no different.

A week later, Hiram had a decision that he could be comfortable with. He'd thought and thought and slept on the ponderings of selling his mine and what mineral holdings he owned. If the energy company wanted to buy his company, he would sell under one condition. He'd made his mind up and had discussed it with Clinton.

"If we sell, I want control of how they mine. No strip mining on my land or yours. Strip mining just tears the land up, pushing dirt into holler fills and ruining the creeks and streams. I hear of a new method of mining which will be more destructive then strip mining. They are talking about removing whole tops of mountains. They call it mountain top removal. I don't want that, Clinton. This has been our home since we were little, and I know I can't stop some people from letting coal companies do strip mining on their land, but we can ours." Hiram was quite for a few minutes.

Clinton said, "You've loved this farm. And I can see why. Poppy and Mommy loved it too. Poppy was a good caretaker of the soil, and Mommy backed him all the way. I'm leaving everything up to you. You will do right."

Clinton shook hands with his brother and drove down the Troublesome Creek road to Slonetown. He had an appointment with his banker.

Hiram told Dora about his decision and smiled at Mattie as she listened in.

"If we sell our mines, I'm quitting work. You all can travel to other states if you like. See some of the places we've only heard about. I don't like to travel myself, but you all can. It might be good for Mattie."

Hiram grinned at his daughter as she smiled her crooked smile.

Dora walked over to where he sat. She put her hands on his shoulders and said, "I'll not travel unless you do, Hiram Daniels. I've got more than I ever expected to have and Joanna, Ceora and Lundy are doing well now since they finally grew up. Jesse will take all the time I can give him. I want him to get the best education money can buy. I was held back because of taking care of my brother and sisters, but if I had to, I would do it all over again."

She sat down beside him on the sofa and rested her head against his chest. Hiram caressed her hair. Mattie looked on. Dora raised her head and gazed into Hiram's eyes.

"I'm a happy woman, Hiram. My life is complete." Then she rested her head again. Hiram was happy too.

Hiram drove to town to see his lawyer. He didn't hesitate

to tell his lawyer how to draw up the papers. He spoke to his friend about every detail, from wanting control over the management of mining to what kind of mining.

"Only deep mining would be allowed on our property."

The lawyer started by dictating to his secretary how to draw the documents up.

When he got to the stipulation on what methods of mining to be allowed, he paused then said, "To whom this document presents: only site preparation and the deep mining method is to be allowed on Mr. Hiram Daniels and Clinton Daniels' property. This document will be binding to said energy company, to all heirs of Hiram and Clinton Daniels, and to the Daniels Brothers Coal Company."

His secretary typed away as she listened.

Hiram shook hands with Mr. Johnson and left for Sissy's hardware store. She was waiting on a customer as he walked through the door. Sissy was showing her age. Since Grant died, she been worrying how to keep her businesses running. She couldn't hire any help anymore. Nobody wanted to work like they used too. Too much give away from the government . A lot of the younger people of draft age protested while smoking marijuana all day. Some dressed in flowered shirts and bell bottom pants saying as they held their fingers up saying, "Peace. Make love, not war." Cities in other states had riots in the streets. Things had changed so much for Hiram that it hurt. He would never have thought the world would ever get into this kind of a mess. A new president had been elected, Ronald Reagan. The talk was that he was going to create new jobs. Hiram was all for that. Other jobs beside mining coal needed to start up here in River County.

He hugged his sister and smiled at her as she hugged him back.

"Hiram you look so happy," She said, letting go of him.

Hiram smiled and said, "I'm going to buy all your stores out after we sell the mines. I'm going to retire and let someone else take care of my business for me. Might buy me a farm down in the Blue Grass. Don't know yet."

Hiram picked out a few things he might need at the mine and around the farm and laid them on the counter. He thought back on the old days and how change had developed River County. Slonetown had four service stations, a pool hall, a theater, a post office, two banks, two churches, three hardware stores, a high school and grade school and a library. A new Chevrolet car dealer lot was right in the middle of town. There were three barber shops where men would hang out telling tales of old times while whittling on pieces of cedar wood or swapping knives. The old courthouse had been remodeled. A county jail sat by the creek side. There was a drug store and two doctor clinics, one on each end of town. Five grocery stores in town helped to keep the county fed. There were two hotels, a dime store, a shoe cobbler and two clothing stores lining Main Street. Two restaurants stayed full from Monday until Saturday. On Sunday, everything closed down.

Hiram paid Sissy for what he bought and drove home. Today, he felt satisfied with his life. He arrived home just in time for supper. He thought about the crew of men he'd passed on his way home. They were working on a new drive-in screen to show movies on. "Just another place for teenagers to hang out and get into trouble," he thought, as he walked into his living room.

People were living good in River County, better than they ever had. There was a coal boom happening, and a person could almost sell black dirt. Yes, times were changing.

The mine was cleaned up and ready for production again. Hiram really didn't want to go back to work, and neither did Clinton. But they had to wait on the energy company. After a hard day in the mines, Hiram worked until dark in his garden and flower beds for Dora. She kept her flower beds in first class shape. Hiram enjoyed planting and tending a garden. He always picked fresh bouquets for Mattie and Dora. Mattie would smell the flowers and smile her crooked smile. Hiram would grin and pat her nose. He placed Dora's flowers on the wooden table near the bar cabinet. It was the middle of April, and the hillsides and pastures were grown over with young dogwood and redbud trees. They were in full bloom. Hiram couldn't even see his mine site because of the blooming trees.

Hiram retired to bed early. He wanted to rise before daylight to start back to work at the mines. Before he knew it, Dora's white rooster crowed as loud as he'd ever heard. He turned over and watched Dora breathe as her chest rose and fell lightly. He always liked to watch Mary Liz and Alice Marie as they lay in bed. He felt sorry for himself for a minute but then he thought just how lucky he'd been. God had blessed him with three fine wives and five wonderful children. He made it possible to survive a bad case of pneumonia and a roof fall where he thought for sure he would not survive, but he did. He heard Jesse whimper from his bedroom, so he rose and walked down the hallway to see if he needed anything. The young lad lay covered in his daybed. His little body was sweating. He pulled down the quilt and placed a sheet over him. "Too hot for a quilt," he thought as he looked down into the child's face. A sense of pride swelled up in him. This was the last child he would father, and he had big plans for him. He never could make Cullen understand respect and responsibility that a man should have. He helped Cullen and his family a lot, financially speaking, but he'd given up on him of ever taking enough pride in himself to be well spoken of. He wondered again where he went wrong raising him. The rooster crowed again, so he went into the kitchen to fix breakfast.

After breakfast, he drove his work truck toward the mine site. He hadn't been there two minutes when a brand new Ford F-250 pulled into the parking area and two men got out. One was wearing a suit with a white hard hat. The other man was dressed in work clothes.

They introduced themselves to Hiram. Clinton pulled up and joined Hiram as they all shook hands.

The man with the suit said, "My name is Derick Manners. I'm the manager of the Pittsburgh Holding Company, and we want to buy your mining company. I stopped by the court-house yesterday. Your lawyer showed me the documents you had him draw up for me, but I don't like the stipulations you included. If we buy you out, we want freedom to mine the way we want to."

Hiram watched the man's face as he talked. Mr. Manners was a middle aged man with slightly balding hair. He held his hard hat in his hands while he talked. His eyes were black, his skin color a tanned brown. He sported a small mustache. His build was medium, and his hands were large and a rosy color. Hiram could see right off those hands had never done hard labor. He had what Mattie would call dishpan hands. The other man just listened while Manners talked.

Hiram looked down the hill towards his house then back at the city slicker and said, "I was born and raised here, and my parents lived out their whole life making a living here. They worked hard taking care of this farm until they weren't able to no more. Me and my brother here took over after they were gone. I've owned this land ever since my mother passed away. My life has been here, and I've got loved ones resting there on the dogwood point that you can see."

He pointed his hand in the direction of the graveyard and

began again. "That is our terms; take them or leave them. It really doesn't make any difference to us."

Hiram watched Clinton as he shook his head in agreement.

The manager and his foreman walked to the truck and spoke in private. The manger was pointing in different directions while his foreman listened. The foreman nodded his head and the two men walked back to where Hiram and Clinton stood.

Mr. Manners turned to Hiram and said, "I think we'll make a deal with you. I do want to ask a favor of you though. Will you show my foreman the mines and go over the acres of minerals with him?"

Hiram shook hands with the suited man, not changing expressions at all. He said, "Me and my brother here will help you in any way we can to get you started right. And we'll be watching to make sure you stand true to our bargain."

The manager smiled and said, "Meet me at the courthouse this afternoon. We want to start operations as soon as next week."

The foreman walked toward the drift mouth and peered back inside the mine opening as Clinton talked to him. After this, the manager and his foreman drove off the hill and turned down Troublesome Creek.

Hiram and Clinton talked for a while, then they drove to Slonetown to see their lawyer. Mr. Johnson was sitting at his desk, fiddling with a hand full of papers, his eyes searching for something that seemed to be hidden from him.

Hiram spoke, "Grayson, we've made a deal. The energy company manager came to see me and Clinton today. They are probably here in town now. We got what we asked for. I'm going to give you a bonus when the check has cleared the bank."

Hiram grinned at the young lawyer as he sat down in one of the plush chairs that lined the room. Clinton did the same. Hiram was glad for his brother. He would have enough money now to quit work and do what he wanted to for a change. He and Susanna worked hard for what they had and endured many hardships and troubles during their marriage. Hiram was going to give Sissy her part of the money. Even though he'd paid Clinton and Sissy for their part a long time ago, it just seemed fitting to give them more. He was thinking of Lee John's children and Reldon's girls too. He would make it right with them also.

Mr. Johnson rose from his chair and said, "I'm ready, Hiram. Let's go and make you boys multimillionaires."

He put on his hat as he twisted out the door. Hiram and Clinton followed him to the courthouse, then to the county clerk's office and met Mr. Manners and his foreman. All five men stood in front of the clerk as they discussed the signing of the legal document. Hiram signed the paper first, followed by Clinton. Then Hiram's lawyer scooted the paper in front of the suited man. He read the document and signed his name. Hiram watched him write. It was some of the fanciest handwriting he'd ever seen.

Mr. Manners looked at his signature again and handed the papers to Hiram's lawyer. Mr. Manners showed Hiram the check he'd made out for twenty-nine million dollars. The coal company was to pay off all the debt Hiram's company was carrying. Hiram had never heard of such a large amount of money before. He glanced at it hurriedly. He didn't want to seem overwhelmed by the large amount. He showed the check to Clinton, then watched his lawyer record the document. The county clerk notarized the paper and recorded it in one of the large books that rested on the shelves that circled the entire room. Hiram and Clinton shook hands with Mr. Manners and his foreman and headed for the Bank of Slonetown. He walked to the counter and laid the check in front of the young teller. Her eyes widened as she gazed at all the zeros in the amount section.

Finally, she said, "How do you want this deposited? I'll have to get our bank president to show me how."

She quickly went into the side room and appeared again with an older, gray-haired man following her.

He approached the counter and said, "Hello," to Hiram and Clinton. "How may I help you?" Hiram knew the bank president, but he hadn't had any dealings with him other than acquiring a loan from the bank when he and Clinton began mining.

"We want to deposit this check in our names. I want an account in my name and one in Clinton's. Equal amounts in each."

The banker was excited. He smiled and showed the teller what to do.

"Give each man a savings account book and open each a checking account."

Hiram corrected the teller. "No, we already have a checking account. We won't need another."

The teller looked toward the banker for instructions. He smiled and nodded to the girl as she nervously wrote the amount in each account book. Hiram and Clinton weren't a bit nervous. They already had quite an amount in savings, and Hiram hardly let his balance get under a hundred thousand dollars. He and Clinton were wealthy now, but he didn't want to change. He wanted to be a humble man just like he'd been all of his life.

After all the transactions at the bank he and Clinton both paid their lawyer. Mr. Johnson's eyes lit up as he looked at his check. He smiled and shook both their hands and went into his office. Hiram told Clinton he'd be down to his place tomorrow, then he headed for Troublesome. He watched as the creek flowed towards Slonetown. He felt sad as he drove along. Plastic pampers hung from the willows and small sycamore trees. Hiram couldn't understand why people upstream threw their garbage into the creek. People made garbage dumps in the head of several hollers instead of hauling it off or burying it somewhere like in the old days. "Back in the day, everyone had an outhouse where they buried all their unwanted trash then filled the hole when a new toilet was built." Troublesome Creek was filling up with silt from all the strip mining. The swimming hole where the one room school used to be stayed filled with rocks and debris. The water in Turner Branch ran red and yellow.

Hiram felt bad by the time he reached home. Thinking of all the destruction of the water ways and the hillsides didn't bode with him too well. He sat down on the porch and looked towards Rolly Joe Mountain. He wondered how long the mountain would be safe from the mining companies wanting to remove the mountain's top to get at the large reserves of coal that lie underneath the soil.

Rolly Joe Mountain had six different seams of coal underneath the surface. The Whitesburg seam was near the creek bed, followed by the number four seam. Just above that was the four rider. It was not as good. The rider was thicker, but the seam had pardons in the middle that lowered the value of the coal. Number five-a was the next seam, which was not as good as the four-rider seam. The number seven seam was about halfway to the top of the mountain. But just underneath the top of the mountains surface was the number nine seam. This was the prize seam. It ran about six to seven foot or sometimes as much as eleven feet thick of clean coal. He didn't know who owned the minerals on the mountain, but he figured he'd get his lawyer to find out. He walked into the living room where Mattie, Jesse and Dora waited him. He was glad to be home. It'd been a trying day, and he was tired.

Hiram was happy, just laying around doing much of nothing. He did work his garden and had two men mowing his yard and bottom. His bottom land hadn't been farmed in five years. He had them all plowed, and he'd sowed Kentucky 31 fescue grass seed in each bottom. He'd had one of his work hands mow the grass twice a year for hay. He either sold it or gave it away. He loved to sit on his front porch and watch his tractors cut the grass and smell the fresh cut hay. He enjoyed his farm more today than he used to because he had the money to hire all his work done. A lot of times he'd join in the work, working in the heat of the day. He loved to still pull his shirt off and get dirty as he worked alongside his hired help. The dust from the fresh mowed grass did make him cough, and Dora quarreled at him trying to keep him out of the hay fields, but Hiram paid her no mind. Dora still waited on Hiram, hand and foot, taking care of him like she would Jesse. His every need was seen to. Sometimes Hiram grew restless from all the attention she gave him, but he wouldn't hurt her feelings for anything.

She hollered, "Dinner is ready."

Hiram told his help to come and eat. Dora had a large table set out under the shade tree. Her and Mattie had filled it with enough food to feed an army. Hiram sat down and asked a blessing over the food.

Hiram enjoyed his days without having to work all the time. He still piddled around the farm when he wanted to but left most of the work to his hired hands. He'd bought a few small parcels of land down on Lem Wilson Road and was looking at several acres of farmland just west of Slonetown. While discussing the closing deal on one of his new parcels, the owner told him he'd heard that some of Rolly Joe Mountain was going to be on the market before long. Hiram's mind began to ponder on this idea of owning this mountain. Rolly Joe Mountain had been a staple on Troublesome Creek ever since he could remember. He'd crossed that mountain in the summer and the winter while he lived on Graves Creek. He would hate to see the top of that mountain destroyed. He quickly closed the deal on the farm and told the landowner to meet him in Slonetown in half an hour.

Hiram drove back to Slonetown and visited his lawyer. Mr. Johnson sat in his chair overlooking the bustling town. Hiram glanced over the lawyer's shoulder and said, "I can remember when those paved streets were nothing but slick mud in the wintertime and dry dust in the summer. A lot has changed since those days."

Mr. Johnson said, "Hello, Mr. Daniels. How are you today?" He extended his hand for a hefty handshake. Hiram took hold of his hand and squeezed slightly. He still had a reputation of having a firm grip.

The young lawyer looked up at Hiram and said, "Why Hiram Daniels, your grip is a strong as a young man yet." He grinned as he motioned for Hiram to sat down in a chair he'd offered.

Hiram sat down and watched the lawyer take a cigar from his special pack and offered it to Hiram. Hiram waved his hand. Mr. Johnson said, "Do you mind?" holding the cigar towards Hiram.

Hiram said, "No." Hiram was used to people smoking around him, and it never bothered him in the least. The lawyer puffed the cigar and exhaled thick smoke into the air, blowing smoke rings that floated to the ceiling before disappearing. He puffed again and laid the cigar on his favorite ashtray. The ashtray was a see through green with indents for as many as four cigars or cigarettes.

He looked at Hiram and asked, "What brings you to town today?"

Hiram wanted to say something about the rich smell of the cigar and its aroma, but he decided not to. He leaned back in his chair and said, "I hear tell that parts of Rolly Joe Mountain might be for sale. I want you to find out for me and if it is, I'll buy part of it or all of it every acre of that mountain and maybe a few acres surrounding it."

Mr. Johnson grinned and watched Hiram as he evaluated his client.

"I'll get on it today and will let you know by the end of the week." The two men shook hands and Hiram left. He stopped at Sissy's store for a minute, then headed for home.

Mattie was crying when he walked through the front door. Hiram quickly inquired what was wrong. Mattie hugged her father and laughed. "I'm so happy, Poppy. Dora let me cook supper all by myself, and she let me watch Jesse while she worked her flower garden. She didn't even check on me but one time."

The tears fell on her blouse and slacks. Hiram raised her face to gaze into her eyes. He wiped the tears and hugged her as they both checked on Jesse. The young child was sound asleep. Hiram helped her sit down at the breakfast table. Dora walked into the house wiping her forehead. Hiram watched his wife walk to the sink and wet her face as she dried with a towel.

She sat down by Mattie, patted her shoulder and said, "Yep, we got a regular maid right here, honey. She cooked all by herself and took care of her little brother for me. I'm so proud of her."

Mattie began to cry again. She was so full of joy, and it pleased Hiram that his wife was so patient with his special daughter. Supper was good that evening.

After everyone ate, they all sat on the porch and listened to the sounds of a warm summer night. Even though it was already the middle of August, the lightening bugs still filled the air and the swamp frogs croaked. A screech owl hooted from a tree on the hillside. Off in the distance, he could see the top of Rolly Joe Mountain as the sinking ball of sun left twinkles of light sparkling through the trees and around the chimney rock.

Hiram hadn't heard a fox hound on the mountain in a long time. All the old-time fox hunters had died out, and the

younger generation used the mountain to grow dope. Hiram
didn't like what some of the younger teens of today had become. Not many wanted to work the mines or farm. More
than should moved away to other states to work. The ones
who stayed in River County that were educated lived good,
but the rest either worked the mines or lived off the government. This made Hiram mad. As he looked, Hiram did see a
dim light near the Sweetgum Spring. He wondered if someone might be moonshining. Most of the moonshiners had
moved their operations closer to their home. Even some set
up a still in their smoke house or barn. Moonshining wasn't
the thing anymore. Marijuana was, and he'd heard about
harder drugs coming into River County from the larger cities up north. Drugs like cocaine and pills of every sort. No,
Hiram didn't like what this generation was coming to.

He rose from his chair and stopped in front of Mattie and
Dora. He smiled at his daughter as she jumped to her feet
after hearing Jesse cry out. She walked as fast as she could
through the front door, her braces and crutches wobbling as
she went. Hiram and Dora followed her inside.

Chapter 12

A few weeks later, Hiram was awakened by a clap of thunder. His house seemed to shake and windowpanes from the loud noise. The rain poured down as fast as he'd ever heard it. He laid there for a minute while Dora stirred from her sleep. She turned to Hiram with a puzzled look.

"The radio nor TV said anything about a storm today."

The lights blinked on and off, then back off. Jesse screamed from his bedroom. His mother rushed to him. She came back carrying the frightened lad and laid him down beside Hiram. The lights came back on. Hiram rested his hand on Jesse's chest and rolled the boy over. Hiram patted the boy's back, and he quickly went back to sleep. Dora checked on Mattie and brought candles from the kitchen in case the power went out again. Hiram rose from the bed and opened the front door to look out. Troublesome Creek was about to leave her banks. She was as full as he'd seen her in a long time. Trash and logs floated down the creek faster than Hiram could watch them go. He closed the door and got dressed. He put his shoes on and stepped back out on the porch.

Hiram leaned against one of the brick posts. Troublesome Creek was muddy and ugly as the water trickled at the
edge of his hay fields. Water was rising by the minute. He
knew that downstream, Slonetown was probably flooding.
He hoped Sissy and everyone were on high ground. Most
of the time the flood waters just made a mess, but these waters were different. Hiram figured it was a cloud burst. The
ground couldn't hold water like it used to. The strip mining
had disturbed the land, which caused the runoff.

Dora joined him, and her eyes were full of fear as she
watched the muddy torrent rush by.

"Hiram, we might ought to seek higher ground if that water keeps rising," she said, grabbing his arm.

He turned and followed her inside. He woke Mattie and
threw a blanket toward her as she put shoes on. He helped
her to the truck and returned to get Jesse and Dora. He carried the boy, and his wife carried the snacks and blankets.
Jesse was crying again. He began screaming from not being able to see anything. Hiram reached him to Mattie and
then opened the truck door for Dora. He started the truck
and drove toward the haul road that led to the mine. Every branch and ditch line were running at full capacity. Ruts
were washed in the middle of the haul road. The water from
Troublesome was halfway in the bottom between the house
and the creek. It didn't look like a creek now. It looked more
like a river. The tires of the truck were spinning in the loose

mud and Red-dog. Hiram engaged the four wheel drive, and the truck tires dug in with all four tires pulling. Hiram topped the haul road and pulled over so he could watch the creek from safety. Even he gasped as small smoke houses, barns and sheds floated downstream. He watched as chickens and hogs floated by. He knew this was bad.

He wouldn't let Dora see the raging water. She tended to Jesse and Mattie. Mattie didn't realize the seriousness of the flood. She'd never been through or seen anything like this. Cullen and his family came to his mind. He wondered why. He was praying that they were all right. The rain still poured as Hiram watched the flooding waters lap at the edge of his porch. The old house was higher back on a knoll behind Hiram's new one.

He told Dora, "If the rain doesn't stop, it will get in our house."

He sat there helplessly. He wasn't worried about the material of the house, just the contents. His antique furniture and most of his old pictures of his mother and father, grandparents, Mary Liz and Alice Marie, and Ballard and the ship the navy named after him were inside. The looking glass still hung on the wall by the sink. These were things that were priceless; their value could not be measured. He got out of his truck and gazed over the hill. The water was now in his house. The torrent moved the foundation. His home seemed to twist. The water's force was moving the sides and walls, causing them to crumble. The roof gave way first, then the house was washing down the angry stream as the waters picked up what was left and carried it swiftly downstream where the bottoms of hay used to be. He thought to himself "Troublesome was sure claiming her right of way this morning, and then some."

He hated to lose his house, but they could easily rebuild . A lot of his neighbors couldn't.

Hiram asked Dora if everyone was all right. She sobbed softly. Jesse was sleeping in his mother's lap and Mattie's eyes were wider than Hiram had ever seen them before. No doubt she was frightened. Hiram examined the mine site. Not any of the men had come out to work. He hoped everyone was okay.

A small stream of water ran out of the drift mouth. It would have been hard for the first shift to run coal this morning. The new owners of Daniels Brothers Coal Company were doing good. The company employed over one hundred men, and they paid decent wages too. The rain had stopped, and the sun was trying to break through the clouds. Hiram started the truck and slowly drove off the hill towards his old house. The water had receded somewhat but was still deep and rushing. Dora covered her mouth as she pointed at a car floating down Troublesome. The car turned sideways and lodged against one of the many sycamore trees that lined the creek banks. The raging water turned the car on its side, and the car flipped and filled with muddy water before sinking. Dark muddy water rose and waved over the submerged car.

Dora said, "I hope no one was in there."

Hiram put the truck in four wheel drive and drove around the back side of his field to the old farmhouse. He parked in the front yard and began to get Mattie, Dora and Jesse out and into the old dwelling. He built a fire in the chimney to take the chill off the cool air. The rushing water was so loud that Hiram could hardly hear Dora asking him what they were going to do.

He looked at her and said, "We'll be all right here for the time being.

Dora looked scared. Jesse was awake and whimpering, wanting to be fed. Mattie went into the kitchen and started making a pot of coffee. Hiram smiled at her and gave her his okay. Hiram always kept some groceries in the old home place so he could just visit now and then. He walked out on the porch and gazed across the bottoms toward the creek. The wild water had flattened his corn crop and garden and left logs and stumps in their place. All his plank and wire fence was laying on the ground or missing all together. It hurt him as he thought about his loss, but he couldn't imagine how bad the flood was in Slonetown. He worried about Clinton and Susanna. Sissy should be okay. Her store was off the ground at least six feet. He had never seen this much destruction before.

He walked back inside the cabin, and Mattie reached him a cup of coffee. It tasted good and did wonders for his chilling bones. Dora had laid down with Jesse to keep him quiet.

He tried to sit up when his father walked into the room. He grinned at Hiram and spread his little arms wanting his father to take him. Hiram leaned down and nestled the child in his arms and swung him around playfully. Jesse enjoyed the turning and laughed out loud. Hiram did this a few more times as he carried him through the cabin, stopping in front of a family portrait of his parents and siblings.

He studied the picture for a minute then exclaimed, "I'm glad to have this picture left!" Dora came to his side, and they both looked at the portrait.

"Should I start breakfast?"

"If you would like, that will be fine. I'll watch Jesse while Mattie helps you. I want to let the creek go down a little bit more, then I'll put on my gum boots and look around."

He picked Jesse up, carried him into the sitting room and sat in the rocker and began to rock. Jesse loved to rock. He sat perfectly still, almost falling asleep again but never completely going all the way. Many thoughts came to Hiram's mind as he sat there in that rocking chair. Thoughts of his childhood and the way life used to be. So much had changed.

After dinner, Hiram walked down to the edge of Troublesome Creek. A lot of the creek bank was missing. The bank where Hiram had worked for all those years shoring the side bank was gone. Dirt, gouged from the bottom, was showing. A gash had been cut into the side of the bank as if a bulldozer had been at work. Topsoil was gone, and the yellow dirt was showing. The moving waters were still loud, and their sound echoed across the valley.

Hiram couldn't find any of his cattle or sheep. He figured he'd lost them or that they were in the upper pasture. He walked the length of his bottom and saw a body laying where his corn field used to be. He quickly ran to where it lay and stooped down to see if there was anything he could do. The young man was already gone, drowned in Troublesome Creek. Mud caked his face and neck. His shirt was twisted around his chest. Gravel and sand covered his trousers. He only had one slipper on his right foot. The left one was missing . The body had cuts and scrapes on its face. Hiram felt so sorry for the young man. He had known him. He'd worked for Hiram a few times taking up hay. It was Joey Melton from near the foot of Rolly Joe Mountain, from a branch called Hinton Branch. Back when Hiram was crossing the mountain, no one even lived there. Joey's father and mother had bought their place and had a nice house and small farm. Joey's father worked for Hiram in the coal mines until he passed away four years ago. Joey's mother was ill and not able to get around. Hiram wondered where she was.

He walked back to the cabin and asked Dora if the phones were working. The telephone was the only modern thing he'd installed in the old house. She said they were.

Hiram said, "Call the sheriff and tell him I found the body of Joey Melton."

Dora dialed the number, and the rough voice of Sheriff

Ray Dalton came over the line.

"Hello," it said.

Dora reached the phone to Hiram. He took the phone and walked to the porch and leaned against one of the popular posts.

He answered, "Ray, this is Hiram Daniels. We've had a wash-out out our way. About took everything in its path. My house is gone, and I found the body of Joey Melton laying in one of my hayfields. Send someone out here as soon as you can."

Hiram listened for the sheriff to speak.

Hiram heard the sheriff moan before saying, "I'll be there as soon as I can. We got spared here in Slonetown. The water did get in the streets, but the only damage was water damage and mud. I'll see you and about half an hour."

The phone line clicked as Hiram replaced the receiver.

Hiram waited for the sheriff. He walked down to the edge of the creek bank again. He'd already covered Joey's body to be as respectful as he could under the circumstances. Large sycamore trees were uprooted and had fallen across the creek. The moving water was still swaying the trees and limbs as the water flowed just below the tree trunk. Some of the sycamores had fallen back unto the bottom land. Great gouges of dirt and black-top were washed away downstream or had landed in Troublesome Creek. Hiram located the car he'd seen floating. It didn't have anybody in it. His mind went back to the year Mary Liz was drowned. He wondered if someone might be underneath the car and hung on something. He heard a truck coming, and then he got a glimpse of the vehicle. It was the sheriff. Hiram walked back to the roadway and threw his arms up, flagging the sheriff to stop. Sheriff Dalton pulled the truck into Hiram's yard and got out.

He walked around to the side and shook hands with Hiram.

"How ya' doing, Daniels? My, you all have had a flood out this way. Nothing like this in Slonetown," he said as he looked toward the creek. Hiram told the sheriff to follow him. The two men waded mud and water to the spot where Joey's body lay. Hiram uncovered the body for the sheriff to see. His face turned white. Then he turned to Hiram and wiped his forehead. Perspiration had formed there.

Hiram watched the lawman turn around towards the creek. Ray Dalton was a little on the heavy side. He weighed a good two-fifty and was built low to the ground. His thighs were as round as Hiram's midsection. His hair lay mostly on the sides. What hair was on the top of his head was thin. His eyes were what Hiram noticed the most. They were set close together. When the sheriff looked straight ahead, one would think he was crossed eyed, but he wasn't. His belly shook as he picked up the sheet that covered the dead body. He wore his gun belt hanging from way below his waist. The way he wore his belt made him look unkept. He hadn't shaved today, and his face was covered with a thick growth. Hiram wondered how anyone could have a full beard like that and not have a lot of hair growing on his head. Hiram noticed Ray's feet were huge as the sheriff paraded back and forth to his truck. He radioed back into town for the coroner to come and do his work. Dalton sat down on the step side of his truck and wiped his forehead again. Hiram asked him if he could get him a drink of water or something.

"I'll take a pop, if you have one."

Hiram walked to the cabin and soon returned with a twelve ounce Royal Crown Cola. The sheriff drank almost half the bottle before he took it away from his mouth. A trickle of the beverage slowly ran down the corner of his mouth and disappeared underneath his chin.

Hiram told him he was worried about the people that lived above him.

"There is old man Thomas Kittle. He lives alone and almost crippled. And there is Mrs. Melton. I guess she might be all right."

Hiram told the sheriff he would drive up the holler and see if he could help anyone.

The sheriff finished his pop and said, "Get in with me. We'll go together."

He swung his short frame around the step side and climbed into his truck. Hiram got in on the passenger side. The sheriff let out on the clutch and drove the truck up Troublesome. He had to swing the truck around several roadblocks where road culverts were washed out. Hiram bounced from his seat several times as the truck drove over rough places. Sheriff Dalton stopped at Thomas Kittle's place, and he and Hiram got out of the vehicle. They walked up the small hill that led to the old man's place. Hiram knocked on the door. He heard a movement inside the house. In a few minutes, the curtain rolled back, and Hiram could see the face of Mr. Kittle as he peered through the windowpane. He disappeared. The front door opened, and he stepped out on the front porch.

He cupped his hand to his ear and said "What's wrong Hiram. Is anything wrong?"

He looked up at Hiram and then looked at the sheriff.

Hiram bent down closer to his ear and said, "Nothing's wrong. We were just checking on you to see if you were all right."

Evidently, the old man slept right through the storm. He smiled at Hiram and said, "I'm glad you came by. Come again sometime."

Then, he turned and slowly made his way back inside his house. He didn't realize the destruction the water had caused. Hiram was glad he was all right.

He and Sheriff Dalton drove on up towards Rolly Joe Mountain. The widow lived just at the foot where the steep started. Hiram could see that the storm had blown down a few giant oak and beech trees. The tops of the trees were twisted together and twisted around each other. The rain had not hurt the mountain though. Hiram could not see where any soil had washed or slipped away. Hiram could hardly recognize Widow Dorothy's place. Her meager house and smoke house were missing, and Hiram feared the worst. Sheriff Dalton exited his truck and radioed Slonetown to ask his dispatcher to send one of his deputies to him.

"Also bring along a search party to start looking for survivors."

He hung his mic on the radio and walked over to where Hiram stood.

Hiram was trying to figure out in his mind where the house used to sit. After measuring the distance using his memory he said, "Her house sat right here where this small sink hole is now. Her out building over on that knoll is the only thing that is left of her place. No doubt in my mind she is drowned."

Hiram lowered his head as he jumped the branch where a small stream of water ran off the hill.

The sheriff followed him and exclaimed, "This is the worst flood I've ever seen in River County. You walk the creek bank if you will. I'll head up this branch and see what I can find."

Hiram nodded his head, and the two men separated and walked in different directions. Hiram walked down by the creek bank as he looked at the destruction the flood had left behind. Gravel and sand filled the water holes that used to be ten to fifteen feet deep. The creek banks were missing a large portion of their soil. Roots of downed trees were sticking jaggedly out of the rich bottom land. Deep slices of dirt were missing from the roadway, with part of the pavement hanging over the creek. Hiram had never seen such devastation in his lifetime. He figured a lot of lives had been lost.

He didn't find anything or anybody after walking close to a mile downstream. He turned and walked back to where the sheriff's truck was. The sheriff was bent over something just above the branch. Hiram walked to where he stood. Hiram could see the rib cage of a cow protruding through the sand and gravel with most of the animal covered.

He said, "That's Widow Dorothy's milk cow. She called her Old Moss. She was getting old and probably not able to run out of the way of the raging water."

Hiram folded his arms across his chest. The sheriff asked if he'd found anything. Hiram shook his head 'no.'

"I'd say the cloud burst happened here in the head of Troublesome Creek, right there on that mountain. The water kept getting larger and gaining strength as it passed each mile down this valley. We'd better go down stream and see if we can find anyone. I didn't see any houses as I drove in."

Hiram wondered if Clinton and Susanna were all right.

He said "I've got a brother that lives below the schoolhouse. Let's go."

He climbed into the passenger's seat, and the sheriff started the motor and drove over the washed out valley. He figured most of his neighbors had lost something in this flood. The last swinging bridge at the schoolhouse was gone. Hiram gasped as they rode by where the school used to stand. The building was gone, and the play yard was washed away. Even the stump of the old sycamore was gone. The giant tree had been gone for a couple of years now. It died of diseases after the lightning strikes had weakened it. Hiram felt a lifetime of memories flare inside him. Memories from long ago. Memories of love and joy that he enjoyed as a child and dances that had been held there through the years. He was sad to see it missing.

The sheriff drove on downstream where more small hills were. Hiram could see where the wild waters made a path around the foot of the hills leaving paths of debris. His eye caught a glimpse of what looked like a body laying halfway up the hill where a curve on the hill began.

He said, "Stop! I think I see something."

He rushed out of the truck and ran toward what he saw. The sheriff was right behind him. Hiram reached the body first. The sheriff was breathing hard when he arrived. The body lying there on the ground was Widow Dorothy. Her body was covered in a light coating of mud. Her lifeless eyes stared up at him. Her body lay halfway twisted toward the creek bank. Hiram felt a little anger at first that the helpless had to die this way. But he soon calmed down knowing the Lord had His own way, and His way was always the right way. He looked on down the creek toward where Clinton and Susanna lived. He started walking toward their place.

The sheriff walked back to his truck. Hiram looked over

every inch of the mud and debris. He was looking for anything that resembled a human being. He didn't find anything until he arrived at Clinton's place. Clinton's house was gone.

Hiram became very emotional and yelled, "Clinton, can you hear me?"

He waited a minute and he yelled again. Clinton's barn was still standing. His heart leaped for joy when he saw him appear in the hallway of the barn. Susanna was standing beside him. Hiram let out a shout of praise to the invisible God that he knew existed. He ran towards the barn, and he and his brother embraced slapping each other on the back. Hiram let go of Clinton, opened his arms and pulled Susanna between him and his brother and the three cried tears of joy. When the sheriff walked up to them, Hiram could see tears in his eyes too.

Hiram said, "Sheriff, this here is my little brother and his wife, Susanna. Clinton is one of the best preachers in these parts."

The sheriff shook hands with the couple and stepped back.

Clinton finally spoke as he looked at the destruction.

"The Lord giveth and the Lord taketh away. Blessed be the name of the Lord."

Hiram knew that Clinton served the God of Abraham.

Hiram told Clinton and Susanna to walk to the house, and Dora would fix them something to eat and get them cleaned up.

"My house is gone too, but the old home place is still standing."

He watched as they walked toward his farm. Clinton held his wife around the waist. Hiram thought as they walked along, "The Lord watches over his servants and His mouth-pieces." He'd heard Clinton say that many times when he began to preach his sermons. Yes, Clinton was a mouthpiece for God and a good and faithful one.

Hiram and the Sheriff waited for the rescue squad and volunteer fire department to arrive and helped move the bodies that they knew about. Hiram figured to himself that there could be a lot more. He was feeling sort of sick at his stomach. He felt like he might pass out, so he sat down on a rooted-up tree as waves of nausea overtook him. He'd seen so much death and dying in his lifetime. More than enough. The sheriff came over to where he sat.

"Mr. Daniels are you okay?" Hiram was pale in the face. His eyes looked watery.

He looked up at the lawman and said, "I'm weary. I've been through a lot in my life. I've lost mother and father, brothers and wives. But the hardest thing I've went through was losing my son. He was a war hero, you know. They named a battleship after him for his bravery."

Hiram told his story with sorrow and great pride. The sheriff must have felt sorry for Hiram, because he put his hand on Hiram's shoulder.

The sickness passed, and Hiram rose from his seat and said, "Come on, Sheriff Dalton. I'm hungry, and the weak trembles almost got me down. Let's go to my place. Dora will have supper fixed!"

The two men got into the truck and headed for Hiram's place. The men talked about life in general as they traveled along. The sheriff told Hiram about his childhood and the way he was brought up.

Sheriff Dalton waited for Hiram to exit the vehicle before he followed him to the porch. Hiram pointed out to the sheriff about where his boundary of land lay.

"This farm has been in the Daniels hands since before the Civil War. My grandpa Jennings fought for the North."

Hiram opened the front door for the sheriff and introduced him to Dora and Mattie.

"This is Ray Dalton, High Sheriff of River County."

No one addressed an official by that title anymore. That was the old way. Now they just called them 'sheriff'. Clinton and Susanna had already met him. Hiram motioned the lawman toward the supper table. He pointed to the wash basin by the stove. After each had washed their hands, both took a seat at the table. Hiram began to tell Ray about the old days.

"Mommy used to set this very table with food so good that a man could hardly sit still and eat it," he said proudly.

Dora passed out new plates and silverware. Clinton and

Susana had eaten with Dora and Mattie. Dora poured a glass of milk for both men.

Mattie walked into the room and asked her father if she could sit down and listen as the two men talked.

"Why, yes. Is that all right, Mr. Dalton?"

Dalton grinned and nodded his head. Mattie loved to sit and watch everyone else eat long after she was through. Hiram grinned as her crooked smile reached from each corner of her mouth.

Dora brought dish after dish and set the table: half runners beans cooked with salt back, fried taters, a bowl of gravy, a pone of fried corn bread and fried chicken with blackberry dumplings rounding out the meal . Hiram asked Clinton to hold a small prayer of thanks, and the two men began to eat.

"You won't find a lot of store bought food here on my table. No hotdogs or hamburgers, things like that. I believe in real food."

The sheriff wasn't bashful as he ate two heaped plates full. Then he ate some of the blackberry dumplings.

He said, "Mrs. Daniels, these are the best dumplings I've ever had, and I've ate a lot of them. But these are the best!"

This pleased Dora. Hiram was pleased too. He liked the sheriff and was glad he was sitting at his table. Hiram pushed his plate back, and he and the sheriff joined Clinton in the sitting room. Clinton chunked the fire in the old chimney to take the chill off the evening air.

As the men sat talking, Hiram told the sheriff he'd seen tides before but nothing like this. "The 'fifty-seven flood was pretty big. It got up in my bottoms, but it was nothing like this."

The sheriff rose to his feet and said, "I've got to be going. You've been a lot of help today, Mr. Daniels. Keep yourself and your family safe. The rescue squad will probably work through the night and will be out here tomorrow and maybe the next day. Thanks for the hospitality."

He grabbed his police hat and walked out the door. Hiram and Clinton talked well into the night. Mattie sat listening to them until she rubbed her eyes raw. She hated to give into sleep worse than anyone Hiram had seen.

Dora and Susanna were in the kitchen cleaning and washing dishes. Hiram could hear Dora tell Susanna they would have to build a new house.

"But you are staying with us until you get settled and on your feet again."

They came through the kitchen door, and she showed Susanna where she and Clinton could sleep.

"Me and Hiram will take the loft room tonight. Mattie will sleep down here in Sissy's old bedroom."

Hiram felt pride for his wife. He loved her more every day. She was so good to him, waiting on him for his every need, pulling his socks off at night and half dressing him when he got out of bed in the morning. Sometimes, Hiram felt kind of guilty, but was always thankful for what she did for him.

They went to bed tired and worn out. Hiram didn't know what tomorrow would bring, but he figured there would be more bodies recovered. He felt for Clinton. More wakes to preach; more friends to bury. He said a prayer for Cullen and his family, wondering how things were with them. He listened to Jesse breathe, as his little chest rose and fell. Soon he fell asleep.

Chapter 13

The next two days were hard on Hiram. He drove over to Ben's Fork to check on Cullen and his family. At the mouth of Ben's Fork, where the creek joined Cody, a stack of driftwood and material lay bunched together under what used to be the bridge. Two by fours and roof rafters, along with debris from upstream, clogged the creek's path. Ben's Fork had decided to make a new right of way by washing out half of the bridge and took tons of rich bottom land downstream with it. Hiram couldn't get across the bridge, so he drove back upstream to a low water bridge. He got out of his truck and moved debris from the concrete slab and continued to meander his way to his destination. He arrived at Cullen's house an hour later in a trip that normally would have taken but ten minutes from the mouth of the streams joining.

Hiram stopped in front of Cullen's place and looked at the house. It was still standing, to his surprise. He hadn't figured there would be anything or anyone left. Hiram was glad but wondered how Cullen's house was left while others were gone. Hiram knocked on the front door and stepped back. A groggy headed lad opened the door and peered out at Hiram. The young lad didn't recognize his grandpa.

Hiram said, "Is your father home?"

The boy, Bradley, rubbed his eyes and Hiram heard Ruby open the door wider to ask the lad who it was.

She looked at Hiram and smiled.

"Why Hiram is that you? Come in, come in," She said as she opened the door wider and stepped out of the way.

Hiram smelled pee as he entered the doorway into the living room. Heads lay sleeping underneath sheets. Cullen and Ruby still had five children at home. The seven older ones had moved to different parts of Indiana to live and work. The oldest girl, Stella Fay, had married well and was living good in Nashville as a country music star. The rest were doing all right. Hiram was glad they decided to move away from here and away from their parents. Cullen didn't raise his children to work. He had lived off welfare, commodities and government assistance all his life.

Hiram asked Ruby where Cullen was.

"He's in jail in Slonetown. The sheriff arrested him Monday morning. I didn't have money for his bond. Weren't that much, but you know, Hiram, Cullen spends it as soon as he draws it. We barely get by most months."

She watched Hiram as he looked around the house. Dirty dishes were still in the sink from last night. Part of breakfast still sat on the stove. Britches and shoes sat by the coffee table and beds and dresses hung over the couch. He could hear snoring from the back bedroom.

Ruby said, "Look over the mess, Hiram. Seems like every time you visit, everything is piled up. You know I've tried. I wanted Cullen to stay in Indiana, but he wouldn't. There was plenty of work up there, and the children could have had a future there. Here all they want to do is follow in their daddy's footsteps, drinking and raising cane or growing dope. I've had a hard life Hiram."

Hiram did feel sorry for her and the younger children, but the older ones could do better.

He told her of the destruction the tide had done on Troublesome and all the debris he found at the mouth of Ben's Fork.

"You all have been spared. How long will they keep Cullen in jail?"

He looked at Ruby, waiting for an answer. She told Bradley to wake the other children.

"I don't know. I guess until the trial or someone goes his bail."

Hiram dug his billfold out of his front pocket and reached her two hundred dollars.

"I'd say his fine will not be over fifty dollars. Use the rest for food and things you need for the house."

Bradley looked at Hiram for a minute then asked, "Are you our grandpa?"

Hiram felt strange, having grandchildren living this close to him that didn't even know who he was.

Hiram grinned at the boy and said, "Yal, I'm Hiram Daniels, your grandpa. I'd like for you all to come and visit me sometime. It is time, I think."

He bid them farewell and left. He drove back down to the low water bridge and headed across and turned in the direction of Betty's Troublesome. He took notice of how much destruction the storm caused. The water had done its damage after dark. He was sure there would be bodies washed down the creek. He didn't want to see anymore. Groups of men were clearing away fallen tree stumps with chain saws and axes. He crossed the hill down into the Troublesome valley and headed for Slonetown.

He went straight to the sheriff's office to make a report on what he saw. The sheriff was sitting at his desk looking at papers. He raised his head and smiled at Hiram's entrance.

"Well, what can I do for you this morning?" He reached his hand out to shake.

Hiram shook his hand and said, "Looks bad over on Bens' Fork right where it joins with Cody. Have you heard of any more deaths?"

The sheriff pointed toward a chair for Hiram to sit down.

"Yal, they told me about two more from Troublesome. Two children were washed away and are presumed drowned. Not found their bodies yet."

He laid the papers down and leaned back in his chair.

Hiram asked him about Cullen. The sheriff asked Hiram, "He's your son ain't he?"

Hiram turned his head toward the sheriff.

"Yal, he's my son by my previous marriage. I don't know where I went wrong with him. All of his kin from way back were moonshiners and bootleggers, but most made a decent living and even some quit their evil ways and joined the church. How much is his fine?"

Sheriff Dalton smiled at Hiram and said, "Nothing. I'm going to let him out this evening because I like you Mr. Daniels. I'm going to let him go. He's been in here for three days now. You want to talk to him?"

Hiram wanted to in the worst way, but he figured Cullen would just argue with him, so he told the sheriff no.

"I've got something else I need to attend to. I'll get up with him later."

He rose from his chair and walked out the door into a crowded street. The flood waters hadn't bothered Slonetown much, just left a little mud here and there. He drove straight home. He found Dora and Mattie cleaning house.

The next day was Sunday, but Hiram didn't take his family to church. The roads were still too muddy, and some were washed out too bad. He decided to stay home and help Dora do the housework and cooking. A big dinner was prepared, and he hoped Clinton and Susanna would come by to eat. Clinton had converted his smoke house into a dwelling place. Clinton had divided the little building into a kitchen and bedroom. It was small but efficient for the purpose.

Clinton and Susanna did come by to eat dinner. Clinton

told Hiram he'd been in a funeral every night since the flood.

"A total of six people were drowned, including two children."

Hiram watched his brothers face as raw emotion escaped from deep inside him. His expressions went from hope to sorrow when he spoke about the two children that were lost. He cried when he mentioned them. Hiram could hardly hide his emotion from Clinton, so he turned away. After supper, Clinton and Susanna drove back to their place. Hiram and Dora went to bed early. A busy day was sure to come tomorrow.

Hiram was up early the next morning, waking to the sound of a bulldozer working nearby. He washed his hands and face, then walked out on the porch of the old house. He saw a bulldozer and high-lift moving dirt and debris off the road. The high-lift was lifting what was left of a culvert. Hiram got Dora up to start breakfast, and he walked to where the dozer operator stood and looked the situation over.

Hiram said, "How are you this morning?" extending his hand.

The dozer operator shook Hiram's hand and said, "I'm wondering what to do with this mess," pointing to the mud and drying soil.

Hiram said, "I want to donate my equipment and money to fix our roads back to normal. You get on the shortwave and tell the county judge."

Hiram had his heavy equipment stored in Slonetown at a

warehouse.

"You tell the county judge I'll drive there after breakfast. Have men to operate the equipment and bring the culverts, and we'll rebuild the bridge where the one room school used to be."

The dozer operator climbed into the county truck and began to call the judge's office. Hiram walked back to his house and ate breakfast.

Within two workdays, Troublesome Creek was looking better. The road was coming along. A new culvert was installed, and a work crew was repairing the bridge. Hiram and Clinton cleaned the bottoms of rock, tree stumps and trash. He used one of the dozer operators to make a new house seat for his new house. He told Clinton they would work on getting his place back to normal tomorrow.

By the first of December, Hiram's house was under construction. Clinton's was almost finished and under roof. Hiram figured Clinton and Susanna would be able to spend Christmas in their new home. Hiram, Dora, Mattie and Jesse would spend Christmas with them this year. On Christmas Day, word came that the state had sent Cullen to Danville to the insane asylum. He'd been drinking so bad Ruby couldn't get him to stop. The social services sent him down there to dry him out. Danville was an institution for crazy people, not for sots, but Ruby didn't know what else to do. She apologized to Hiram when she and all of her children appeared on Clinton's doorstep that morning. The weather was warm for Christmas, about sixty degrees. Clinton welcomed all of them in for dinner. Ruby had two children in diapers. Patsy was the oldest girl and Colbert was the oldest boy that still were at home. Hiram noticed how much Colbert looked like Cullen.

After dinner, Ruby told Hiram and Dora how they had been living.

"If it wasn't for commodities and handouts, I don't know what we would have done. Cullen bootlegged some, but since Perry County was voted wet that cut down on our sales. The state has a new thing coming out this spring called food stamps. We can sign up on them then. That will get us by until Cullen can get out. Hiram will you sign him out when the time comes?"

Hiram was very upset with his son. He gave him money all the time, but he wasted it. He didn't want to upset Ruby, so he said he would. He pulled his billfold out of his pocket, opened it and reached Ruby three one hundred dollar bills.

"Take this and buy food and some new clothes for the children. I'll have a crew over to your place and fix the damage the flood caused . I'll hire your Patsy and Colbert to help us here at the house. Dora can use the help, and Colbert can help the carpenter crew. How long did you say they are going to keep Cullen?"

Ruby took the money and thanked Hiram.

"Until spring, I guess, unless you call down there. Someone will have to go down there and pick him up. I tried to get him to quit drinking, Hiram, but he wouldn't listen. You know how he is when he gets ahold of moonshine."

She waited a minute then started again, "He'd been making liquor for two whole months. He got to drinking so much each day, and it got out of control. He's weak, Hiram. He loves whiskey better than anyone I know."

Hiram agreed with her and she got up to leave. Ruby hugged Dora, Mattie and Susanna and left with her children following behind her. Hiram couldn't help feeling sorry for her and her children. Cullen hadn't supplied her or her children with a living or upbringing.

It was only a month after Christmas when the word came that Cullen's son had been killed in a car wreck near the mouth of Ben's Fork. Colbert had been drinking, his mother told Hiram, and the car went into the creek, pinning him underneath the vehicle. Colbert drowned in the muddy waters.

Hiram felt so sorry for Ruby when she told him. Here Cullen was in Danville, and she was all alone. She'd have to bury her son without his father.

Hiram and Dora both cried along with Ruby. Hiram made his mind up then and there. He would go to Slonetown and see if he could get Cullen released. He told Dora his plans and drove straight to the courthouse and stopped at Sheriff Dalton's office. He opened the door and walked into the large room. The sheriff's office was inside the courthouse beside the County Clerk and County Attorney's office. The sheriff smiled as Hiram walked into the room. Sheriff Dalton sat behind a large wooden desk that shined as if it was new. Whoever cleaned the courthouse each day did a good job.

The sheriff motioned for Hiram to sit down. He said with a grin, "What can I do for you, Daniels?"

Hiram never did ask for favors from any politician. He didn't like to be involved in county or state races. He did vote for president when there was an election. He'd been voting in all the presidents' races since President Kennedy.

Hiram sat down, looked around the large room and marveled how high the ceilings were. He noticed the pictures on the walls. He knew some of the past sheriffs of River County but had only liked a few. He said, "One of my grandsons was killed in a car wreck last night at the mouth of Ben's Fork. The boy's daddy is in the asylum in Danville. They had him admitted to dry him out."

Hiram looked away for a minute. When he turned back to the sheriff he asked, "I wonder if you can use your influence to get him out."

Hiram dropped his head and turned toward the wall. The sheriff reached for the phone and dialed the County Attorney's number.

"The sheriff talked to the voice on the other end for four minutes, then hung the phone back on the hook.

"Your son will be home tomorrow after noon. You'll have to pick him up in Danville though."

Hiram smiled at Ray Dalton and shook his hand saying, "If you ever need a favor from me let me know."

He rose from his chair and walked out the door to his truck and drove home.

Hiram told Dora that Cullen was to be released tomorrow.

"I want Lundy to drive my truck to Danville to pick him up. Do you reckon he'll do that for us?" Dora took his hand and squeezed it. She knew Hiram was very upset. This was the first family member he'd lost in years.

Dora said, "I'm sure he will, Hiram. He thinks the world of you. I'll call him and ask him."

She went to the living room but soon appeared back at the table. "He'll be here first thing in the morning."

She hugged her husband and held him.

She let go and continued to fix supper. While she did that, Hiram called Ruby to tell her that Lundy was picking Cullen up tomorrow.

"You ride down there with him, if you will. Dora and I will watch the children. I'll come by and pick them up in the morning."

Hiram walked back to the table and sat down in his chair. He turned to Dora and said, "We'll have to call Stella Fay. She will want to come in."

Dora shook her head and said, "Yes, we will. Is she in Nashville, you reckon, or on the road?"

Hiram looked toward her, "She probably will be home

at this time of year. Most of her shows are done in the summertime. I heard her new song on the radio. She sure has a Daniels' voice. I love to hear her sing."

He stopped and then said, "But she sings the wrong songs for me. I love the old mountain Regular Baptists songs."

He didn't say anything more until after supper. As Dora washed dishes, Hiram stared into the fireplace.

The next morning, the weather was wet. Rain had poured most of the night. Troublesome Creek was raising a little. Hiram was up early starting breakfast. He thought of Mattie, and he figured she was ready to come home. Cassie kept her about once a week at her place in town. Mattie loved staying with her half-sister, but after one night she was ready to come back to Troublesome. He placed the food on the table and woke Dora to eat. He heard a knock on the front door. It was Lundy. Hiram offered for him to eat, but he declined. Hiram reached him the keys, and Lundy told his sister goodbye and headed for Ben's Fork to pick Ruby up.

Hiram finished breakfast and followed Lundy out the front door with Dora right behind him. He opened the front car door for Dora, and they drove toward Ben's Fork.

Ruby had the baby ready and the other children too. Hiram gave Lundy a hundred dollar bill and told him to buy what they needed on their trip. He watched them as they drove out of sight. Then he loaded the children into his car and drove back to his place.

Dora held the baby as they drove along. The other two

girls slept on the trip back to Troublesome Creek. Hiram was tense, but he figured everything would be all right after Cullen came home. This might make him think about all the wrong he has done in his life. The death of his child might change him. If it didn't, Hiram didn't know what would. Hiram pulled into his lane and everyone got out and went inside. All except Hiram.

He sat in his rocking chair, staring at Rolly Joe Mountain. He'd heard tales about a large mining company from Alabama making plans to mine the old mountain, striping it's top and leaving the mountain top laying scattered all over the hillside. It hurt Hiram to even think about it. His wife had the radio on in the kitchen. Hiram sat down in his rocking chair A song begin to play. Hiram caught his self-patting his foot against the porch floor. The radio announcer said this is a new song by Stella Fay Daniels. Hiram rocked as the music and words came over the radio speakers.

One bucket at a time; one bucket at a time,
I'm carrying Troublesome Creek away
one bucket at a time.
Some people don't like it; they say it's a crime,
Cause I'm carrying Troublesome Creek away
one bucket at a time.

I started at Ary then I moved North,
I've just about got all of the dirt

moved away from Dwarf.
It won't take me long if I stay in line,
And keep carrying Troublesome Creek
away one bucket at a time.

Now Fisty and Emmalena and Carrie too
But when I get to Slonetown, I don't
know what I'm going to do.
For if the sheriff catches me, he will give me some time,
For carrying Troublesome Creek
away one bucket at a time.

One bucket at a time; one bucket at a time
I'm carrying Troublesome Creek away
one bucket at a time.
Some people don't like it; they say it's a crime,
Cause I'm carrying Troublesome Creek away
one bucket at a time.

Dora called again that dinner was ready. Hiram grinned as he walked inside to eat.

That evening, Lundy drove Ruby and Cullen by Hiram's place. Hiram didn't know what to say to Cullen, and he didn't like not being able to discuss his grandchild's wake. Cullen's face turned a light pale as he shook hands with his father. Hiram wept, and so did Cullen. Finally, Hiram hugged his son and held him for a few minutes before turning him loose. Cullen could not face his father. Cullen turned and walked back to the truck and opened the door and slid in on the passenger side.

Ruby looked at Hiram and said, "This is going to be hard on him Hiram. He cried most of the way home. I'll let you know when the funeral will be."

Hiram never liked that word. 'Wake' seemed more appropriate than funeral, but Hiram let on like he did not hear his daughter-in-law. Ruby turned to Dora and smiled then she left.

Lundy asked Hiram, "Do you want me to bring the truck back here tonight, sir? We've had a long trip and I'm tired."

Hiram shook his head and said, "No, you go on home after you drop Cullen and Ruby off at their place. You can bring the truck by tomorrow. I appreciate this, Lundy."

Hiram watched the young lad walk to the truck and get in. Hiram's mind was thinking as they disappeared down Troublesome. He leaned against the porch column as the truck vanished out of sight.

For the next three nights, Clinton was out every night and day, preaching wakes across River County. Hiram felt sorry for his brother, but when Hiram spoke to him about it, Clinton said, "This is my life, Hiram. The Lord pays me for the job He called me to do it. I don't take money from anyone, because that is not our way. You know how Preacher Silas and Brother Lonzo went night after night, through the rain, the snow, whether they felt like it or not. That's the life of a minister and the rewards are great. Since you've joined church you'll understand what I'm talking about."

After the wake, the undertaker took the body of Cullen's son and placed it in the hearse. Then the procession made its way to the dogwood point to where all the Daniels kin were laid to rest. Hiram had gotten a crew to cut all the large trees to enlarge the graveyard. It was filling up fast. Headstones were covering spaces where Hiram could remember bare spots used to be. After the dismissal, Cullen and Ruby walked down the hill to Hiram's house. Hiram stayed behind. He wanted to just sit, look around for a while and think on days gone by. Hiram thought about the hardships he endured on this piece of land he called home. Things the land had given and things the land had taken. Finally, he said to himself, "I guess everything works out about even, some points I gained and some points I lost."

He wept awhile and turned to walk down the hill toward home.

Months had passed. The winter was cold and wet most of December and January. February and March were warm for the time, so he planted a large garden. He had thirty-one heads of black angus cattle that grazed the hill side pastures. He'd rebuilt his white plank and wire fences. Up on the high flats, he left a few split rails just to have them around. He'd bought all the land that consisted of Rolly Joe Mountain. Took half a year for his lawyer to search the deeds and find the owners and relatives that owned the land. His lawyer traveled to over a dozen states to get the deeds signed. The total acreage of Rolly Joe Mountain was just a little over fifty-five hundred acres. Giant red oak and black oaks grew high on the mountain, along with huge scaly and slick bark hickories. Popular swags were full of the trees plus black walnuts that were worth a small fortune. But Hiram had no plans of logging his land, and he was going to fight with all he had to keep any one from mining its majestic peak. Engineers said the number nine seam of coal was one of the largest in the eastern United States. He could double his investment any day he wanted to. The mountain's cost and the lawyers' fees came to five million dollars. Hiram thought it well worth every penny he'd spent on it.

Hiram was happy again. Cullen had joined Sandgap Church, and he'd turned over a new leaf. He was different as daylight and dark from what he used to be. Hiram had never seen as much of a change in any one as he saw in Cullen, and Hiram was glad. He'd lived to see something that he figured he would never see. When Cullen gave his experience to the church, he told of how hard it was for him to get forgiveness.

He said while crying, "I've been as mean as any two men. One of the worst sinners of all time. I think the Lord took my son to make me realize my sins. And I prayed a long time before God would hear my cry."

Sisters shouted, preachers preached, congregations cried and children wept as the Spirit worked that day like Hiram had never seen, not even when Clinton joined. He remembered back when his mother read the Bible aloud to them. He remembered her reading, 'The chief of sinners make the best Christians.' And Cullen had been the worst.

But his happiness was not for long. Hiram received an urgent call for him to come to Slonetown to meet with his lawyer. He told Dora after supper to be ready.

"We'll have to make a trip to town tomorrow."

Hiram sat on the porch at the old house until just before dark. He held Jesse in his lap. The young lad had fallen asleep. Hiram picked him up in his arms and carried him to his bedroom and laid Jesse on the bed. He covered him with a sheet. Hiram joined his wife in the living room. She talked to him about the garden and her chickens. He really didn't pay any attention to her. His mind was on his lawyer and what might be his need to call him to his office. He didn't sleep much after he and Dora retired for the night. When he did sleep, he dreamed all night about losing something, but he couldn't quite see in the dream what it was.

He woke with a start. Jesse was crying. He jumped out of bed to see what was wrong. Jesse was sitting up in bed, rubbing his eyes as the tears fell. Hiram comforted the boy until his mother came and took him in her arms. Hiram started breakfast. Mattie appeared from her bedroom. Hiram turned the radio on to hear the morning news and weather report. The news was that coal mining was booming. The weather report was sunny days for most of the week. Hiram was glad. It had rained for most of March and April and May had set in dry. Hiram finished breakfast and set the table. He yelled for Mattie that the table was set.

Dora carried Jesse to the table and sat down with him still crying. Hiram figured he'd had a nightmare. Mattie came and took her place. Hiram asked a blessing over the food and they all ate in silence. After breakfast, Dora swiftly did the dishes while Mattie sat with her younger brother. Mattie loved children. Hiram watched her as she talked to Jesse and told him stories about Slonetown.

Hiram washed his face, shaved and readied his self for the trip to town. He used the new looking glass every morning. Dora had bought three new mirrors, but Hiram refused to use any of them but one. He preferred this one.

Hiram walked behind Mattie to help her if she needed him. Dora carried Jesse. Hiram opened the door for Mattie and helped her into the back seat of the car. Hiram opened the door for Dora and held Jesse until his wife could take him. He started the new Chevrolet Suburban and turned right down Troublesome Creek toward Slonetown.

Slonetown was busy. Cars and trucks lined every parking place and lot. The lot near the bank and courthouse was full. The sidewalks were full as people walked from store to store, getting haircuts or just doing business of some kind.

Hiram told Dora to take Jesse to the barber shop for a hair-cut. Mattie walked along beside him. At the lawyer's office Hiram opened the front door and motioned Mattie to go in-side. Mr. Johnson had built one of largest office buildings in town. It was made of colored brick. The building's lobby had chandelier hanging from the ceiling. Hiram led Mattie to the elevator, and they stepped inside. He told her to push the button for the second floor. The elevator jumped lightly as it started its accent and stopped with a jolt at the second floor. Mattie was so excited that her gums were showing from her wide smile. A bell sounded, and the elevator doors opened. Hiram helped Mattie across the doorway. He turned right, stopped at a large door, opened it and they walked into Mr. Johnson's office. He told the receptionist what his business was. The young lady rose from her chair and disappeared into another room. When she walked back out, she showed Hiram and Mattie where to sit.

Mr. Johnson sat in his wide mahogany chair, and he smiled and greeted both Hiram and Mattie with a handshake. Mr. Johnson had done a lot of legal work for Hiram over the years. He had helped Hiram in several cases, and they had become good friends. Hiram liked him and respected him.

"What can I do for you?"

The young lawyer leaned back in his chair and smiled, his teeth showing. Mattie looked around the room admiring the pictures.

Ralph said, "A large coal company has been snooping

around and even gouging loose dirt in places. They are wanting to mine coal."

Hiram cleared his throat and said, "Do they have a leg to stand on?"

Hiram pointed at the map hanging on the wall.

Mr. Johnson squinted his eyes as he looked at the map then he said, "They do own the minerals, Hiram. They bought the mineral rights on that mountain back years ago. They have the deeds recorded in the courthouse. I've looked at the deeds several times to see if I could find a loop-hole, but no luck so far. And the new legislature in Frankfort has passed a broad-form deed to the effect that a coal company can enter your property and mine their minerals and then leave, only paying you for damages. We need to vote some of the representatives out of office."

He threw his hands in the air as he stared at the map. Hiram grunted and then turned to his lawyer, but he didn't speak.

Hiram finally said, "Suppose I put up 'No Trespassing' signs. Will that help?"

Mr. Johnson said, "No, Hiram the law is on their side. The only way we will be able to do anything is make a trip to Frankfort and speak before the Department of Permits. I'll go with you and represent you."

Hiram flinched and walked toward the door as Mattie halfway rose from her chair.

He turned and said, "I'll figure something out. I'll get

back with you."

Hiram helped Mattie to his car and drove to pick up his wife.

Time passed and, before Hiram knew it, it was Decoration Day. He bought five hundred dollars of silk flowers for the dogwood point graveyard. Dora helped him arrange all the flowers. Hiram had a huge bunch for his two late wives and for his mother's and father's graves. He placed a large arrangement on Ballard's grave. He walked to the lower end of the graveyard and gazed up-hill to where the flowers lay. He told Dora, "They look good," then he cried.

He and Dora helped Mattie walk down the hill.

July came in hot and dry. Hiram's garden didn't do a bit of good. It was the worst dry spell he'd seen in a long time. The blades of corn were curling up, begging for a drink of water. Pasture grass was turning brown and would crackle when walked upon. The soil dried and caked, cracking open the bottom soil. Tree leaves on the hillsides were drying and curling too. Rain crows hollered every morning, but there hadn't been rain for thirty-eight days in a row. Hiram kept count because of dogdays. He knew if July set in dry or wet the whole month would be the same.

Fogs of the morning were thick and cool but soon burned off revealing a blue sky and a sun ball that was especially hot. The heat waves lifted off the hillsides as great waves on an ocean before filtering into the blue skies. The days were long and dry. Rattlesnakes and copperheads crawled about in search of water. Hiram had killed several near his barn. Gray foxes had a rabies outbreak again. The Department of Fish and Wildlife dropped poison biscuits to control the outbreak. Hiram had heard packs of coyotes yelping from the top of Rolly Joe Mountain. He could hear them from his front porch as he sat relaxing during the evening time.

He woke early one middle July day to the sound of heavy equipment. He walked out on his porch and looked toward the mountain. He could see a yellow bulldozer pushing dirt as if it was making a road on the mountain side. He quickly put his shoes on and drove his truck to the foot of the mountain, dismounted and hollered at the dozer operator. He finally got the operator's attention, and the man stopped the dozer to see what Hiram wanted.

Hiram said, "This is my land. Who gave you permission to do this?"

The operator stopped the engine and replied to Hiram.

"Why, I'm just doing my job. The coal company sent me here to build an access road." He waited to see what Hiram was going to say. Hiram walked around to the front of the dozer and stood in the middle of a mound of dozed dirt with his arms crossed, defiant as he could be. The dozer operator didn't know what to do. He finally climbed down from the dozer's seat and called on his short wave radio. It wasn't long until the company foreman and two other workers were trying to talk Hiram into moving. But Hiram wouldn't budge.

He said, "I bought this land, and there is nobody going to mine it as long as I can prevent it."

The foreman had called for the sheriff. Sheriff Dalton arrived a half hour later. He approached Hiram and shook hands with him.

"Hiram, we are at an impasse. They claim they own the mineral rights, and I don't want to take you to jail. Won't you come with me, and we'll drive to town and see if your lawyer can get an injunction to stop the coal company for a while."

Hiram knew the sheriff was right, but he didn't want to own up to it.

He said, "Sheriff, make them wait until tomorrow to work. At least until I can see what I can get done."

Sheriff Dalton talked to the foreman. The foreman didn't like the conversation and used a few bad words. Hiram's temper was getting the best of him as the situation dragged on. Finally, the foreman threw his arms in the air, got in his truck and slung gravels and burned rubber as his truck sped down the highway. The dozer operator and workers left too. Sheriff Dalton talked awhile and told Hiram to stay out of trouble.

Hiram answered, "I will. I'm going to town just as soon as I get dressed."

Hiram and his lawyer met at the courthouse and appeared before the circuit judge. Judge Carson was and old friend of Hiram's. Even though they were good friends, the judge made few rulings because of favoritism. Most of the time he ruled by the law. Judge Carson sat in his office looking over legal papers. Ralph shook hands with the prestigious old man. Judge Carson then rose from his seat to shake Hiram's hand.

"How are you doing Hiram?" the judge smiled warmly toward him, then he motioned for Hiram and his lawyer to sit down. He sat down in his chair and leaned back with his hands and arms folded behind his head. Hiram noticed how gray the judge's hair had gotten. He'd only been judge for two terms now, but the job was taking its toll on his friend. Hiram watched him as he and his attorney discussed the problem Hiram had. The two men used terms that Hiram didn't understand. Hiram's attorney quoted several past rulings concerning the state's high court.

Judge Carson listened as his mouth grimaced at the corners where his lips met with his chin and upper lip. Finally Judge Carson lowered his hands and arms and leaned forward on his desk, clasped his two large hands together and said, "I can give you a temporary restraining order prohibiting the coal company from entering your property."

He looked at Hiram as he talked. He further said, "But this is only temporary. Hiram you'll have to go to Frankfort. You'll have to appear before the permit processing body and speak your piece before them, if any of the state legislatures will listen. They are in session right at this minute. If you are lucky, you might persuade the legislative body to change the rules on the coal company plans of mining under the broad-form deed method. I doubt they will change because of the state's revenue they collect from each county. Severance tax brings in a lot of money for the state you know."

Hiram shook his head in agreement and turned toward his lawyer. Ralph asked Hiram if he was willing to make the trip to Frankfort.

"You'll have to do the talking. Why you think the state needs to change the method of mining under the broad-form deed and all the hollow fills and mountain top removal practices."

Hiram's face flushed, and he could feel his skin tingle at the very thought of standing in front of the legislative body of Kentucky and speaking in front of such a large crowd of men and women, most of whom were lawyers and men of renown. People who had proven their worth of being able to speak eloquently and make speeches as though they were born for this very reason. His insides shook as he thought about the thought.

Finally, he said, "For the need of Rolly Joe Mountain to be left intact and to save its integrity, I'll go."

He rose from his chair and thanked his friend, shaking hands with the judge.

Judge Carson replied, "The injunction will give you only two weeks to work with. I wish you luck. You will need it."

A week passed, and Hiram was up early to make the trip

to Frankfort. He was to meet Ralph in front of the hotel in
Slonetown. He kissed Dora and Mattie goodbye, walked to
his truck and headed down Troublesome toward town. He
thought about all the things that had befallen him over the
years as he drove along. He wasn't nervous anymore. He had
fought for what was his all his life. It had often been trying
times to make a living in these rugged mountains. God had
paid him well by blessing him with much. He'd lost battles
from famines and pestilences. He'd lost family members
to death. "But I've emerged stronger each time death took
one of mine," he thought as he drove along the newly paved
highway. His truck traveled smoothly as the trucks big diesel
engine whined its power to make the dual wheels turn on
his new 'dooly.' He passed a line of eighteen wheelers on
their way to haul coal. Horns honked as the big rigs moved
to their destination. He pulled into the parking lot, parked
and locked the truck doors, then crawled into the passenger's
side of Ralph's Suburban. Hiram liked the smooth ride the
Suburban produced. He noticed the greenness of the mountainsides as the landscape slipped by quickly. He'd never
been to Frankfort before, and he actually looked forward to
it.

Soon, after an hour's driving, the mountains became far-
ther apart. Large valleys along the Red River were wide and
long. Bottoms of corn were up about waist high. Hiram liked
the large bottoms. High rock formations were located high
on the mountain tops with cliffs that looked to be over one

hundred and fifty feet high. Hiram thought, "That's higher than the chimney rock atop Rolly Joe Mountain."

Soon, the landscape changed again to little rolling hills and then the bluegrass region of horse farms. Horses of all sizes picked grass that grew in fenced in pastures. The plank fences were all white.

"Frankfort is not too far from Lexington, Hiram. Another half an hour, we'll be where the Governor and the state house is."

He watched Hiram's expression as Hiram looked the landscape over. Hiram didn't say anything. He just stared ahead looking from one side to the other when something caught his eye. Ralph exited off of Interstate Sixty-Four to the exit that led into the city limits of Frankfort, Kentucky's capitol.

Hiram said, "I'm glad you know where you are going. I was lost as soon as we entered the city limits of Lexington ."

The two men laughed.

Hiram didn't like big city life and all the traffic . He looked out his side of the Suburban as Ralph drove through Frankfort. Ralph maneuvered around cars, trucks and pedestrians. Hiram felt uneasy, so the two men talked little. Even Ralph was nervous. He kept watching the red lights and hearing the honking of horns. But he managed to drive right up to the capitol building. Hiram looked in amazement at the size of the building, with its columns and steps. Ralph stopped the Suburban for a minute then drove on down to a parking garage, engaged the parking brake and opened the door and got out. Hiram slid out his side.

Inside the Capitol building, Hiram and Ralph waited for a chance to see the governor. But the governor never showed. Ralph told Hiram that they had better go on to the State Department of Mines and Minerals room.

Hiram said, "You lead the way."

Hiram kept up as the two men walked down a sidewalk to a smaller building. Ralph led the way inside. He stopped in front of two large, windowed doors with letters painted on the windowpanes. Ralph opened the door for his client, and Hiram walked inside. Ralph motioned for Hiram to take a seat.

"We'll have to wait for the director to call our case. So, just relax."

He slumped down in his chair and crossed his legs. Hiram sat down and looked the room over. The room was spotless and smelled very clean. The wooded walls shined liked they had been polished, and the ceilings were tall and high.

A young woman walked into the room and called out, "Is Hiram Daniels here to represent his case against Puma Coal Company?"

Hiram's lawyer raised from his seat and motioned Hiram to follow him. Both men followed the young lady into a conference room where several men in suits sat around a large table.

Hiram stood as his lawyer introduced the pair.

"My name is Ralph Johnson, and this is my client, Mr. Hiram Daniels."

One of the men told them to be seated and said, "Have you brought proof why this coal company should not be allowed a permit?"

He looked over a stack of papers and pulled out one. It was the letter Hiram had written the permit board trying to stop the strip mining on Rolly Joe Mountain. The director's eyes scanned the letter before giving it to the man that sat next to him. This man read the letter too.

The director said, "Well we'd better get this hearing started."

He first introduced Hiram and his lawyer. Then he introduced the coal company's president and his company of lawyers. Hiram knew the coal company would spend money and a lot of it to try to mine Hiram's land, and mine it the way they wanted to. Hiram had already agreed to give them permission to deep mine the minerals on his land, but if he could, he planned to keep his surface intact.

A water pitcher sat on the table directly in front of the panel. Hiram wondered where his and Ralph's pitcher was, but he reckoned they weren't counted to be worthy of a water pitcher. He wanted a cold drink of water very badly, but he wasn't about to walk to the end of the building to get a drink from the water fountain. He wet his lips and stuck a cough drop into his mouth, then offered Ralph one. The lawyer took the wrapped cough drop, carefully unwrapped the wrapper and inserted the red, cherry flavored drop into his mouth.

The director spoke for at least ten minutes about the process that Hiram couldn't understand but Ralph hopefully could. That's why he paid him large sums of money to take care of his affairs. The Director invited the coal company to present their case.

A large, suited man rose from his chair and began to speak.

"We hope this permit body will examine the plan we propose today and grant Puma Coal Company a permit to mine the coal minerals on Mr. Daniels land holdings. We plan to strip the land using the mountain top removal method, which is the only method to remove the number nine seam of coal. Then mine the number seven and number four seams the same way, by using the strip mining method by contour and auger mining. Our proposals will include a valid plan for reclaiming the surface to its original shape. The sowing of grass and planting pine and locust trees will cover what few scars we leave on the surface. We plan to hollow fill two sites and close off the branch water and build two silt ponds to catch silt that may wash from the mined area. The mined coal will produce a sizable amount of revenue for the state. Severance taxes the state collects will build new roads, and the state can use some of the taxes for education purposes. The broad form deed gives us a right to mine our coal holdings, and we'll pay Mr. Daniels tonnage for every ton of coal we haul from his land. That includes a monetary figure for damage of his property."

The man waited for a minute and conferred with the other lawyer that sat beside him. The president didn't speak.

Finally, the suited man spoke again.

"The mining laws are on our side!"

He sat down in his chair and glanced at his law partner. He also gazed at the coal company's president. The director told Hiram and his lawyer that they could speak now.

Ralph rose to his feet and began.

"We are here today to save a valuable mountain range that is known to the residents of River County as Rolly Joe Mountain. This land is owned by my client, Mr. Hiram Daniels. Mr. Daniels was a miner himself and mined coal for a living for years. When he mined coal, he mined in a responsible manner. He took the mineral without disturbing the surface much at all. This method he used is called deep mining. Deep mining cuts a hole in the side of an area and extracts the coal out of the heart of the surface without damaging the surface of the land. On that basis, we are asking the mining permit be denied."

The director turned his head toward Hiram and asked, "Mr. Daniels do you want to speak? We have a letter from you describing your property and giving the reasons why this coal company should be denied access to their coal."

Hiram listened as the director talked. At the offer, he rose to his feet and said, "My name is Hiram Daniels, and I'm from River County. I live on my farm that has been owned by the Daniels for over a hundred years now. I own more than five hundred acres of bottom land and hillside alike. Prime land; farming land. Land that has kept my family alive by feeding all my relations through thick years as well as the thin years."

Hiram cleared his throat and started again. He felt weak in his knees, but he spoke on.

"My folks worked and raised five children, and I have raised five, or almost five. My youngest son is five years old now. I've worked my farm and still do, but not as much as I used too. I made a small fortune mining my coal and I bought land all over River County, including Rolly Joe Mountain. In my younger days, I helped make moonshine liquor on that mountain. I've hunted ginseng on that mountain for I don't know how many years now. I met a supernatural being there one night when I was just a young man. I still don't know what it was, but it was real. The beauty of that mountain is not to be compared to any place else in Kentucky. It has the highest peak in our state. It is picture perfect in the spring with its wild mountain laurel and wild honeysuckles bloom-ing, along with the redbud and dogwood trees."

Hiram waited for a minute then continued.

"There is one thing that Rolly Joe Mountain has that I've never heard of or saw anywhere else in the world: a white honeysuckle bloom. At least twenty honeysuckle bushes bloom white instead of the normal orange. To kill this bush that may be the only such plant in the whole world seems selfish to me. Just for a few dollars, or yes maybe even a million dollars. But at what price will there be to the mountain itself when the same coal company can mine their coal by deep mining and not disturb the surface?"

Hiram started to sit down but rose again and spoke.

"God made Rolly Joe Mountain the way he did, in the beginning. It has never been logged or mined. There are yellow poplar trees that are over two hundred feet tall, along with virgin forests of red oak, white oak and the remains of chestnut trees that once stood king over these forests. A lot of loggers have wanted to harvest my timber, but I refuse to sell any of it."

The room was quiet after Hiram took his seat. He was getting a little emotional after speaking of something he cared for so deeply. More deeply than he even realized until now. Right at this moment, he felt a closeness to his roots that he'd never felt before. His mind was thinking about a million things all at once. All the memories he had of this place he called home came boiling to the top and was about to boil over. He searched the room for comfort and to hide his thoughts as he sat there. The director finally spoke and thanked everyone present. He thanked the coal company's president and their lawyers and thanked Hiram and his lawyer before saying, "We'll take everything that we've heard here today into consideration and make our decision by next Tuesday. Everyone involved in this hearing will receive a letter from the Department of Mines and Minerals."

He began to file the stacks of papers he had in front of him, storing them away in a tan folder. He rose to his feet and walked down the hallway and disappeared behind a closed door.

Hiram and Ralph shook hands and made their way toward the door that led outside. They got into Ralph's Suburban and drove toward home. Hiram smiled when the mountains came in view as they drove through the Red River Valley in Powell County. In his mind he was thinking, "How could anyone leave their home for any reason?" He couldn't wait to get back to Troublesome Creek.

Hiram watched that Tuesday morning as the mail boy drove into his driveway. The mailman stopped in Hiram's cement driveway, then dismounted and walked toward Hiram. His hand was full of letters.

The carrier reached the mail to him and said, "You have a certified letter that has to be signed for, sir."

Hiram watched the young man as he smiled at him. He was no older than twenty years old and slim. His youth showed from his build to his close cut hair and his flailing arms. He was dressed in a regular pair of Levi's and a light blue shirt with the Postal Service logo embroidered just above his shirt pocket. Hiram smiled back at the young man and quickly signed the form and reached the return receipt back to the mailman. The young postal carrier turned and left Hiram staring at the envelope he held in his hands. His eyebrows lifted upwards as he gazed at the return address.

Hiram opened the letter and began reading. It said:

Mr. Daniels,

This letter is to inform you that the Department of Mines and Minerals has made a decision concerning the mining of your property by the Puma Coal Company. After much deliberation we have decided not to issue a permit to the said coal company to strip mine or use the mountain top removal method of extracting coal minerals. I want to congratulate you for the speech you gave in front of this hearing body last Monday. I could only imagine the loss you would feel if the coal permit had been issued. Nonetheless, we will issue a permit to the coal company so they can deep mine their mineral if they choose to.

My best regards to you sir,
Brown Ledford
Acting Director

Hiram almost cried as he walked towards his house. He could hardly wait to show Dora and Mattie. He picked up Jesse and kissed his rosy cheek as he walked inside the door. He was so happy. His battle was won.

Dora read the letter as the phone rang. It was Ralph Johnson. He'd received a letter in the mail also. Hiram could tell his lawyer was happy too. Hiram walked outside to the porch.

Holding his five-year-old son, he pointed toward the mountain he'd fought for.

"You don't know enough of what I'm talking about but one day you will," he said, shaking the boy on his hip.

Hiram couldn't hold Jesse too long because of arthritis in his left shoulder and elbow. He sat down with him in his favorite rocking chair. He'd bought two new rockers and a settee for Mattie. Hiram was happy in his old age. He thought, "My bones feel awful old today, but this victory makes me want to jump. For a man of eighty-seven years old I've seen a lot in my lifetime. If this is to be Troublesome's last sunset then I have lived a full life."

Life was peaceful for Hiram after that day. Every evening he'd sit in his rocker and gaze at Rolly Joe Mountain and listen to the sounds of Troublesome Creek. One evening, he brought a pen and notebook with him as he sat rocking. He began to write a letter to his youngest son, Jesse. Hiram figured more than likely he wouldn't live to see his young son grown and, just in case he didn't, he wanted to make sure Jesse knew just how important Rolly Joe Mountain was to his father and his family. He began his letter like this:

My youngest son Jesse,

The son of my old age, that God blessed me to live and see born. I love the very mention of your name. You mean so much to me. You are the one to carry on the Daniels name with pride and distinction. Your image is near mine, with your black curly locks and blue eyes and even your young mannerisms are fashioned after mine.

Rolly Joe Mountain is to whomever that appreciates natural beauty and desires to preserve the past for future generations. It is beyond explaining. My dear mother, Mandy Daniels, your grandmother, loathed the very appearance of the mountain, but your grandfather loved the mountain as I do like his own life.

You will inherit enough wealth to live your life ever how you choose. But I want you to remember that these mountains have been home to the Daniels family for centuries and must be preserved as close to nature as possibly can be. It is not an impossible task to ask my own kin to respect my wishes. If it were, I would not ask this of you. You will be grown and educated before you see this letter. My lawyer and faithful friend, Mr. Johnson, will make sure that it is not opened before that time.

So, I leave you with these few words.

Your Father,

Hiram Daniels

Hiram made several trips to Slonetown that fall. He wanted to make sure his lawyer would heed to his instructions pertaining to his wealth and property holdings. He hid a copy of the letter he wrote to his son and the deed to Rolly Joe Mountain inside a locked deposit box at the bank. Hiram also hid the five dollar gold piece that Ballard carried with him during World War Two. Whenever in town, he always made a point to check on Mattie, who was now living with her sister and aunt Sissy. Hiram knew she was better off near Cassie's clinic because of her bad lungs. It took all her strength to fight bouts of bronchitis and pneumonia. Hiram worried about her most of the time.

Every evening, Hiram loved to sit in his favorite rocking chair and watch his young Jesse play on the porch or front yard. Hiram loved to listen to the sounds of the last swamp frogs and crickets as they sang their evening tunes. One of his favorite past times was watching the sun ball sink down behind Rolly Joe Mountain, bringing a graying dusk to the Troublesome Creek valley. Nothing could bring more happiness to Hiram then evenings like these.

This particular evening, Dora found him sitting in his rocking chair. Hiram seemed so at peace with himself.

She waited a minute before she said, "It's time to come in Hiram. It's supper time!" She called a couple more times, but Hiram didn't respond as he usually did. She touched his shoulder, and she began to sob.

She thought to herself, "A good life has ended, and a great tongue has been made silent. Surely God passed by Troublesome Creek this evening."

The End